ISBN 978-149596

Copyright © Ben Blake

The author has asserted their moral rights under the Copyright, Designs and Patents Act 1988, to be identified as the author of this work.

All rights reserved. No part of this publication may be reproduced, copied, stored in a retrieval system, or transmitted, in any form or by any means, without the prior written consent of the copyright holder, nor be otherwise circulated in any form of binding or cover other than that in which it is published and without a similar condition being imposed on the subsequent purchaser.

This is a work of fiction. Any resemblance to any real persons living or dead is entirely coincidental.

Cover art by Mark Watts

For Josh and Emily Watts

"Families are made in the heart."
(C. Joybell C.)

Ben Blake is on Facebook at
https://www.facebook.com/benblakeauthor

Follow Ben's blog at http://benblake.blogspot.co.uk/

Or email him at ben.blake@hotmail.co.uk

Also by Ben Blake

The Risen King
Blood and Gold (Songs of Sorrow volume 1)
The Gate of Angels (songs of Sorrow volume 2)

Troy

Volume One

A Brand of Fire

O'er our victim come begin!
Come, the incantation sing,
Frantic all and maddening,
To the heart a brand of fire,
The Furies' hymn,
That which claims the senses dim,
Tuneless to the gentle lyre,
Withering the soul within.

Aeschylus

Book One   Blood Red Roses

Chapter One

A Thessalian Field

The great boar turned at last just beyond the woods, in a wide vale sprinkled with the crimson droplets of anemones.

The chase had lasted half a day by then, and the heroes and princes of Greece were strung out across the hills like ants in the sun. Fewer than half of those who had roused the beast from its peace in the wood remained to fight it when it turned, and those were all tired beyond reason. Many of them didn't get their spears down in time.

Castor, the heir to Sparta, was picked up on a tusk and tossed thirty feet through the air, a broken leg flapping like a torn sail.

Chaos reigned after that, as men struggled to bring the points of their spears to bear on the rampaging animal. Atalanta shot the creature but missed its eye, and her arrow did nothing to slow it. A bronze knife, thrown by no less than Theseus of Athens, whipped over the boar's shoulder and buried itself in the thigh of Telamon, who gave a fearful bellow as though he was a beast himself. He took a step forward and fell over.

The boar was upon him in an instant, mouth gaping to reveal rows of curved yellow teeth.

It ran straight onto another man's spear, driving the bronze point deep with its own rage and momentum. Even then it didn't stop attacking. It began to chew along the ash length of the spear, impaling itself more with every convulsion but also coming closer to the man at the other end. The air was filled with grunts and drops of porcine sweat. The animal reached the middle of the spear and was stopped, foiled by a crosspiece of wood put there for just that purpose. It roared and thrashed even harder.

Then ageing Theseus was there, driving with his legs to thrust his own spear deep into the boar's flank. A moment later the young prince of Mycenae, Agamemnon, did the same from the other side. And then everyone joined in, ramming spears from all angles while the pig screamed and flailed in utter fury, until finally it made a strange coughing sound and died.

The men let go of their spears cautiously. Behind them Atalanta came up, an arrow still half-drawn and her eyes sharp. But the boar didn't move. Arms wiped sweat from faces, and a few men found the energy to smile.

"Well," Theseus said finally. He turned to the man who had first impaled the creature. "That was good work, Peleus. Artemis herself couldn't have done it better."

"Is it possible," Telamon demanded, sprawled in the grass a short distance away, "that one of you *kopros* eaters might actually help me up?"

*

Boars represent war, and death. They should perhaps have remembered that, those kings, before they gathered for the hunt.

An hour later the chariots had started to come up, bringing the men who had fallen behind as the chase wore on. There were great names among them: some titans of the past, others giants whose time was yet to come. Among the former was Atreus, the High King, stooped and worn now like an old sandal, attended by three pretty handmaidens who rode a chariot of their own. He was stopped and almost completely bald: not one of them was more than seventeen. Most men thought they were for show, a boast for all men to see. Surely Atreus had no use for young women now except to look at, and stir faint memories of the days when blood ran hot in him and the colours of the world were bright and clear. Nobody said so aloud though, or if they did they whispered it behind a cupped hand, and only to trusted friends. Carefully.

The gods gave the House of Atreus pride, men say, but not wisdom. They had given them temper as well, and that was one thing about the High King that had not diminished with the years.

The younger men included three who were judged too young to join the hunt proper, but old enough to ride with the followers, and see the chase unfold. One was Atreus' younger son Menelaus, the younger brother to Agamemnon, a good charioteer but a soft spear, or so the murmurs said. Alongside him rode Telamon's towering son Ajax, a man so big he drove his own chariot because the horses couldn't pull him and someone else besides, not for any distance. A careful distance behind these two came a slim youth with brown hair, nondescript compared to red-haired Menelaus and the looming form of Ajax. He was from a tiny island in the west. His name was Odysseus.

Behind all these came the wagons, each one drawn by eight sweating horses and burdened with sacks of grain and amphorae of wine, great barrels of figs and olives and nuts. Servants leapt down and began to lay out tables, covered with embroidered cloths. Others went to the boar with skinning knives in their hands, only to be stopped by Atreus.

"Let the priest do his work," he said. "We can wait a little longer for our meat."

The priest was a servant of Apollo, an old man in a once-resplendent white robe now spattered with mud thrown up by the chariot wheels. He had tried to wipe it off and only smeared the stains instead, making them worse. As he moved forward a new arrival dismounted from his chariot and went to join the other kings, limping slightly on the uneven ground.

"King of Messenia," Theseus said, inclining his head.

The smaller man nodded back, just as minimally. "Lord of Attica. I see you are well."

Theseus smiled a tiny smile. "I see you couldn't keep up."

Nestor didn't rise to the taunt. He was almost a decade younger than Theseus, and could have kept up well enough if it hadn't been for a tummock of grass that snagged his foot and turned his ankle over. Theseus probably knew that anyway. He was just taking his chance to score a point.

It was remarkable, really. Thirty years ago Theseus had been the darling of all Greece, famed for killing the terrible Minotaur of Knossos and throwing down the Minoan civilisation there, almost alone. He'd entered the maze of tunnels beneath the palace and slain the priests and their awful monster, and then slipped away unseen. In the ensuing chaos people fled the city, convinced their bull god had abandoned them, and Theseus found King Minos unguarded and killed him in his own throne room.

On his way home he'd abandoned Ariadne on Naxos Island, tossing her aside now her usefulness was done in a gesture of magnificent contempt.

Then he met Atalanta.

She was famous too, the Arcadian princess who refused to conform. Neither her parents nor their priests could make her obey. Atalanta liked the outdoors, not scented baths and weaving. She dressed in a chiton like a man, and ran or climbed with the boys, and she refused to be caged. Finally her parents gave up trying and just let her run free. By the time she was twenty she was as good a hunter as any man in Arcadia, fleeter of foot than most and better with a bow than anyone in Greece, man or woman. She'd refused a dozen offers of marriage by that time, some from princes of other lands. Her father the king, knowing it was impossible to force her against her will, only shrugged and let her go her way. People began to say she must have sworn an oath of virginity to Artemis, and would never allow any man to touch her.

She and Theseus met when both were hunting a lion in Boeotia, not far from Mount Helicon where the Muses dwell. They were in their prime then, strong and proud, ready to abandon whatever they were doing to go chasing after a beast that rumour said was unusually fierce. Neither spoke of it often, but it was known that they'd killed the lion and then spent a week together, sleeping under the stars and going where the mood took them. They'd been together ever since, though Atalanta had never slept under a roof as far as Nestor knew. Still, her hand on Theseus' shoulder now stopped him, and with a shake of his head the Athenian turned from Nestor and moved away.

Beyond them all another man stepped down from his chariot, this one dressed not in a chiton but a shirt and kilt, and wearing boots instead of sandals. His brown hair was cut short, barely an inch from scalp to manicured end, more like a slave than a free man. Nestor nodded to him too and went to stand with Peleus, not far from Odysseus and the other younglings.

"Kalapogma Apollo," the priest said. Murmured conversations came to an end around the field. His voice was slightly nasal, giving each word a whine as it entered the ear. "Hear now your servant Archilaus! I come to you with head bowed, in all honour, in the names of the kings and lords gathered under your light today. Heed my words, Lord of the Bow!"

"Theseus doesn't like you," Odysseus murmured, almost in Nestor's ear. The crackle of a votive fire bowl being lit would have kept anyone else from hearing him speak. "Why?"

"Theseus doesn't like anyone who can add two numbers and get the same result every time," Nestor answered in an undertone. "He's great fighting bull kings, but not much use with his brain, our Theseus. I think it's mostly fat between his ears anyway."

There was a pause, and then Odysseus whispered, "You told him that, didn't you?"

It was hard not to laugh. Odysseus was easily the cleverest of the younger nobles in Greece, though he was still young and naïve enough to think he could speak openly in a gathering of lords and not risk being overheard. Still, it was a shame he'd been born to the king of tiny Ithaca, and not as heir to Mycenae or Sparta, or to wealthy Argolis. He might have changed the world, if he'd been born there. As it was, hardly anyone would listen to Odysseus even when he spoke wisdom.

"I might have said men like him were the past in Greece," Nestor said, "and men like me, who can think, are the future. Men like you too. Now be quiet, there's a good lad. I want to listen."

The woody smell of burnt frankincense wafted over the assembled men as the priest went on speaking. "Send us your favour, Lord of the Sun! We await your word!"

He bent and slit the boar down the middle. The curved knife was whip-sharp, but even so he had to saw it back and forth to penetrate the think skin of the animal at his feet. Innards spilled out onto the grass. An attendant stepped swiftly up and wafted the bowl of burning frankincense under Archilaus' nose.

The priest's eyes flickered and he fell to his knees. He had gone pale with that inhaled smoke, and his hands trembled as though palsied. He blinked and his irises were missing, leaving only the whites of his eyes, and when he spoke the nasal whine was gone and his voice throbbed from deep within his chest.

"From this moment the world turns towards war," Archilaus said. Or the god said through him, in truth. "There will be glory and sorrow unmeasured by mortals, and amidst it shall be the son of the man who first impaled the boar, a warrior ten times greater than his father."

Afterwards, even years later, Nestor swore that when the priest fell silent a breeze soughed across the valley, ruffling the hair of the silent men. There was no other sound. One by one heads turned towards Peleus, standing at Nestor's side in the wide circle; Atreus and his sons, Theseus with Atalanta by his shoulder, even the stranger in his kilt and boots. It was a great pride for a man to have a renowned son, but a great sorrow to be so insignificant that your get outshone you. What Archilaus had said was a curse. Nestor looked at Peleus and saw, to his surprise, that the big northerner was smiling.

"A toast!" Peleus cried. He strode to the nearest table and scooped up a cup of wine, already watered by the servants. "To my son, who will grow into a warrior to outshine us all. To Achilles!"

The breeze sighed once more, and then time resumed its steady tread, the sun moving across the dome of the sky.

*

"Castor will be all right," Tyndareus said. The king of Sparta was old now, and hadn't even tried to keep pace with the hunters through the long hot morning. "He's a fighter, that boy of mine. A little thing like a broken leg won't stop him for long."

"Of course it won't," Nestor said. He knew well enough how many men died from injuries like that, but then so did Tyndareus, and it would be impolite to point it out. Castor was his only son, the one man who could succeed Tyndareus when the Fates cut his thread and Hades took him, as he surely would before long. Nestor knew how he'd feel if his own firstborn, his only son, was taken from him. Or no; he didn't know how he would feel, couldn't know, because the gods saved such suffering for the men who endured it, and others could only guess and shiver and hope such darkness never blighted their lives.

Thrasymedes was a son to make his father proud, nine years old now and growing straight and strong. He'd never be an Ajax, but then who was, apart from storied Heracles? Nestor felt his heart would burst whenever he looked at the boy. To lose him to such a thing as a broken leg… he made a warding sign against evil and shook the thought away.

But Castor's leg had been more than merely broken. It had been *snapped,* cracked in half like a mast torn in two by a storm wind. Nestor had seen it flapping as the chirurgeon heaved him onto a board for treatment. If the boy lived he was always going to limp, every day of his life. He'd never fight, never win glory in battle as Greek kings were expected to do.

Enough of this, Nestor told himself firmly. *Put such worries aside. Castor will live or he will not.*

The lad was missing now, probably deep in the opium sleep, but Telamon was back among the lords and he was, characteristically, angry. It never took much to rouse the lord of Salamis' temper, and being spitted by another man's thrown knife was more than enough to do it, even without the boar all but goring him as he lay helpless. The big man sat on a bench with his injured leg stretched out in front of him, swathed in bandages, and drank thirstily from a wine cup filled at regular intervals by a servant. The level of the water jug nearby hardly seemed to move at all. Telamon was going to be drunk as Dionysius soon enough, but nobody was about to tell him to stop.

Nestor's mind wandered back to the priest and his prophecy. *A warrior ten times greater than his father,* Archilaus had said, and perhaps it would be so. Nestor didn't recall that he'd ever seen little Achilles, so he couldn't judge. But the boy would be about seven or eight now, a year younger than Thrasymedes yet old enough for his abilities to have begun to show. It might be worth making an enquiry, if he could do it discreetly.

It was the other thing that worried him though, the first statement Archilaus had made. *From this moment the world turns towards war.* There were always wars, of course, one king battling another over the disputed placement of a border or some minor insult given by a royal cousin the year before. Or when one king went looking for plunder, for that matter. For whatever reason, there had been less of it since Atreus became High King. Arguments tended to be resolved in council now, and fighting men earned their glory overseas, as Theseus had done on Crete thirty years ago, and Jason in far-off Colchis.

Perhaps the war would come in Egypt, where the pyramid-kings' control was not as firm as it had once been. Raiders had won booty and captives from the coast of the Nile in recent years. In former times that had been a sign that Egypt might slip into one of its periods of internal strife. That would mean chaos in the trade markets, especially for wheat, but Nestor couldn't really see how the Greeks would be dragged into any fighting.

Certainly the war wouldn't come in Colchis; Greeks couldn't even get there now, between the dangers of the Hellespont and Hittite control of the land routes, through their client kings. It couldn't come in the west either, simply because there was no nation there strong enough to stand against the Greeks. There were only cities, Hesperian or Etruscan for the most part, none of them able to exert control more than a day's walk from the walls. That left only Greece. Did the priest mean that the Argives would turn on themselves? Perhaps the lords of Mycenae were going to lose their authority. It would be worth watching events unfold.

Nestor was still thinking that as his gaze drifted along the line of kings and princes, past Atreus sitting flanked by the sons who now towered over him, to the stranger in his kilt and fine-spun shirt.

"It's nearly time to eat," Peleus said then, stepping into the midst of the group. The air was heavy with the smell of roasting pork, and Nestor's stomach rumbled at the other man's words. "But first, we have with us today a guest, come all the way from windy Troy. He has asked to speak to you all, and I believe we should indulge him in this."

The stranger stood and bowed to Peleus. "My thanks, lord of Thessaly, and those of my king, at whose command I come. I am Antenor."

Now *there* was a name Nestor knew. Antenor was king Priam's closest advisor in far-off Troy, his chief helpmeet, and not a man well liked in Greece. It was Antenor who set the transit duties for goods that passed along the Trojan road, avoiding the treacherous waters of the Hellespont to the north. Set them too high, as any Greek merchant would tell you. He was said to be a shrewd and tough man, and he was here, with this hunt of kings in the hills of Thessaly. Nestor could think of only one possible reason for that.

"Bind my tongue," Theseus said before Nestor could speak, "this is about Hesione, isn't it? Again."

On his bench Telamon had gone very still, wine cup held halfway to his lips.

"The lord of Attica is as perceptive as we were told," Antenor said smoothly. "Age can wither muscles, but the mind endures longer, they say."

And Trojans can make any words sound like honey from the lips of gods, Nestor thought. It came of haggling with merchants from all across the Greensea. Sometimes it seemed the meanest of Trojans could dicker with kings from any other land, and most likely sell him a pig in a sack for more gold than the kingdom could afford.

"This is indeed about the lady Hesione," Antenor said. He moved into the centre of the circle, left empty by Peleus. "The king's sister has been held captive in Greece now for nearly ten years. Priam is of the opinion that this is long enough. He wishes her back."

"He can't have her," Telamon growled. "Besides, she bore my son. Would you take her from her child?"

"Why not?" Antenor answered. "You took her from her father."

Telamon dropped his cup and started to struggle to his feet.

"Enough," Atreus said from across the clearing. Nestor thought he looked like a man already walking with death. It wouldn't be long now until glowering Agamemnon was lord in Mycenae, but Atreus' voice at least was still firm. "Peleus our host has granted this man the right to speak. Whatever we think of that decision, we will respect it. Sit down, Telamon."

"I will not give Hesione back! What would –"

"Sit down," Agamemnon said, and his voice was even harder than his father's. Telamon broke off and then sank back to his bench, looking surprised that he'd done so.

"I am grateful," Antenor said. He bowed to Atreus, more deeply than he had to Peleus. "My lords, we Trojans realise that women are treated differently here in Greece. You regard them as spoils of war. A glance at your history reminds us of that. Perseus took Andromeda from Joppa against her will. More recently Jason took Medea from Colchis, against her will. And more recently yet my lord Theseus here stole Ariadne from the palace of Knossos, again against her will... and then abandoned her on an island before he even reached home."

"What would you suggest I should have done?" Theseus asked. He sounded honestly bewildered. "Bring her home to my father's palace? A snake sleeping in my own bed?"

He hissed then, turning to Atalanta who had just dug the tip of her knife into his thigh. She withdrew the blade and studied the scarlet tip. "If that was your concern, you shouldn't have taken her from Knossos in the first place, Theseus. I never did like what you did to her."

"I would never do it to you," he said.

Her answering smile was brilliant, even on a woman past her fiftieth year. "You never could. I do not depend on you, king of Athens."

It was well known that Theseus had asked Atalanta to marry him twenty years before. She had refused, but taken him to her bed nonetheless. So things had remained, with him periodically asking for her hand and she rejecting him, refusing to be tied to any man. Watching them from across the circle of men, Nestor wondered how many married couple shared the love he could see in the pair. He didn't think there would be many.

"As I was saying," Antenor resumed, "we Trojans view women in a different way. We give them rights, powers alongside men. It is our queen Hecuba who will decide who her children marry, and it's she who intercedes with the gods on the city's behalf. Things are the same in her homeland of Lydia. Cultured men do not treat women this way."

"Weak ones do," Leonteus snapped.

There was laughter at that, though the king of Pieria hadn't meant it as a joke and seemed briefly discomfited by the reaction. Antenor let the amusement pass, though Nestor thought his skin reddened slightly.

"Priam asks that dignity is served in this," the Trojan went on. "He asks that Hesione be given back, to resume her life in Troy as the princess of the city she was born to be."

"No," Telamon said bluntly.

"Perhaps we might discuss other matters," Nestor said, breaking his silence. He thought he might know why it was Antenor who had come to ask this time, and not the usual lower-ranked official. "Such as the levies charged for use of the Trojan Road."

"Perhaps we might," the Trojan allowed. "After we have seen evidence of some goodwill."

There was a silence. Every man in the valley knew what lower transit duties would mean for their country's merchants, and therefore for the royal treasuries: more gold. Every king in Greece always needed gold. They turned a blind eye to piracy if it brought coin into the cities: some even went with the raiding parties with scarves tied across their faces, then denied being there if a diplomat came to protest.

"Some compromise might be possible," Atreus began.

"No," Telamon said again, cutting across the High King. His face was red with anger. "How many times must I say it? Hesione was taken as a fair spoil of war. She belongs to me and I will not hand her back like some mewling weakling."

Antenor stared down his nose at the big man. "There was no war. The princess was taken by pirates raiding the coast."

"He's calling me a reaver," Telamon said, appealing to the crowd. "And don't forget, I wasn't alone that day. I sailed with Heracles himself. Would you call the son of Zeus a pirate?"

Partway around the circle, Tyndareus muttered, "Bind my tongue, but I wish you'd shut up about Heracles."

He wasn't quiet enough, and the words carried. Telamon started to get up again. This time his son Ajax took a step forward too. Schedius spoke before they could go further.

"Handing Hesione back to Troy will make the Greeks look weak in the eyes of others," he said. His eyes gleamed under thick black brows. "There are cities around the Greensea that wait for us to falter. This is not about one woman, whatever Antenor might wish us to believe."

"Which cities?" Antenor asked. "I know of none which can stand with Troy. None which control trade routes as rich as ours." He turned to Atreus. "I ask for your judgement, High King. Is a single woman's fate more important than the friendship of mighty Troy?"

Atreus studied him for a moment, then shook his grizzled head. "You are asking the wrong person, Trojan. I am High King, but that doesn't grant me authority in all affairs. This is Telamon's decision to make –"

"Then no," Telamon said.

"– and however coarse he might be in council," Atreus went on, "I cannot change that."

Antenor looked at the king of Salamis.

"No," Telamon said. "I won't hand her back. By the dog of Egypt! Not for all the wealth of Troy, I won't."

"Then that closes the matter," Atreus said. "Though I would be pleased to discuss trade duties with you, Antenor, if your time allows."

The Trojan bowed once more. "My time is yours, High King, until my own lord calls me home."

His time might be, but Antenor would make no agreements today, Nestor was sure. He'd want to make sure Atreus understood that Greek intransigence over Hesione could be met with Trojan stubbornness over trade prices. But Antenor knew how to be subtle. He'd smile and say all the right things, like any glib-tongued Trojan, and then go home without giving anything away.

The meeting began to break up, most of the men heading towards the big fire and the boar sizzling above it. Odysseus lingered though, leaning down to murmur again into Nestor's ear. "That's a clever man, I think."

"Antenor?" he asked. "Yes, he's a devious one. He must be, to have thrived in Priam's court. They're all snakes in the east, but Trojans most of all."

There weren't many clever men in this field, in truth. Odysseus was one, Antenor another with his measuring eyes. Atreus was canny, and there was Nestor himself. The elder son of the High king, Agamemnon, might be shrewder than his broad farmer's face might lead a man to believe; Nestor wasn't sure of him yet. But Theseus was a fathead lost in past glories, and the memory of a Greece which had changed and left him behind. Telamon was a braggart and a drunk; and Peleus a fool, for thinking he could let the Trojan speak without causing antagonism. Most of the others were just warrior lords, men who let their muscles do the thinking and couldn't read if you cut their index fingers off. Men from the past that Theseus longed for, and who hadn't yet realised it was gone.

It had to be gone. Greece couldn't continue as a land of fighting men and pirates; at least, not only as that. They had to learn to build, the way Priam and his predecessors had built Troy into a city of fable, or as Minos had once made Crete into the cultural hub of the world. Here and there they had begun to. Tyndareus had a palace of gardens and courtyards, and Atreus was turning Mycenae into a mercantile city with large new *agora* for merchants to trade in. Nestor was trying to do the same in Messenia, though it was harder there, at the edge of the Greek homeland. But they were the only ones. The rest of the kings preferred to go on as they always had, bickering and snapping at each other, feral dogs with inflated egos and obsessed with their own pride.

Theseus and Atalanta passed him, making their way towards the fire. As they walked Nestor heard the old hero say, "I'll not ask you again. From now on I will take what you offer, be glad of it, and ask no more."

Nestor couldn't help smiling. There was hope for even the most stubborn of Greeks if the ox-brained lord of Attica could learn that a woman sometimes knew her own mind, and would not be swayed from it. The Trojans all knew it from early childhood. Perhaps the Greeks would understand it one day too.

His stomach rumbled. Nestor turned and headed for the roasting boar, to feast and drink cups of watered wine, and swap lies with the other kings about hunts and women and war, in the hour the gods gave them before Castor died.

Caesura

I was not there that day in Thessaly, when the boar fell to Peleus' spear. I heard the tale later, when I had grown to an age when my elders thought me worth talking to. When some thought so, at least. There are always men who cannot bring themselves to regard a hollow-chested youth with a club foot as a proper man at all, who turn away rather than speak as though feebleness might be catching if they open their mouths.

I became a storyteller, and then people talked to me.

Every king wants his name remembered. They build palaces for their sons and burn the houses of enemies, all to make a mark on the world. They etch their names in silver and have them carved into stone, and still it's not enough. Still they want more. When the sky shudders to the echo of their name, chanted by multitudes, then they might be content. But I doubt it.

As a teller of tales, I was sometimes given a place in the *megaron* of a king. A long way down the table, or across the hearth, far enough away that the lord and his cronies could pretend not to see me – but close enough to hear. That was how I learned what had happened on that hunt. I heard it in Atreus' hall, and in Nestor's in the west, and Peleus' own poorer palace to the north. Later I heard it told in Mycenae again, seated on the same bench as when Atreus spoke, but this time it was his sullen son Agamemnon who told, short days after his father had been laid into his tomb.

It was there, too, that I heard of the death of Theseus, leaping from the cliffs of Attica into the sea three days after Atalanta passed in her sleep. She was several years past fifty by then: a good age for any woman, but remarkable for one who slept in the open from choice. Atalanta was not a woman who took easily to imprisonment. Perhaps that was why Theseus loved her so. He longed for the one bird he could never catch. Happiness is elusive for such men.

I've long thought I should write a play about their story. A hero king, home from slaying the dreadful Minotaur; and the free-spirited maiden who takes his great heart and ties it on a thong about her neck. Perhaps I will, one day, if the Fates spare me and the seasons are kind.

But this is a greater tale, the story of the age. There has been none greater since Zeus threw down his father and the time of the Twelve Olympians began. It is the story of what flowed from that day in the Thessalian meadow, the events which came down through time to fall upon mortal men. Is it bad luck or good, to be fated to live in such times? I have heard the tale told in a hundred halls by a thousand tongues, and I do not know. Perhaps Zeus himself does, the Lord of the Black Cloud on his throne atop Olympus. Or perhaps not, for even the gods are subject to Fate, not masters of it.

This is a tale of the fall of kings, the ruin of empires and of pride. A tale too of love and honour. And for much of its length it is *my* tale, the story of how a crippled boy went from the lakes of Magnesia to the walls of Troy, to the halls of kings from Greece to Phoenicia, and who knew the men who walked with gods on their shoulders. Achilles, Hector with his voice of thunder, Diomedes shining like silver in mud. Agamemnon, king of kings, and great Ajax hefting his oblong shield, and Paris staring down from the wall at the chaos his recklessness had brought. I remember Helen, first demure in Sparta and later standing forth in Troy, proud as Aphrodite with the golden apple in her hand.

And I remember Odysseus, an ordinary man standing usually in a corner or half in shadow, speaking little but always watching, watching, and smiling his wry smile.

I knew them. I spoke with them, and they with me, and I heard the thrum of the gods in their words and saw divinity glimmer in their eyes.

I am Thersites. I will tell you of Troy.

Chapter Two

In Blue and Gold

The city stands on the flat top of a ridge, a hundred feet above the surrounding plain.

To the north lies the Hellespont, the treacherous water that leads to all the riches of the Euxine Sea, and wrecks the ships which try to reach them. It is only a mile wide, but currents swirl under the choppy surface, and rocks lurk well out from each shore. Beyond lies Thrace, and a different continent. Thrace is a land of top-knotted warriors in savage clans, endlessly fighting over arcane matters of honour only they understand.

Westward is the Greensea, thick with the sails of trading ships. Many of them come to the Bay of Troy. Some were built in Egypt, some in Cyprus or Phoenicia; most, however, are Greek. They may carry goods from far-off lands, but their timbers grew in groves in Salamis or northern Magnesia, and their captains learned the sea in the gulfs around the Greek coast.

South, and the river Scamander flows through a gorge that leads back to Mount Ida and the woods and meadows of the hills. Grass grows all year round there and the sheep grow fat, their wool the finest in Anatolia. Towns have sprung up along the valley, filled with Trojans and others; the greatest of them is Zeleia, on a crag high above the water.

East are hills thickly carpeted with shrubs and thorns, and offspring trees that curve their branches to the ground and plant seeds where they touch. Deer multiply there, hunted by wolves slinking through the screens of branches. There are a thousand paths and none is ever the same from one year to the next. Men who travel there return speaking of shadows half-seen, figures moving behind a veil of leaves, or voices that murmur in empty glades. The spirits of trees and streams are fewer now, harder to find, but they have not left the land entirely.

And in the middle a wide, grassy plain, fed by three rivers: Scamander, Chiblak and Simois. Between the mouths of the latter two lies the city's ridge, the mound of Hissarlik, an outcrop of rock surrounded by marshy grassland. Atop it the city sits, a place of towers and turrets, walls and concealed gates. From the outside, to a sailor as his ship noses into the great bay, the tops of those towers seem to hold up the sky.

The Greeks say the walls of mighty Mycenae were built by Cyclops, an army of artisan giants in the long-ago. If true then the walls of Troy must have been built by gods – perhaps by Pallas Athena, the patron deity of the city; or by Ipirru, god of the sun and of horses.

Horses.

They are the wealth of Troy, the pride of Troy, the source of the city's influence and fame. Trade along the Trojan Road brings coin by the bucket, and textiles bring more, but horses outshine them both. The plain teems with them, hundreds of untamed *tarpans* roaming in herds, sustained by the lush grass that grows in earth kept fertile and black by the shifting, reed-lined Scamander. The Trojans let them breed wild and then rope and corral them, harnessing their wildness until they make the finest chariot horses in the world. The kings of Hattusa and Egypt send for Trojan animals when their own herds are depleted, and the price paid for them is higher even than the topless towers.

Today the northern wind is blowing, the *Meltemi* that turns the Hellespont into chop and pins merchant ships to the beaches of the Bay of Troy, unable to move north to open water. The horses have taken shelter south-west of the Scamander, behind the double lines of willows and tamarisk that line the low banks. They know the wind might blow like this for days, perhaps weeks, and are resigned. They are used to it.

They are used to people passing by too, and they only flick their ears when a line of chariots runs by on the other side of the river, wheels rattling on the packed-earth road.

*

Really, a man's heart could burst with pride.

He never liked it when his son went away. His eldest son, the one he suspected every father loved best, because he was the first proof of a man's virility. You never admitted it though, never let your other children feel less loved. As a king the pressure was greater yet, because what you could and couldn't show was constrained by the twin chains of duty and honour. You made do with few words, an occasional gesture, and hoped they were enough.

Because of that it was a comfort to see that the councillors felt his son's absence too, and the city's wider population. They might not love him, not the way a father did, but there was always a sense that Troy was holding its breath, and praying, until the heir came back home.

He was home. Citizens had poured into the streets to chant his name, and now it rose like a cry to the gods from ten thousand throats, echoing off stone: "Hector! Hector! Hector!"

The sound carried clearly here, in the *megaron* of the king's palace in the Pergamos, the great citadel of Troy. The palace had been designed to allow views of the lower city from its balconies, but to keep out unwanted noise. Still, when every citizen of Troy was in the streets and shouting, solid stone couldn't have kept it out entirely. Nor would Priam have wanted it to. It proved how much the city loved the man who would next be king.

The main doors to the throne room were closed. They were inch-thick cedar from Phoenicia, enamelled with a diamond pattern in the royal colours of blue and gold. They would not stand up long against attack, but what enemy could reach here, into the living heart of Troy? Even mighty Heracles had balked at that prospect, when he and the villain Telamon had come twenty years before. But the doors were decorative, not defensive. A soldier stood at each side, both wearing breastplates in the yellow lacquer of the Palladians; it was their turn to stand guard today.

The Palladians were going to strut about this for days. They had stood the watch when Hector came home.

People still trickled into the chamber though, through a small door set discreetly behind a statue of Tarhun close to one corner. The god was shown with one hand raised high, clutching a thunderbolt as though about to cast. As a child Priam had been afraid the statue would come to life and throw that bolt at him; it was that realistic. He used to touch it to make sure it was still stone, then snatch his hand back. The fancy had passed quickly enough, of course, but he still touched the statue whenever he entered the *megaron,* these days to invoke the blessing of the god on all he tried to do here.

"I've tried to be a good shepherd to my people," he said to the person standing beside him. "Have I succeeded?"

She rolled her eyes in theatrical amusement. "You have. As I've told you before. And if you ask me that one more time, my dear, I will have to swipe you with a flyswatter."

Priam snorted. He'd loved her a little from the first time he saw her, this bold-faced wife of his, and she'd never betrayed a trust or shaken his faith in her. He still didn't know if she'd loved him from the start, though. She wouldn't tell him. When he asked – which he rarely did, now – Hecuba just smiled an enigmatic smile and changed the subject.

She loved him now, as much as he did her. He had come to understand, with age, that the details didn't matter.

Someone rapped against the doors from the far side. The two Palladian guards looked to Priam and waited for his nod, then unbarred the doors and swung them open.

Hector stood framed in the centre of the corridor, a large man still wearing a cuirass lacquered in the royal colours, the blue and gold smeared with dust from the road. His sandy hair was damp from being confined under the helmet held by the straps in one hand. Beside and behind him was another man, smaller, half hidden by the prince. Priam couldn't see who he was.

"Father," Hector said. His voice was deep and sure. He stepped into the *megaron* and went down on both knees, hands on the floor as he touched the tiles with his forehead. He was heir to the city; one day Troy would kneel to him, and its treasuries and sanctuaries open their doors at his approach. But that day had not yet come, and until it did there were formalities to observe.

"Rise," Priam said, and let himself smile. There was a limit to formality, after all. "And welcome home, son."

Hector sat up and then stood, all in one smooth motion. He'd always been an agile child, and training had made the man even more athletic. And he didn't seem to have suffered any injuries while he was away. Priam's eyes searched and found nothing. He began to relax a little.

"It's good to *be* home," Hector said. "We were so far east by midsummer that I half thought I wouldn't be back before snow closed the mountains, and left me trapped in Hattusa. I came back so quickly that I doubt word of the battle will have beaten me here."

He paused, no doubt waiting to be asked what had happened when the Hittite army finally brought the Assyrians to battle. Hector did love his tales of war. On another occasion Priam would have been happy to let the court listen while Hector reminded them of his prowess in combat. He'd have enjoyed hearing the story himself, in truth, but not this time.

"Who," he asked, sitting a little straighter in the throne on the shallow dais, "is *that?*"

Hector didn't bother to turn around. "That is Mursili, Father. A Hittite, from the Royal Workshops."

Priam could see he was a Hittite. It was that which had caused his surprise, but to hear the man was an artisan as well… "The Hittites have taken to sending their craftsmen to Troy?"

"The king permitted me to bring this one," Hector said. "As thanks for my part in the battle at Emar. He's an ironsmith, Father."

An ironsmith. The brown little man only stood with his head down, not offering the obeisance but respectful in his bearing despite that. Priam stared at him and thought rapidly.

This explained a good deal, and raised other questions at the same time. Hector must have fought like a dozen demons in the service of the Hittite king to be allowed to bring a worker of that marvellous new metal to a western city. Without knowing any details, Priam knew his son must have gained real glory in the east. But even so, the Hittites guarded their ironsmiths jealously; for years, it was only in Hattusa that iron could be worked at all. Nobody else knew how, and the Hittites had lamed their experts so they couldn't flee.

The secret had leaked out, back when Priam's father Laomedon had been a young boy. But it was still devilishly hard to mine iron and then smelt it, and Troy had never been able to do so for itself. Iron came through the city from time to time, carried on galleys or loaded onto wagons, but that was all, and it was how Hattusa wanted it. The Great King would tolerate an ironsmith in Babylon, and another in Ashkelon if the rumours were true, but nothing else. Troy itself was nominally a tribute city, under Hittite protection and sworn to send help in various wars, and the empire definitely did not want its half-subject, half-allies to grow strong enough to become rivals.

As thanks for my part in the battle, Hector had said. That meant he had asked for an ironsmith and his request had been granted. Urhi-Tešub must be weaker than any king in Hattusa had been for a century. Priam studied his son and received a faint nod, a signal that there was more to the story than had been said. Well, that was wise. The rest could be spoken later, with fewer ears to listen. He looked significantly at his wife.

"Hector," she said. Hecuba rose and went down the single step to the floor, the hem of her gown trailing on the tiles as she walked. "It wouldn't stain your manhood to kiss your mother, would it?"

He grinned and bent to brush lips against her cheek. "I'd hug you, but I think I ought to bathe first."

"You should," a very tall man said, from the left of the dais. "You reek like an unwashed stable hand."

"Laocoon!" Hector exclaimed. He strode across to clasp the taller man's forearm. "How are the gods treating you?"

Laocoon smoothed the front of his white robe. "Athena smiles on me, as always. I knew you would be home today."

"A prophecy?"

"Auspices only," Laocoon said with a slight smile, "but I've learned to interpret them well."

"You should, at your age."

"Pup," the priest said, laughing with the rest of the room. "Put on a white robe, and I'll take you into the sanctuary and see if you take to the paths of wisdom as readily as you take to those of war."

"The temples already have one of my children," Priam said. "Please don't try to seduce my heir."

The laughter became uneasy, then dwindled. Everyone knew that Cassandra had been given in service to the priesthood because she wasn't good for anything else. She became hysterical when she was touched, even by her siblings, or her mother. Priam's was the only hand that didn't frighten her. That made it impossible to arrange a marriage for her, or use her as an ambassador to foreign kings. A bride of Ipirru was all she could be, and even if she wasn't a very good priestess, what else was there for her?

Thinking of marriage made Priam glance at his wife again, and he nodded towards Hector in silent suggestion. *Tell him.*

"I have found you a wife," the queen said.

Her son raised his eyebrows. "Without consulting me?"

Hecuba made a dismissive gesture. "We've talked about it enough, in the past. Frankly you should have been married four years ago at least. You're twenty-six, Hector. Do you know how many princes are still unwed at that age?"

"Quite a lot are, in Hattusa," Hector said. He wasn't smiling, and the room was still silent. "I told you who I wanted to marry."

"Andromache," she said promptly, "from Thebe-under-Plakos. And I told *you* why it was difficult. Eetion is a good king, and a loyal friend to Troy. But Thebe is not a major city. There are greater powers to consider in the world than a small town south of Mount Ida."

Hector nodded. "I realise that."

"Then you understand."

"Perhaps," he said. "Who did you choose for my bride, Mother?"

"Andromache of Thebe-under-Plakos," she answered, and smiled. "Whatever the realities of the world, I do try to fight for my children, you know."

Hector laughed aloud, and the room laughed with the relief from tension. The prince strode to his mother and lifted her off the floor, her dress swirling as he spun and kissed her on both cheeks. When he set her down her braided hair was awry, and Priam noted with amusement that a flush had coloured her skin. It wasn't often that Hecuba was put out of countenance, but she was now.

"Are none of my brothers here for this news?" Hector asked. "Or my sisters? None of them came to greet me?"

"Cassandra rarely leaves her temple, and Troilus is with his horses," Priam said. "You know how he is; he forgets everything else as soon as he reaches the stables. Paris was supposed to be here though."

Everyone in the room knew what that meant: Paris was off with another of his young women, one more body to tease and arouse, and then discard. That was one prince who would find it very hard when he was married, and couldn't please himself where women were concerned.

"So no one came?" Hector asked, and deep slow voice or no, he sounded crestfallen.

"I did," someone said languidly, from the back of the crowd. The throng of nobles parted to reveal a man leaning against the tiled wall, arms folded across his chest. Hector let out a shout of delight. "Aeneas! Why didn't you speak before, you dog?"

"I thought I'd better wait," the other man said. He was almost of a height with Hector, though slimmer in build. "You Trojans can be dreadfully sensitive when outsiders speak uninvited."

"You're not an outsider. You married my sister."

"Speaking of whom..." Aeneas said.

Hector followed his friend's eyes, then laughed again as a woman stepped from behind a pillar. "Creusa! You look wonderful, sister. I swear, you grow lovelier every season."

"Flatterer," she said, and then screamed in pretend terror as Hector seized her too and spun her around, just as he had his mother. "Put me down! You know I get dizzy when you do that!"

Creusa was hardly lovely. Priam only had two daughters, and when one was a delicate reed who flinched at sudden sounds and hated to be touched, it meant the other was doubly important. Creusa had always been destined to wed a prince from one of Troy's ally cities. The trouble was that she was simply plain, with a broad farmer's face and long nose, and hair that straggled no matter what lotions were used to wash it. She was kind and loyal, but what prince valued those assets above beauty?

Aeneas had. Two years ago he'd come to Hecuba to ask for Creusa as his wife, a request like lightning from a clear sky. Everyone had been taken completely by surprise, nobody more than Creusa herself, who for days had refused to believe it. Handsome Aeneas, one of only two men who could match spears with Hector and not be stomped flat in moments? Asking for her hand? It was too unlikely to be believed. Priam had struggled to believe it himself, in honesty, and Hecuba had accepted Aeneas' offer with almost unseemly haste.

Aeneas had called her *the best of all Trojan women,* and when she stood at the altar to speak her vows, Creusa had been as beautiful as any too. Priam held that memory dear, a touchstone in difficult times.

"I hope your judgement is accurate," he murmured to his wife. "That Thebe is the right city to bind to us now."

Hecuba sniffed. "Your siblings all died before they could marry, husband, in battle or in sickbeds. I brought you a link to Lydia, when we wed, but every city in Troas and many beyond have been too long without that connection. Whatever I chose for Hector, someone would be disappointed."

"Let us hope," he said, "that it doesn't go further than disappointment."

"Tend your own affairs," she said. Her tone was still warm, so he knew she wasn't really warning him, but the words were still blunt. "You administer the city and look to our defences, and let me worry about marriages and the temples. I haven't done so badly, before."

"No," he agreed, smiling a little. "No, you haven't."

She had done wonderfully, in fact. Aeneas had helped, with his startling wish to marry Creusa, but that was only part of it. Hecuba had seen Cassandra taken in by the sanctuaries, when no temple had really wanted to accept such a timid creature. She'd used Lycaon's love of travel to turn him into an ambassador for Troy overseas; he was in Cyprus now, dickering over lower prices for copper from the great mines there. The lad was also married to Eshan, a minor princess from the Hittite court, and minor or not that was a considerable diplomatic coup. Very few Hittite noble women married outside their own people. Priam couldn't remember the last time one had wed a lord from the coastal cities.

Now Hector was to marry Andromache, strengthening Troy's links with Thebe-under-Plakos again. It had been too long, as Hecuba said. That it fulfilled Hector's own wish at the same time was an added benefit. His marriage would leave only Troilus, who would make a good husband if he could stop thinking about horses for three minutes at a time, and Paris. Troilus ought to be easily dealt with. Find him a wife who didn't mind that he came home late and smelling of horse, and they would both be happy.

Paris, Priam and Hecuba's youngest, much-loved child, was probably going to be a problem. The silence in the room a moment ago was proof of that: everyone knew what he was like. Show him a pretty girl and all sense left him. Show him another and he forgot the first to go bounding after the new conquest. Some men were fools for money, others for power or glory, but it was saddest of all to see a man be a fool for lust.

Hecuba was wrong about one thing, though: not *all* Priam's siblings had died. One still lived, though in captivity far away. And it was lust that had led Telamon to steal Hesione, twenty years ago now.

Priam still hated to think of that. His sister had lived half her life in a foreign land, held prisoner by a pirate and raider who used her as he chose. She'd borne him a son, soon after her capture, though no children since. Priam thought that meant she'd found a way to defy him, at least in that one thing. To keep a small part of herself from him.

She had used to bring him flowers, when she was very small and he was learning the spear. He still remembered her toddling in the mud of the training yard, an anemone held in her tiny hand.

Antenor was in Greece again, trying to secure the return of Hesione. He hoped to gain the trust of other Argive lords, who would in turn persuade Telamon to hand her back. Priam didn't hold out much hope. Too many efforts had been rebuffed, and the Greeks had never changed their position by one inch. It was Telamon's choice to make, they said, and if he refused that was an end to the matter.

There would not be an end while Hesione lived. Priam would keep trying, and Hector after him would try. And if the Argives still refused, then Troy had other weapons it could use.

"People are noticing," Hecuba murmured to him.

He came to himself again, a smile forming on his lips without the need for him to think. He didn't need to ask what his wife meant. The courtiers and lords gathered in the throne room had become aware that Priam's thoughts were elsewhere, and the talk had quieted as they waited to learn why. Even Aeneas was looking, just from the side of his eye, but then he often did that. A clever lad, the Dardanian. He'd be a good support for Hector when he was king.

Priam stood and went down the step to the *megaron* floor to rejoin his son, and the conversation picked up around them once more.

Chapter Three

Lachesis Measures

She ran from him, darting sure-footed through shadows of maple and hazel – but not too fast. He always kept her in sight, hunting her laughter through the trees until she let him catch her in a glade above a small stream, shining in the midday sun.

His hands were strong on her hips, but she twisted her lithe form and dashed her lips across his, still laughing.

"By my eyes," he said, "you'll be the death of me."

"Not me," she said. Her laughter stilled as the gift of her people came to her, soft yet insistent. "That woman is yet to come."

He'd been about to pull her to him, but at the words he paused and drew back. "What do you mean?"

"I... don't know." She put a hand to her head, as though to wipe away the faintness she felt. A moment later she was smiling again. "Did you run me down just to talk?"

He grinned, and this time did pull her to him and kissed her, his other hand already untying the belt of her dress. He laid her down in the grass among snowdrops and purple gladioli, sunshine falling on her face as she closed her eyes.

*

Afterwards they lay side by side, one of her legs resting between his, their clothes dotted around them.

"Look," she said presently. "A cloud shaped like a wolf."

"A wolf?"

"There, can you see its snout? It's about to pounce on that sheep there."

Paris squinted at the sky. "A sheep that has no legs, it seems. Hardly difficult to catch."

"As I wasn't?"

"I'm no wolf," he said.

"All men are wolves." She shook her head and pointed again. "That one looks like a boat. One of the Greek galleys, sailing the endless sea."

"The sky *is* endless."

"So is the earth," she responded. "That one's shaped like a lyre."

"Or the horns of a bull," Paris said.

She turned to look at him. "You see? Men are wolves. Always thinking about war."

"I'm not thinking about war. Bulls don't always mean battle. You're thinking of boars."

"So contrary today," she said, smiling a little. "Perhaps I should have hidden among the trees and let you blunder about alone, calling my name until light drained out of the day."

For answer he tangled a hand in her hair and kissed her, and as always she lost herself in him. They were still kissing when he touched her somewhere else and she shivered all over, moaning against his teeth.

"Perhaps you should," he said, teasing her.

Oenone shook her head, her quicksilver mood shifting to serious in an instant. "There's something about you, city bred though you are. My sisters disapprove, they say I should find a mate among our own kind, a mountain man. But I only feel truly alive with you."

He studied her with hazel eyes. *Witch hazel eyes,* she thought a little wildly. *I am a woman of the streams, tied to running water for longer than a thousand lives of men. I hardly remember what I was before. I'm the one who is meant to captivate and enthral. But this prince of Troy has turned all that back on me. He's taken my heart, not I his.*

Not I his.

"You're more alive than any woman I've ever known," he said finally. "Living on this mountain has given you something special. Joy, energy: I don't know. But you glow with it."

"Does that mean you love me?"

"I love you." He ran fingertips down her bare leg, making her shiver again. Grass prickled at her back. "What did you mean, earlier? About a woman yet to come?"

"I don't remember."

"Oenone," he said.

She sighed. Love was the greatest joy she'd ever known, like summer sunlight playing on a still pool. But when Paris made demands his love became annoying, like thorns under the skin. "I saw it, that's all. When you said I would be the death of you."

"Saw what?"

"That a woman will be," she said.

After a moment he grinned. "I'll die because of a woman? There are worse ends, I suppose."

She reached up to brush brown curls away from his forehead. "Don't joke. I can't bear it."

"So what will she do?" Paris asked, still joking. "Torment me to death in a pillowed bed? Knife me in my sleep?"

"I don't *know!*" Oenone cried. "I never know! You might never meet her, or hear her name. But what she does will affect you, one day."

"Well, then," he said. His smile had gone at last. "I'll be sure to keep a wary eye out for her, I promise."

That wouldn't matter. Nothing mortals did could affect the threads of the Fates. *Clothos spins, Lachesis measures, Atropos cuts the thread.* They did their work with cold efficiency, never hearing the cries and pleas of those desperate for more life. A man yearning for a single minute so he could tell his wife she was loved. A woman praying that her baby live through the next hitching breath. None of it mattered, or changed what the three Fates did.

She couldn't explain that to Paris. Or rather, she could explain but he would never understand. City folk didn't, men most of all. They were too set in their rigid ways, the patterns of thought that solidified as they grew until they might as well have been cut in stone. They built a city and called it permanent, forgetting the lesson learned by the men and women who lived amidst the wild; nothing is permanent. Everything changes.

Even the mightiest fall.

She wanted suddenly to be back among her people in the deep forest, where axes had never thudded into wood. There was peace there, the calmness of thousands of uninterrupted years. Sometimes at night she would float in her stream and listen to the singing of the dryads, gentle spirits dancing in their glades in the darkness. They would startle if she came close, so she just lay and listened, and watched the stars wheel above her.

She'd never found that sort of peace with Paris. He was too hot a man for that, too caught up in his own emotions and whims. Oenone knew she wouldn't hold his heart for long. She didn't need the gift of prophecy to foretell that.

But he was mortal, and would age and die while the dryads still sang, and Oenone still dwelt in her pools and streams. *Long,* for him, was a mere instant for her. He was here now though, and she reached up to cup his face in her hands and kiss him again, then stroke the inside of his thigh with her toes. He reacted as he always did, all that fire and passion rising up in him, and shortly after Oenone was swept away and she didn't think about endings anymore.

*

The king's palace stood at one side of the Pergamos, the great citadel at the northern end of Troy. On three sides the roof of the lower stories formed balconies outside windows on the upper floors. On summer evenings it was possible to sit and drink wine while looking over the Bay of Troy, or westward over the plain teeming with horses. Usually Priam sat to the south, above the city itself, letting the palace shelter him from the wind.

This evening not even that was possible. The *Meltemi* had been blowing hard for nearly a week, and his bones were too old to enjoy sitting in that chill wind. Servants had closed the light summer shutters and set lamps around the room. A brazier sat in front of the fireplace, occasionally grumbling to itself as the wood within crackled as it burned.

Hecuba had gone to her own quarters, with her own servants. Probably she was planning Hector's wedding. It would be soon, Priam knew: a chariot had already been sent to inform Eetion that the prince of Troy was home, and his bride was now expected. Marriages, and so alliances, were the domain of the queen: those, and the sanctuaries. Priam had always been content to leave them to his wife, while he busied himself with trade, and when necessary with war.

"Tell me," he said. "What should we be wary of, now we know Andromache is to be your wife?"

Ucalegon steepled his fingers and said nothing. He was a good advisor, the kind who knew when to speak and when to shout, and most of all when to stay silent. A rare gift, that. By the wine tray Hector poured himself a quarter cup, watered it heavily, and then came back to his chair before he spoke.

"Not the Dardanians," he sat at length. "Marrying Creusa to Aeneas was a clever move. As well as making them both happy."

"Obvious," Priam said.

Hector nodded. "Not the Lydians either, since Mother came from there. The only difficulty I can see would be the Trojans from outside the city."

"I agree," Priam said. "Your solution?"

Hector shrugged. "Leave it to Mother. This is her affair."

"And if Andromache proves less adept at dealing with those affairs than your mother is?" Priam asked. "You must know it for yourself, son, so you can teach her. Or teach another wife, if Andromache should die. You may have to do this when both the queen and I have gone to the next world. So bend your mind to the task. What is your solution?"

Hector nodded again. He'd had time to bathe now, and had changed his armour for a plain shirt and equally simple kilt and boots. The fading yellow of bruises showed below the cuffs and hem, marks of a hard campaign in the east, but if he was weary it didn't show. The young were resilient. The young and very strong could deal with almost anything, and Hector was very strong. Sometimes he almost seemed made of stone.

"In this case, the solution is for me to go see Pandarus," Hector said. "I can go tomorrow, spend a day with him and still be back in Troy before Andromache can set out from Thebe-under-Plakos. He's no fool, and he trusts me – as I do him. But this is going to be a problem soon, Father. A lot of Trojans live outside the city now. Keeping them content is harder every year."

"You expect trouble?"

"Perhaps not in the way you mean," Hector said slowly. He sipped from his cup. "I can't see an uprising, if that's what you ask. But Zeleia has two thousand citizens now, and Pandarus is something close to a king in his own right there, just as much as Eetion is in Thebe. Leris and Mela are thriving. Even on the edges of the plain of Troy towns grow every year; I remember when Bunarbi was a tiny fishing port. Now five hundred souls live there."

"What would you do about it?"

"I have no idea," Hector said frankly. "It's a new situation, one we haven't faced before. Troy has always been one city and a few settlements scattered around it. Now there are Trojans from the Hellespont to Mount Ida, and as far east as the Granicus. They're loyal to the city, but in fifty years they might not be. Do you have a suggestion?"

Ucalegon leaned forward slightly. "I suggested that royal cousins be placed in the towns as children. When they grow they would be governors, in the name of the king of Troy."

"That could work," Hector said, after a moment. "As long as they're clever enough to govern well, and while the supply of royal cousins holds out."

Priam smiled. "Make sure you and Andromache have many children. It seems you'll need them."

Hector returned the smile, but didn't answer. He never talked about the women he'd known, or in this case that he would know. Unlike Paris, who couldn't seem to touch a woman without boasting about it the next day. It was hard to stay angry with Paris for long, though; even the women rarely managed it. He would give a self-deprecating smile, and the old laughter would glimmer in his eyes, and suddenly it was impossible not to forgive him.

"There is word from the west," Ucalegon said.

Hector looked up. "My aunt?"

"No good news on that score. Telamon still refuses to let her leave." Priam's brows had drawn down. "I sent Antenor back to Greece a month ago, to speak with the kings one by one, in their own halls. It might be possible to cultivate some support that way. Though I hold out little hope."

"She has been there twenty years," Hector said. His deep voice had become rough with anger. "Half her life. We treat our horses better than that brute Telamon treats her."

"I agree," Priam said. "Which is why, if he fails to gain support, Antenor is to inform the High King that duties on

Argive goods using the Trojan Road are to be raised by half. More than that for olive oil and wine."

"Good," Hector said. "If they won't behave like civilised men, we shouldn't treat them as such."

"And if the taxes bring no response?" Ucalegon asked over his steepled fingers. "If the Greeks are enraged, rather than chastened?"

"Then we've lost nothing," Hector shrugged.

Priam was looking at the councillor closely. "What is it you fear, my friend? Will they attack us?"

"They might," Ucalegon allowed. "An Argive fleet could burn Bunarbi, or Leris in the south. That would hurt us as much as raised taxes hurts them. Nobody wins in such a dispute." He folded his hands and sighed. "Oh, never mind me. I'm just trying to think of all the possibilities."

"They would be fools to attack Troy," Hector said. "One sight of our walls and half the soldiers would flee back to their ships and row for home as hard as they could. We are not an easy fruit to pluck."

"We would also have Hittite support," Priam said. "Your new stature with Urhi-Tešub will stand us in good stead, if the Argives are stupid enough to challenge us over this."

"Paris," Ucalegon said, choosing his words with obvious care, "believes we should consider a raid on Salamis, if the taxes fail. So does Antenor."

Hector wasn't likely to pay much attention to anything Paris said, of course. The eldest brother had little except contempt for the youngest. The smiles and mischievous eyes that charmed so many women worked no spell on Hector. But he'd listen to Antenor's ideas, which was undoubtedly why Ucalegon had added that name too. It was a shame that Antenor was the same age as Priam, and wouldn't be there to offer advice to Hector when he became king: not for long, anyway. Most of that burden would fall on Ucalegon, who was a decade younger.

Priam hoped he could find a way to bring Aeneas to the city more often. The young king of Dardanos was cleverer by far than Ucalegon, or Pandarus in Zeleia; as wily in fact as Antenor himself. If Priam had realised that a little earlier he would have made it a condition of Aeneas' marriage to Creusa that they spend each summer in Troy. But he hadn't, and now Aeneas didn't want to leave his little city on the Hellespont, so another way would have to be found. He and Hector had been friends since childhood. There must be something that would persuade Aeneas to come. Priam made a mental note to speak with Hecuba about it. Perhaps the priests she dealt with would have an idea.

"A raid in Greece would be a last resort," Hector said now. "It could be done, from a simple military standpoint. Especially now we have Phereclus here from Colchis, to build us ships to match those of the Euxine Sea. I could lead it myself easily enough."

"No," Priam said. "Bad enough that you must fight for Hattusa when our liege lords call. I will not send you to raid the Greek coast as well."

"Aeneas, then," Hector said. "Or Pandarus, for that matter. But only if all else fails. Taxes might not inflame the Argives to war, but an attack on their homeland will."

"Telamon is old," Ucalegon pointed out. He'd formed his fingers into a pyramid again. "Old and fat. He cares for nothing but wine and spilling his seed in whores. A raid on Salamis will enrage him, but it need not spur him to action. We don't have to worry about him."

"We don't have to worry about this matter at all, for the moment," Priam said. "It's a suggestion only, one I'd like my son to think on before Antenor returns from Greece."

He wondered, actually, whether it might be wisest to accept the loss of Hesione and move on. The gods knew, Argives had taken women from foreign lands before. To them it was nothing out of the ordinary. Andromeda from Joppa, Ariadne from Crete, Medea from Colchis: even their father-god Zeus had taken one, turning himself into a great bull to seize Europa from Lydia and carry her away to be ravished. There was hardly a city in the world that had not lost a queen or priestess to the raiding Greeks.

But it was different when it was your own sister. Priam heard those other names as only that, words without faces to go with them, no stories and characters at all. No tug at his heart. He'd known Hesione though, had grown up with her in this very palace. When she was very small he used to bring her flowers from the meadows, and she'd accept them with grave solemnity, as though he was a suitor declaring his love. She was gentle, a compassionate soul, and his own spirit bled to think of her caged by a tyrant far from her home.

But Hector barely remembered her, and to his children she would be just a name like all the others, words without faces to go with them. Hardly something for Troy and the Greeks to argue over.

He would talk to Laocoon, he decided. The Seer gave good advice, although usually Priam had to sacrifice a ram or spend the night making offerings at Athena's temple before he heard it. Still, the guidance of the gods could be a good thing, as long as it didn't go too far. Troy was Priam's to rule. He would not give that up even to a goddess.

He sipped his wine, almost as heavily watered as Hector's, and wished his bones didn't feel so cold. Outside the *Meltemi* went on blowing, its voice like children crying in the dark.

Chapter Four

A Bit Less Green

"Where do you want to go?" Isander asked. He was almost dancing and didn't care. "Gorka?"

"Anywhere," the farmer's son replied. He blinked a little as they emerged from the shade of the barracks and stepped into open sunlight. "As long as there's drink later, I don't mind."

"We'll make a soldier of you yet," the third man said, clapping him on the shoulder. He looked almost indecently relaxed, though a gleam of excitement shone in his eyes. "Look for the wine and women first, and then the food. I think you'll do all right, farmboy."

Isander was a little in awe of Nikos, if truth were told. Gorka had grown up on a farm in the north, and Isander himself in an eastern village so small even its neighbours had forgotten it. But Nikos was a city boy, raised right here in Olympia where the king lived, almost in the shadow of the sanctuary where the great Temples stood. He didn't gawk as his two friends did when they walked past a minor backstreet market, or choke over food lightly dusted with spices he hadn't tasted before. There was always something for Isander to wonder at here, but Nikos had seen it all before.

Still, Isander couldn't help laughing at the other youth's worldliness. "Leave the wine and women until later. We can do *anything!*"

"I know," Nikos said. He was pretending to sound wearied but his smile gave him away. "I was there when the captain told us, remember."

If Isander was a little awed by Nikos, he found Socus almost overwhelming. The commander of the king's soldiers was a bluff, seasoned man, capable to his bones and impatient with foolishness. He'd fought in battles across half of Greece, mostly against bandits or on the borders against barbarians, but once or twice against rival countries. The High King forbade that, but everyone knew it still went on, if only on a small scale. Socus had fought in border clashes against both Messenia and Arcadia, and once had crossed the Gulf of

Corinth on a cattle raid in accursed Locris to the north. They were the sort of actions a king could deny, blaming outlaws and pirates instead, even if he'd taken part in the attack himself with a cloth wrapped around his face. Barracks rumours claimed Thalpius had done exactly that, though no one had seen him close enough to be sure.

Socus they *had* seen, usually in the thick of the fight, and he'd come out with nothing more than minor scars and a reputation for competence.

"I wish I'd been there," Isander had said, soon after he came to the city. "When you fought the Locrians, I mean. I hate them."

"How many have you met?" Socus asked.

"I never met one, but –"

The blow caught him on the side of the head, knocking him to the ground before he even saw it coming. Isander had landed jarringly on his hip and stared up at the captain in shock.

"You hate people you've never seen?" Socus had said dryly. "Don't waste my time with your stupidity, boy. Twelve laps of the yard. And remember, the Locrians are just like us, except," he turned away, "perhaps with a little more sense. Now get your feet moving."

Isander had never spoken before he thought since. Not in front of the captain, anyway. In front of his friends didn't count. Especially on a free day; the king was getting married today, and the recruits could do as they chose.

"So where shall we go?" he asked again.

*

In the end they went to the *temenos,* the sanctuary, to walk around the shrines and see the great Temple of Zeus, as large as most of Isander's village back home. He had to crane his head back until it creaked before he could see the tops of the pillars. Temples weren't really his idea of fun, but he supposed he ought to behave with a bit more maturity, now he was almost fully trained. It wasn't like he was a boy anymore.

Still, it *was* his first free day since he'd come to the city, and the recruits had all been given two silvers to spend as they chose. It wasn't every day that a king got married, after all. So the three of them went to the Theatre for half an hour, but the play was boring, some rubbish about a man talking to his dead father, not realising that it was only a ghost. That might be fine for sophisticated city folk, but it was deathly dull to a village youth, or to a farmer's boy. Nikos said he was enjoying it and wanted to stay, but it didn't take much persuading before he followed the other two outside.

At the market Gorka bought an amber pendant for his girl back home, ignoring Nikos' comment that she'd have forgotten him long before he could hand it to her. Even Isander thought the necklace looked cheap, but he held his tongue; Nikos' teasing was enough without him chipping in as well. After that they listened to a small band in the gymnasion, which had been given over to performers for the festival; there was only a drummer, a flautist and a man playing the pipes, the *auloi,* which Isander knew were fiendishly hard to learn.

And all of them bought little terracotta figures an inch high, to be inscribed with prayers or curses and thrown on the soil of a fresh grave when the time came. Soldiers were a superstitious bunch. They always wanted a curse figure handy for when they needed it.

They went to the *heroon* then, the shrine to the hero Pelops. Long ago Olympia had been oppressed by Harpies, flying women who ate only raw human meat. They swooped down and carried off whoever they chose, children usually, and consumed them on mountain eyries where men couldn't go. Pelops, king at the time, begged Zeus for help, and the Lord of the Black Cloud told him where he could find a pair of pegasi, winged horses. They were dangerous beasts, unwilling to be yoked, but Pelops mastered them and harnessed them to his chariot, after which he took to the skies and shot the Harpies down one by one, so saving the city.

Pelops was the icon of the warrior ideal, in Elis. Every young soldier dreamed of matching his exploits, his *Kleos*; the glory and fame won in battle. Why else be a fighting man at all, if not to aspire to that? But it was hard to stay long in the shrine, feeling as though Pelops might be watching from the other side of death. The three youths poured a libation of wine over the altar, bowed, and went back into the sunshine.

As evening drew on they ate rabbit with garlic off long skewers, and honey pancakes with sesame seeds. It was natural, after that, for them to find a tavern and order some wine. They ended up in a trader's den outside the walls, not far from the river Kladeos and the long line of masts strung out along the near bank. It was full of labourers and sailors, nearly all of them so drunk they could hardly stand, and in some cases had already collapsed on the rush floor. A pair of burly men were busy hauling them outside, where they threw them down by the back wall and abandoned them to the caprice of the Fates.

Nikos had been here before, it transpired. He wriggled through the crush of bodies until he reached the bar, shared a murmured conversation with a flat-nosed man there, and handed over something that glinted in the smoky lamplight. Shortly afterwards the three young men were allowed through a heavy door into the rear room of the inn, which while busy wasn't as hideously packed as the front room, or as raucous. They found a rickety table in one corner and sat down.

"Wine for three, I think," Nikos said. He stretched out his legs under the table. "And one of you is paying."

Gorka did, bringing three cups and a pottery jug back from the bar. They were all wearing plain chitons, but citizens tended to walk small around soldiers, even half-trained ones. Isander had noticed that before. Perhaps they gave off an aura that others could sense, if not precisely see. At any rate, nobody barged Gorka or tried to filch the wine as he wound his way back, and moment later the three friends clinked cups together.

"To king Thalpius," Nikos said. "May he have long life, many children, and find honour in death."

"And be happy at night with his wife," Isander added, which made Gorka grin and Nikos laugh so hard he had to take a gulp of wine before he spilled it. A couple of men looked around, and seeing nothing of interest went back to their drinks. Isander could hear a lyre playing somewhere in the room, but between the square pillars and the crowd he couldn't see where.

"Who are those?" he asked, pointing with his chin.

Nikos turned his head to look. "Those are the reed girls, my country friend. Don't you have them in mud country?"

"We have them," he said, feeling his face redden, "but I don't remember them looking like that."

That was a pair of women, one of them red-haired, in chitons they had surely not bought from any normal tailor. Isander had never seen a hem cut so high, or a neckline slashed so low. It left a lot of flesh on show. He flushed further just thinking about that. A third girl came into view as he watched, leading a man by the hand towards a small door set in the far wall, hazy with smoke from the nearby fire.

"The tavern keepers sometimes let them use rooms over the bar, and look for custom inside," Nikos said. "Especially close to the docks. It brings the customers in. The girls get to work in the warm, and they each have a room – a cubby, really – where they can sleep."

Isander nodded, and took a sip from his cup to conceal the fact that he was looking at the red-headed woman again. It wasn't a common shade among Greeks. Certainly not in flyspeck villages far from the capital, too small to have a name or for it to be remembered, even if they had. *We have reed girls,* he'd told Nikos, but that wasn't really true. They'd had one woman of pleasure, who took her favours from settlement to settlement but never went into any of them for fear she'd be attacked. The men went to her outside, in a barn perhaps, or whatever other building was available. Isander had never worked out how they knew she was there. Nobody ever seemed to speak of her, they just knew, and slipped away unnoticed when they had the chance.

He found his gaze drawn back to the redhead again.

"Put your eyes back in," Nikos grinned, "before someone treads on them."

Isander buried his face in his wine cup to hide his blushes. He knew the other youth was only teasing, but it was still embarrassing, even with Gorka the only other person to hear. Gorka was like a stone, he might hear things but he never spoke of them. He smiled a little at Nikos' jest though, and Isander sought for a change of subject.

"So you think we'll be sent out to fight before winter?" he asked. "The recruits, I mean. Not just us."

Nikos shrugged. "Some of us might be. Those who are furthest along, and aren't likely to put other men in danger through their own inexperience. Which means about one in five of us, I expect."

"Are we that bad?"

Gorka leaned forward slightly, always a sign that he was about to speak. If the others went on talking he would just lean back again, and keep his silence, but they knew him and waited for his words. "I practiced with one of the Guards two days ago. I managed to last about five heartbeats against him. Once. The rest of the time I did even worse."

That quieted them. Gorka was the biggest of them and probably the furthest along as well; it was sobering to think they might be so far behind the more seasoned men. They were learning fast, though. Isander couldn't believe how much stronger he was now, after only two months of training. Life at home hadn't been easy, with firewood to cut and chores to do, but in the few weeks in Olympia his body had strained and grown hard.

That brought another topic to mind. "Are either of you going to enter the Games next year?"

Gorka was a good wrestler – more than good – but he only smiled and shook his head. As for Nikos, his grin nearly split his face. "Not me. I'm a good archer, but there will be better at the Games, and a lot of them. Why? Are you thinking of putting your name in?"

"Maybe," he admitted, embarrassed again. The Games came every two years, and he thought he was too young and green to stand any chance at all, even in the lightweight wrestling. But the experience would stand him in good stead in two years' time, or four, when he might actually have a chance at a wreath. It was something to aim for, anyway. In training he was decent with both spear and sword now, and with the shoving motion that drove his shield into an enemy's face and knocked him backwards, but he was outstanding in hand to hand combat. He could throw men much heavier than he was with ease.

"Patience," Nikos said. He poured them each another cup of wine. "Just wait, my friend. The Games are always there, every two years. You've no need to rush. Wait until you're a bit less green before you set yourself against the finest wrestlers in Greece."

There was sense in that advice. Nikos usually did speak sense, in fairness: he was much the wisest of the three. *The least green,* Isander thought wryly to himself. But sometimes he didn't want to wait until he was older. He wanted to be out doing things *now,* when he was hardly more than a stripling. Hadn't Theseus gone to find his father when he was younger than Isander was now, and slain Sciron the Outlaw, and then wrestled Cercyon to his death? Isander especially liked that latter tale. And had not Perseus defended his mother from unwanted suitors when he was barely an adult at all?

Isander didn't speak those things aloud, even to his friends. Socus would laugh himself into spasms if he heard them: Gorka and Nikos, though they were close, wouldn't be able to stifle their guffaws either. Better to keep some things quiet. But still, sometimes now was better than later. His eyes slid towards the red-haired woman again.

He couldn't see her at first, and assumed she must have taken a man upstairs while Isander was hiding his face in the wine cup. Five men were dicing behind where she'd been standing, every toss of the cup greeted with shouts of delight or groans, according to how the pips fell. Isander knew enough not to be tempted by that, at least. On his second night in barracks he'd seen one of the recruits lose every coin he owned to older soldiers, and while Isander couldn't prove it he was sure the men had cheated, somehow. Luck just wasn't as consistent as they made it seem.

Inexperienced youths new to the city were easy prey. He'd understood that, and kept himself wary. The red-haired woman came into view from behind one of the stacked pillars, chiton riding on the curves of her hips.

He drank down the wine in his cup at a gulp, making Nikos raise his eyebrows in surprise. "Are you expecting a drought?"

Isander didn't answer. He pushed back his stool, and standing he went over to the woman with red hair. He felt as though every eye in the tavern was on him, and laughter bubbled behind every lip, but he didn't stop. Without the wine he might have slunk away, his nerve failing him at the last moment. With it had the nerve to approach the woman, and not flee even when she sensed his approach and turned to him.

"I'm Isander," he said. His voice sounded strangled, the words hardly recognisable. "Could you – I mean, would you mind…"

He tailed off, wilting under the amusement in her green eyes. But she smiled, and taking his hand she folded it in hers. "Aren't you just the prettiest young man I've seen today? And a soldier, by the look of you." She leaned in, so he could smell the musky perfume she wore, and whispered in a voice that curled his toes, "And I *do* like soldiers."

"Enough to come upstairs?" he asked.

She ran a single finger down the line of his spine, making him shiver helplessly. "You have the coin? Four coppers and I'm yours."

"I have it," he said, and showed her. She didn't take them straight away, an Isander had expected. Instead she leaned in and kissed him, quite thoroughly, while his two friends hooted encouragement from their table (which he really could have done without) and several other men whistled good-naturedly. When she drew back Isander felt giddy. He swallowed and still felt strange.

"I'm Meliza," she told him. "Come upstairs, then. I'll show you all the faces of the gods."

He thought later that she must have known then it was his first time. But she didn't say anything, blessedly, in that room full of tough drinking men. She took his hands and led him to the little door, walking sure-footedly backwards between the tables, and kissed him again at the bottom of the stairs beyond them. When they parted Meliza led him up the rickety steps and into a windowless room, furnished only with a narrow pallet with a sheet thrown over it. Isander closed the door, his heart beating wildly as Meliza bent to light a lamp, her chiton riding up as she did so. Isander gulped and hoped she wouldn't notice.

She turned then, and gave a slow smile that nearly stopped the hammering of his heart completely.

Chapter Five

The Weaving Streets

The road ran thirty feet above the rushing Scamander, here where the gorge was narrow and steep. In spring snowmelt on Mount Ida swelled the stream into a torrent of foam, washing down branches and stones that rattled together amidst the flow. Periso listened to that muted roar sometimes as he drifted into sleep. Now the river was quieter, but channels of froth still linked the pools that gathered above boulders left from the last flood.

There had been naiads here, before the town was built. Perhaps hundreds of them: when Tros and Ilos founded Troy, the gorge must have rung with the songs of nymphs at play. They were gone now... probably. Periso thought he'd seen one once, though as he turned his head all he'd really caught was a glimpse of long hair and startled eyes, and then a splash as she vanished into the water.

He turned to look up the side of the cleft, to where Zeleia squatted like a wolf looking down on a pasture. From this low down all he could see was the wooden walls, and a guard tower poking over the top. At the foot of the wall cliffs dropped away on three sides. Zeleia was noisy with the rush of water in spring, but it was out of the north wind, and it would be very hard to capture. If anyone was fool enough to try.

"They're late," Hyrca said.

Periso shrugged. "So the road was bad. They'll be here."

"We'll be in trouble if she goes missing."

"Not if she vanishes before she was handed to us," Periso replied. "Stop fretting. You're making me nervous."

He wasn't though, not really. The days when bandits infested the slopes of Ida were gone now. Troy had sent soldiers to clear them out years ago, back when Zeleia was first growing into a sizable town and its new wealth needed to be made safe. Later fighting men had been stationed there permanently, and in the way of things had married and had children, swelling the town further. Periso' father had been such a man.

Now, any report of outlaws was met with a punitive raid within a day or two. The last had been more than five years ago, as far as Periso could remember. Pandarus had led the soldiers who killed half of them and captured the rest, to be brought back to Zeleia and spat upon and reviled. Then he'd had them thrown from the cliff into the gorge. One of them had somehow survived the plunge, and cried for mercy until someone went down and knifed him in the morning.

Of course, the activity that disposed of bandits had also driven away the naiads. There was a price to be paid for progress, Periso supposed. Sometimes it wasn't you who paid. But he would have liked to hear the naiads sing, just once, as light grew back into the day.

Periso checked the straps of his cuirass, then his boots. For the tenth time, at least. Hyrca watched him ironically.

"Stop it," the other man said. "You're making me nervous."

"Very droll," Periso answered.

"If a driver is nervous his horses will sense it," Hyrca said, parroting one of the first things a charioteer learned.

"They'll sense it if I punch you on the nose, too."

"Oh, very friendly," Hyrca responded. "And you're marrying my sister next week, too. Shall I tell her what a brute you are?"

"Althea already knows," Periso said. "She relies on it so I can keep you from bursting in on us for supper every night."

Hyrca grinned, not in the least put out. "Don't worry about that. I know the taste of her cooking too well to risk it."

Periso couldn't help laughing. Althea was a decent cook in fact, perhaps not great but good enough for the wife of a soldier, a man used to eating half-cooked grain and mostly raw meat. And she was pretty enough, and made him feel content when she was there. What else could a man ask for?

Unless he was a prince, who could expect a beauty from far away to be laid at his feet like a prize. It would be easy to resent that, if the prince was anyone except Hector. Periso had only met him once but Hector had known him, remembering his name from the tale of a raid against Thracian rebels in the north. When Hector gripped his forearm and praised his courage, Periso had decided he'd run through Hades itself with Hector there to lead him.

"There," Hyrca said.

Turning, Periso was just in time to see a chariot and wagon on the road further up the valley. He had only a glimpse before they vanished behind a spur, following the road around, but it must be the party he and Hyrca were waiting for. He went to his own chariot and team, taking the time to stroke his three horses and talk to them in a soft voice, easing their hearts. Horses were strong and tough, but their hearts could be fragile. All three nosed at his hand in the hope of treats, but he'd save that for later. Better to feed a horse after the ride than before.

The wagon and its escort came into view again, half a mile up the valley. The sound of the river hid any creak of wheels, so the vehicles seemed to approach in silence until they were almost on top of the waiting men. There were two people sitting in the open-topped wagon, he saw now, both of them women. The one on the right was clad in a plain green dress, with her hair gathered under a soft cap.

The other must be Andromache.

A beauty from far away, Periso thought as the wagon drew to a halt beside him. Thebe-under-Plakos wasn't the far side of the world, but he'd only been further from home once in his life, when he went on that raid in Thrace. As for beauty, Andromache certainly had that. She was tall even sitting down, with smooth skin and green eyes, and bright beads sewn into her jet-black hair. The other woman must be her servant, Periso decided. He went up to the side of the wagon and bowed, not the full obeisance he'd give the king or queen, or even Hector, but a gesture of respect nonetheless.

"My lady Andromache," he said. "I am Periso. It's my honour to lead you to Troy."

"The honour is mine," she said. He blinked, surprised by the graciousness of her reply. Her voice was low and soft. "I'm sure the journey will be pleasant. Will we reach the city today?"

"With the gods' blessing, I believe we will," he said.

The other charioteer had drawn over to the side of the packed-earth road, putting one wheel on the jumble of twigs and small stones that lined the verge. He stepped down as Hyrca went to speak with him. Periso tried to eavesdrop but the water rushing below drowned their words.

"The road is clear?" Andromache asked.

Periso nodded. "Chariots have been running it for three days, my lady, all the way to Troy. Any obstructions have been moved, and any holes filled in. We'll be in Troy by sundown, never fear."

"I would like," she said, "to enter the city standing in a chariot, not seated in a wagon. As a future queen should."

"I wasn't told about that," Periso said. His mouth was suddenly dry. He could imagine how Hecuba, who *was* the queen, would feel about this idea. "Have you ridden a chariot before, my lady?"

"Once or twice," she said, with a smile. "I leave it in your hands, warrior. If my promised husband trusts you to bring me to him, then I shall trust you too. Do as you think best."

"Thank you," he said. As he climbed into his chariot he realised what she had done, with those few simple words: he was going to let her ride into the city as she wanted to. She trusted him. How could a man not give his queen-to-be what she desired, after that?

Troy, he thought, was going to have a good king and queen, when Priam's time came to an end. He prayed to all the gods that Hector wouldn't be angry with him for letting his bride ride in a chariot. He didn't want the prince of Troy to be angry with him, now or ever.

The road led down the gorge, keeping always high above the water. Periso drove ahead of the wagon and Hyrca behind, both men keeping their spears tucked into the side of the car where they could quickly be reached. But there was no need, no hint of trouble as they drove. Periso kept his eyes open anyway. He was not about to lose the lady Andromache before she even reached her new home.

He could see where the spring floods had reached, a line in the gorge below which vegetation and much of the soil had been swept away to expose bare stone. The steep slopes were dotted with poised pools, water clear as the moment it fell from the sky. Streams ran from them to join the Scamander below, some falling the last few feet in sprays as fine as mist.

Periso knew how cold that water was; he'd bathed in it often enough. Water from the mountain springs fizzed on your tongue, all the bubbles of air bursting in your mouth. By the time the river reached the plain it was slow and lazy, full of silt, all the energy sucked out of it by its long descent through the hills. He liked the plain, not least because it was full of horses, but he liked the mountain better. Pandarus said that though Troy was their father, no child wanted to live forever under his father's roof.

After two miles the valley began to widen out, quite abruptly. The walls drew aside and the river between them changed, its plunges and pools replaced by a more sedate flow. It was still strong though: the current here could pull cattle off their feet, even at low water in the summer. Instead of cliffs there were now sloping pastures, dotted with sheep. Periso had spent long hours in those fields as a youth, watching the flocks with a sling at his belt and a spear in one hand. Every boy did, especially if he wanted to be a warrior. If you lacked the courage to confront a hungry wolf at twilight you didn't have the guts to be a fighting man, and you might as well go back to the town and find work as a carpenter, or a miller. Something where the worst danger was a shrewish wife.

Then the valley drew tight again, closing on the river like a noose around a neck. The road climbed a ridge and ran out between two opposing faces of rock, the river gushing again far below. And spread out before them was the Plain of Troy, with the sea shining away to north and west, and the city itself perched on its ridge five miles across the prairie.

Periso reined in, clicked his tongue to tell the horses to wait, and stepped down from the car. He walked back to the wagon and bowed to Andromache again. "I thought you might wish to see Troy, my lady."

She stood, and without waiting for his help she climbed down from the back of the wagon, careful to hold her dress so the hem wouldn't drag in the mud. She went to the side of the road and stood there, gazing out over the land before her. Periso hadn't expected her to do that. He thought it was all right though, so when Hyrca jumped down from his own chariot Periso waved him back.

The wind blew at them, sharp with hints of northern mountain snow, but the sun over Troy gleamed off turrets and walls.

"I'd heard the stories," Andromache said at length, "but they don't do justice to the sight. That men can build such towers astounds me."

"Up close they're even better," Periso said. "And that's where I must take you, my lady. If you will?"

She turned a smile on him. "Does this mean you will carry me in your chariot, master Periso?"

"Not quite yet," he said. "Let's get down to the plain first, past the bumpier part of the road. Hector would hang me from the wall by my ankles if I brought him a bride bruised by the rattle of a chariot."

"But then?"

"Then I think it will be all right," he said. He couldn't help but share her smile. "If you'll keep your husband from skinning me, at least."

She laughed, genuinely amused he thought. "I will, I promise. Thank you. This matters to me."

"Then it matters to me too," he said.

She smiled at him again and went back to the wagon, still holding her skirts out of the mud. Her maid helped her climb up: Periso hadn't heard her name, he realised, but he didn't mind that. He swung back into his chariot and clicked his tongue, and the horses began to move again.

*

There was some sort of uproar building up outside. Mursili hesitated, but there was no reason for him to keep on wasting time in the building he'd been given to use as a smithy. He went to the door, noting glumly how high the lintel was above his head, and headed out into the tangle of curving streets.

Trojan homes were oval, one family living in each half of the building. They entered through doorways on the upper floors, reached by ladders or stone steps cut into the walls. Often walkways ran from roof to roof, providing easy access without need to descend. Up there Mursili thought it must be easy to find your way around the city: Troy was not nearly so big or complex as Hattusa. It should be difficult to get lost here.

But at street level it was easy. The streets were narrow and wove to left and right as they swerved around the oval houses, so there was almost never a line of sight beyond the next wall. The city stood on flat ground as well, which meant there was no gradient to act as a guide. Mursili had managed to lose his way twice this morning as he tried to find the building given to him near the city wall, and had finally done so only by reaching that wall and following it halfway around the city.

He thought he'd hit on a way to navigate, though. The houses were painted in a variety of scenes, some natural and others not, executed often by deft artisans but sometimes by ham-handed amateurs. Almost every building sported some kind of decoration. If he could memorise those, he might be able to find his way back after he saw what the disturbance was.

He walked slowly, letting the citizens flood past him as they hurried towards the main road through the middle of the city. That was straight, at least, and wide enough for laden wagons to pass besides. He couldn't see it though, and didn't try, instead concentrating on the murals. *Antelopes by a stream on the left, then chariots racing on my right.*

The chariots each had three horses. That seemed an indulgence almost beyond imagining to Mursili. Even the ceremonial chariot of the great King in Hattusa only had two. Quality horseflesh was so rare that the King imposed his personal control on the movement of stallions, and set prices as well, a level of control only matched in the silk and gold markets. Horses were bought for the royal family from Scythia, sometimes even from beyond Assyria when relations with that sprawling empire were in one of their easier phases. But the best horses of all came from Troy, from the lush plain spread out below and around the city walls. The King would pay almost any price for new-tamed *tarpans* which had cropped that grass; he'd pay twice over to stop such animals going to Egypt, or Assyria, whose armies might use them against him.

Troy had grown rich through its horses. If there was one place in the world where three horses to a chariot was ordinary, taken for granted, it would be right here.

Two boys boxing on my right, then women performing what looks like a ritualised dance just beyond it... and Mursili came to the back of a crowd, packed thickly across the curved street. He could go no further, and he couldn't see what had the citizenry in such a froth of excitement, even if he stood on his tiptoes. He sighed and started to turn around, and a hand fell on his arm.

"Wait, my friend," the man at his elbow said. In *nešili,* the language of Mursili's own people. The stranger called up to someone on a rooftop, switching to the Trojan tongue Mursili couldn't understand at all. He'd spent most of this morning trying to explain to a thick-witted soldier why the forge building wasn't fit for purpose, reduced to gestures and scribbled pictures because neither of them spoke a word of the other's language.

"Up that ladder," the newcomer said, again in *nešili,* "and quick, or you'll miss her."

Caught off balance, Mursili didn't even think to ask who the man meant. He scrambled up the ladder and found himself on the flat roof of a house, along with perhaps a dozen other people all crowded along the edge, staring down at the wide street and chattering excitedly. Mursili could tell *that,* even if the words made no sense. Several of the Trojans looked him up and down, then turned to more interesting things. This really was a cosmopolitan city, where outlanders were common enough not to be remarkable. Mursili turned to the man who'd accosted him.

"Who are you?"

"I am Phereclus," the man said. "An outlander, like yourself. Oh look, here they come."

Mursili turned to see a pair of chariots advancing up the avenue, one behind the other. Each was driven by a soldier in a light cuirass, and each carried a woman as passenger. The one in the rear car looked like a servant to him. The one in the front was different.

She was wearing a dress with a tight bodice, quite high-cut, and a floor-length wrap skirt. White beads had been sewn into her raven hair. But it was the way she held herself that caught Mursili's attention, not the fineness of her attire. *She looks like a queen,* he thought, but this could not be Hecuba; the high lady of Troy was decades older than this woman. The crowd was going crazy, screaming and throwing seeds of wheat into the air. Mursili couldn't make out what they were chanting.

"Who is she?" he shouted to Phereclus.

"Andromache," the other man answered. "She's to be the bride of Hector."

That name he knew, of course.

The great King called on warriors from all his subject cities, when he had need. Which he did often these days, with the Assyrians probing persistently up from the heartland of their plain, and the Egyptians having rediscovered some of their ancient martial pride. Subject warriors were formed into ancillary companies, sometimes used to support the Hittite spears, otherwise sent ahead to soften an enemy before the main strike. If he was exceptionally good, a subject might be allowed to fight with the Golden Spears, the Hittite elites.

Hector was allowed to fight with the chariots. The best of the best, finest drivers and spearmen in the world. Mursili had never heard of any other outsider given that honour.

At Emar, the mighty battle last summer against the invading Assyrians, Hector had actually commanded one of the two chariot division. An outlander, captain of chariots! It was astonishing. But then Hector sometimes seemed more than just a man, more than mortal. Soldiers said that at Emar he killed twenty enemy spearmen just in the first charge, and splintered their left just when the battle had been turning the Assyrians' way.

When Mursili had been told he was going west, with Hector, he'd expected to find the man full of boasts and bluster, a fighting man who took pride only in warfare and his own skill. Hector had surprised him. The Trojan was a thoughtful, considerate man, easy to trust, and a good companion on the long journey west. Mursili liked him, and *that* was a thing he'd never expected to think of a royal, of any city.

So the beautiful woman in the chariot would be queen of Troy one day. She knew how to look like one already, that was for sure.

"I must get back," he said to the stranger. Phereclus, he remembered. "I have work to do."

"At the smithy?"

That stopped him, and he gave the man a frown. "How do you know that?"

"I followed you most of the way down from there," Phereclus said. "Ucalegon asked me to find you. He seemed to think you were having trouble making yourself understood."

"Ucalegon sent you?"

"He *asked* me," the other man repeated. "Hardly anyone in Troy speaks your language, you know. Hector does, and his brother Lycaon has a few words – not surprising, given that he's married to –"

"Eshan of Hattusa," Mursili broke in. "I remember when he came to the city for the wedding. A great honour for Troy."

"And for Hattusa too," Phereclus said, almost absently. "In my home we know both cities equally, as places of legend."

"Your home?"

"I'm from Colchis," Phereclus said.

Mursili knew that name too. *Surprise upon surprise,* he thought to himself. Colchis was a place of myth itself, a country where the rivers were laced with gold and precious stones washed up on the strands after a storm. A sheep's fleece hung in the water for a season would glitter with gold when it was drawn back out again. It would be a target for every greedy king in the world, except that the Colchian navy dominated the Euxine Sea and the land itself was ringed by high mountains. There was a tale, probably untrue, of a Greek adventurer who had stolen one of those fleeces, a generation ago or so.

More believable were the stories of armies which had vanished in Colchis, or been eaten by creatures which dwelt in the clouds which wreathed those peaks. One Hittite tale spoke of a hero who battled living trees and the spirits of forest glades, fought off mountain spirits, and came home with only a torn-off scrap of fleece to show for his efforts.

He looked at Phereclus, considering his words, and then gave a mental shrug and said, "You're a shipbuilder."

"That's right," Phereclus admitted cheerfully. "Though my pride leads me to insist that I'm a *master* shipbuilder. I wanted to see some of the fabled places of the world, king Priam wanted an expert shipbuilder, and so here I am." He spread his hands. "A common artisan far from my home, just like you."

"I am not," Mursili said stiffly, "a *common* artisan."

"Ah," Phereclus said. His smile faded. "I see. You really are just like me, and just as proud in your own work."

Mursili shrugged. "Work is all I have."

"We can find you something more, here in Troy."

He grimaced. "Your women are so tall it unnerves me."

"Tall, perhaps, but between the legs they're the same as any other women. Just a bit higher up."

Surprised, Mursili was laughing before he realised it. Phereclus had an ease about him that was reminiscent of Hector, though the two men were utterly different in every other way. Phereclus was balding and boasted a slight paunch, hardly the characteristics of a warrior lord. Still, Mursili thought he might be able to like him. It would be pleasant to have a friend in this new city.

"All right, then," Phereclus said presently. "What's got you so angry about your new smithy?"

Mursili drew a breath.

"The forge pit is on the far wall from the slack tub," he said. "How does that make sense? I need to be able to turn from the forge to cool metal *quickly,* at once, not waste seconds striding across the room. Then the work tables are less than two yards from the forge pit, and they're made of wood. Iron requires a great deal of heat and those tables will catch fire. The heat also needs to be vented, but there are no windows above the forge pit, none at all. The tool rack needs to be –"

"Stop!" Phereclus said, holding his hands up as though in surrender. "Enough, my new friend. I can see you know what you need. I'll arrange for you to talk with Ucalegon. Actually," he added, "I'd better be there too, since the Councillor doesn't speak *nešili.*"

"He can arrange for this to be done?"

"Yes. I'd rather deal with Antenor – that's the man to go to if you ever want something done, I swear the man never sleeps. But he's not in the city just now, and Ucalegon is a good enough sort. He did send me to see if I could help you out, after all."

"Thank you," Mursili said.

"And after that, I can start teaching you to speak Trojan," Phereclus said. "You'll pick it up in no time. Meanwhile I think I'll show you one or two of the more… intriguing parts of the city."

Mursili looked at him. "Intriguing?"

"We're back to talking about women again," Phereclus said. "But with these girls, trust me, height is not going to be a problem."

He didn't understand that at first, but then he caught Phereclus' wicked smile and rather thought he did. The smile came back to his lips again. He really did think he could like this man.

Chapter Six

A Shiver of Desire

The palace in Pylos was surprising.
Antenor had expected to find the hall of a warrior king. That was what the Argives were, after all: warriors and raiders, defining themselves by who they killed and what they stole. Their palaces were built like fortresses, with thick walls of heavy stone and cramped corridors, easy to defend. Shafts of light crept in through small, high windows, and only served to make the greyness around them all the gloomier.

Here it was different. The palace stood above most of the city, on a rising coastline above a west-facing bay. Afternoon sun blazed off the water and into the streets, and also through the wide, arched porticoes that formed the seaward side of the palace. They led to a series of small, cleverly placed courtyards, each with a cluster of buildings to house visiting guests, and all bathed in that brilliant sunlight. Beyond those was the palace proper, wide passageways and bright rooms, all of it painted.

If you knew what to look for, you could see where plaster covered the join between an old wall and a new, or where battlements had been reshaped into decorative balustrades. The designers had used as much of the old, martial fortress as they could, when they laid out these new halls. This palace showed that Messenia had money now, and a lot of it. The use of old walls showed they still had far less than Troy.

Antenor had expected Greek martial scenes and he saw enough of those. Men in crested helmets stabbing with spears, charioteers careering through a chaos of struggle: the usual sort of thing. Argives were not imaginative when it came to showing battle. It was the same few images repeated again and again, in hall after hall. The lords didn't want anything new, or daring, they just wanted the same, tired old repetition.

But that was on the old walls, where plaster hadn't been replaced at all. Not on the new ones.

The main entrance hall boasted a mural all down one side, done in the Egyptian style, all the colours bright but the black darker than evil's heart. Three people were being guided into the afterlife by a god with a jackal's head: Antenor thought that was Anubis, but he always mixed up the strange Egyptian gods, and he wasn't sure. One of the trio was a warrior in armour, another was a woman and the third looked like a labourer, which made the meaning plain. Everyone is equal in death. It was an unexpected message for an Argive warrior king to send.

Then there was plenty of Greek art. Athletes competing in their Games, and a Gorgon's head carved into the stone wall with the snakes of her hair writhing out as though to snatch at passers-by. A vase on a plinth was decorated with two men making pottery – an ironic touch, perhaps – while on a wall a painted maiden gave herself up into a lover's arms. Antenor began to feel he was on more familiar ground again.

And then one of the chambers was decorated with a Hittite pattern, circles made up of dozens of concentric rings in red, yellow and green. A line of lions walked around the edge, while near the middle crimson triangles pointed inward. The circles all overlapped, twisting the eye as it tried to follow them. It made Antenor a little queasy. Most Hittite art took the form of bas-relief or sculpture, and he wasn't sure they'd got the hang of painting.

The *megaron* itself had a mosaic floor, a style Antenor had heard of but never seen before. It was popular among some of the western peoples, the Etruscans and Samnites he thought. When he entered he was too low down to make out the design clearly, but he could see it was another pattern, swirling lines of bright colour set against brilliant white.

This was not an Argive warrior hall. It was more like palaces Antenor had visited in Asia, Halicarnassus or even Troy itself. He was more unsettled than he cared to admit, his expectations confounded even before he spoke a word. Antenor was an experienced diplomat and councillor though, and he was sure his manner gave nothing away when Nestor greeted him.

The king of Messenia was old now, somewhere past his mid-fifties according to Trojan agents, and he looked it. Half his hair was gone and the rest was grey, and liver spots decorated the backs of his hands. But his brown eyes were sharp, and his step was firm when he rose from his throne and came down the dais to greet Antenor. A courtesy, that: he was within his right to stay where he was and wait for his guest to bow.

"Antenor of Troy," Nestor said. "Come to discuss transit duties on the eastern roads, I'm told?"

"The matter requires constant attention," Antenor replied.

The king nodded. "Of course. Important matters so often do. Though I'm sure they will leave you ample time to mention the lady Hesione before you leave," an eyebrow rose ironically, "as you so often do."

It was unfair, really. In his younger days Nestor had been among the most admired warriors in Greece, an excellent spearman and the match of any charioteer in the land. Much like the young man behind him, in fact, who looked enough like Nestor that he just had to be his son. But that had only ever been a part of who Nestor was. He was clever, a rare thing among the viciously competing warrior kings of Greece. He thought things through, devised stratagems and twisty schemes no one saw through until it was too late. This light-drenched new palace was proof of how far that cleverness had taken him, and the country he ruled. Messenia could never have afforded it twenty years ago.

The man was both warrior and scholar, and he'd disarmed Antenor in a sentence, laced with a touch of wit.

"I'm sure of it too," Antenor said, trying not to let his discomfiture show. "But perhaps we might observe the formalities first?"

Nestor grinned, obviously amused by Antenor's effort to match his cleverness. He gestured for his visitor to seat himself beside the throne, and the court advisors and flunkies shuffled aside to make room for him.

It was evening before the two men were able to sit together, away from the business of kingship and diplomacy. They took a table on the westward-facing balcony, in the light of the sinking sun. Nestor waved the servant away and served the wine and figs himself.

"I'm amazed by your palace," Antenor said.

"Because it isn't a dreary castle?" Nestor chuckled. "When Diomedes of Argolis was here he kept asking me where I'd found the architects. I gave him a few names, actually. If our investments work out he'll have the money to make this palace look like a hovel."

"Investments?"

"You're fishing, my dear Trojan," Nestor said comfortably. "But it doesn't matter. Anyone in Pylos could tell you. Diomedes and I are putting some money into the western settlements, especially in Sicily. There's a town called Naxos which has hills just right for olives, but nobody has planted anything yet. We're going to ship some cuttings out there this summer."

"Long project," Antenor noted.

"Oh yes, I won't see it come to fruition. My son Thrasymedes will be the one to benefit from the income. And it might be more than just olives. Once the town starts to grow, it won't be long before business picks up. Once we start proper trading, they'll grow as rich as we do."

Antenor sipped his wine and didn't answer. In truth he was quite pleased to hear the Argives were looking west. It might mean fewer raids on the Asian coast, or that of Egypt to the south. There was something restless in the Greek spirit, some unquiet part of the soul that kept pushing them on to the horizon, and then beyond it again. He was happy to see that energy aimed away from Troy.

"If it was up to me," Nestor said quietly, looking out to sea, "I would return Hesione to Troy. I'd send her home in honour, with gifts of friendship. But we Greeks still value war above peace, glory above honour. Telamon will never release her while he lives."

Again Antenor didn't speak. Nestor seemed to be talking to himself as much as anything, so he kept quiet and let him speak.

"We're changing," the old man said. "We really are, Antenor. This palace is evidence of it, and there will be more. Diomedes thinks the same way I do, and so does Menestheus, in Athens. The days when Theseus ruled there like a typical bully-king are done.

"But we don't have the lineage of you easterners. Trojans, Maeonians are more sophisticated than we Greeks. You've have had centuries to learn how to live together, but most of my people still believe you deal with rivals by the sword, and only by the sword." Nestor sighed. "If this had happened in another generation, say in Thrasymedes' time, I think Hesione would be returned. If she'd ever have been taken at all."

"But she was," Antenor said. "And all this talk of change, while laudable, does not alleviate her predicament."

Nestor looked at him. "I can think of nothing that will. You and I understand each other, I think, and Troy and Messenia are better as friends than enemies. So take no offence when I say I will not set myself against Telamon in this. Not when there is nothing to gain, and certainly not while the High King and most of the lesser rulers support him."

"King Priam has instructed me to say that this issue is now linked, for him, with that of trade duties on the Trojan Road."

"I regret that," Nestor said. "I know why he says so, but I rue that it's come so far."

"The fault is not Troy's."

"Nor is it Messenia's," Nestor shot back, with a flash of the fire he'd had as a younger man. "We're both innocent parties in this, but we're not enemies, so don't behave as though we are."

Antenor sighed. "I apologise, my friend."

"Accepted," Nestor said immediately. "But Troy should be careful, Antenor. Here in Greece we say that if you join the dance circle, you have no choice but to dance. Once events spin out of control we sometimes find we can't control our steps anymore. I'm afraid that may be becoming the case here."

He ruminated for a moment, turning his wine cup in age-spotted hands. "Fate never sets the course of a thread before its time, they say. If we're to find an answer, we ought to talk to Odysseus."

"The king of Ithaca?" Antenor asked, taken by surprise. "I had the impression that was a backwater."

"Ithaca is hardly more than a pimple," Nestor agreed. "But Odysseus is much more than that. If you want winged words, my Trojan friend, then he's your man. Odysseus can persuade wolves to eat berries and leave the sheep alone. Don't ever bargain with him. He'll sell you a pig in a sack and you won't realise he made a fool of you until two years later."

Antenor eyed the old king thoughtfully. He hadn't heard that of Odysseus before: all the talk of the soft-spoken man was that he was a shepherd-king, little more than a peasant. It might be that Nestor was trying to distract Antenor with this suggestion. Delay him with a pointless journey west to Ithaca, while Nestor spoke to others and settled matters behind his back.

He didn't like to think so. Nestor was a friend, as far as any Argive king could be considered so. And if this clever man spoke so highly of the intelligence of Odysseus, his words were worth listening to. Antenor filed the comment away, to be considered later. Perhaps a way could be found to watch this Ithacan, see if reality matched the praise.

But it didn't matter for now. Priam and Antenor had planned this journey together, from Pylos to Sparta and Athens, and he wasn't about to change schedule on the strength of one suggestion.

*

Five days later, in Sparta, Menelaus was blunter.

"Telamon sees himself as the last of the heroes," the king said. "He adventured with Heracles, remember, and not just in Troy. They were raiders together for years. Telamon's whole life has been about pride in that. If he gave Hesione back he would seem weak in his own eyes."

Pride, Antenor thought to himself. All the Argives seemed to care about was pride. Nestor might claim they were changing, but if so it was so slow as to hardly be noticeable.

Here in Sparta it was impossible to believe. The city sat in the middle of a plain, where a pair of streams flowed into the river Evrotas. It was ringed by two walls, one inside the other and both protected by a moat. The walls were square and thick, like the buildings inside. The palace seemed to be all dark tunnels and halls lit by a single candle, guttering in the gloom.

Menelaus himself was big and brawny, with reddish hair and heavy forearms. Wisps of fine hair curled out from the collar of his chiton, at the back as well as the front. An Argive warrior lord, in short, all brawn and bristle. He looked quite similar to his brother in fact, the High King Agamemnon, who Antenor did *not* intend to visit during this trip to the west. There wasn't much point: Agamemnon was surly and sour with almost everyone, nearly all the time. When Antenor had gone to Mycenae two years earlier he'd ended up being made to wait for a week, while the High King went hunting or idled his afternoon away in wine. When Antenor was finally admitted he was treated to a long rant about how other peoples never understood the Argives. His ears had ached for days. He didn't plan to go through that again.

Hence this new approach. It had been Hecuba's idea at first, the queen encroaching onto her husband's ground if truth be told, though she and Priam exchanged ideas regularly. Speak to the other kings, those without a direct stake in Hesione's fate and with nothing to lose by negotiation. Try to build a broad agreement, if not to hand her back then at least to discuss terms. It had seemed a good idea, in Troy. Antenor had considered which of the kings might be most amenable, whose help was most useful if it could be gained, and slowly the trip had taken shape.

It had seemed a good idea in Pylos too, until Nestor spoke and it began to seem hopelessly optimistic. Now, in Menelaus' grim palace, it seemed little better than a fool's errand. But Antenor was here now. He might as well play the game through to the end.

"We Greeks thought you unmanly, you know," Menelaus said conversationally. "That day in Thessaly, I mean. When you wouldn't hunt with us."

It was an effort not to stare. This was supposed to be the smoother, more tactful of the brothers. Antenor spoke without knowing what the words would be until he heard them. "I would never have been able to keep up. In Troas we hunt from chariots."

"We knew that," Menelaus said. "But you could have tried. A lot of the older Greeks couldn't stand the pace that day. They still ran until their legs gave out."

You didn't, Antenor thought. Menelaus had been too young to join the hunt that day, and had followed behind on a chariot, just like an easterner. Yet now he sat and lectured, as though to a weakling or a lackwit. It showed a lack of proper respect.

Antenor was a diplomat, sent by a king of considerable power – more than Laconia, for certain, however this blocky idiot liked to strut. He deserved better than cheap insults.

"Argives judge manliness by their own standards," he said, keeping his voice calm. "There are others."

Menelaus shrugged. "None that matter."

The man was a boorish lout, actually *very* similar to his brother. Antenor was wasting his time here. He was preparing to make a polite excuse – some people knew how to behave, after all – when a side door opened and a woman came in.

For a moment Antenor actually thought his eyes were playing a trick on him. He'd heard poets claim that a woman was as lovely as a goddess, but always thought it just a neat turn of phrase, of no more importance than a man who claims his children are the prettiest in Troy. And he'd seen beauty, in the court at Troy and sometimes beyond, in Miletos or Sardis. But this woman was... astonishing. He didn't think he could speak.

Helen, something in his mind gabbled as he stared. *This must be Helen, daughter of old king Tyndareus. The heir, after Castor died that day in Thessaly. Menelaus is king through marriage to her.*

Word had reached Troy that Helen had chosen her own husband, something unheard-of among the masculine lords of Greece. Antenor doubted it, himself. Laconia was the second most powerful of the Argive nations, behind only Agamemnon's Achaea. The High King would not have wanted to see it in a rival's hands, or even those of a younger man, a better warrior and captain of men. It seemed likely that Helen had been... coerced. Persuaded to choose Agamemnon's brother.

Watching her glide across the floor, Antenor was no longer sure. It was hard to imagine this woman being forced to do anything she didn't want to. There was something about her of open flames, something too of the tigress, though that might just have been the mane of tawny hair, bound up in a net but still seeming to flow freely. Menelaus was visibly changed by it. He sat straighter, his expression sharpened to one of immediate fascination, and his eyes opened wider. Antenor hoped he didn't look the same.

"I did not know you had a guest," Helen said. Her voice was very low, and all but smoked. "Will you introduce me?"

She almost certainly had known, of course. The presence of a Trojan emissary in the palace would have been very hard to hide, even if anyone had tried. She was playing some game of which Antenor was unaware. He kept silent, trying to regain some composure.

"Matters of state," Menelaus said with a wave of his hand. His gaze travelled over her body. "You needn't concern yourself."

Watching, Antenor was sure he saw a flash of anger in her eyes – extraordinary eyes, violet and very large, under strong brows. It was gone at once though, and her smile never faltered as Helen laid a hand on her husband's arm. "Will these affairs delay you long?"

"I trust not." Menelaus was riveted by her, even as he strove to keep a semblance of formality. "I may come to you later, wife, if time allows."

It was a dismissal, and this time the flare of fury was impossible to mistake. The throne of Laconia had been her father's and had come to her, Antenor reminded himself: she had made Menelaus king here by her own choice, whether coerced or not. It must rankle sorely that she could now be dismissed like a common maid. Those violet eyes flicked to Antenor and pinned him to his chair, and he was sure he could feel his skin crisping in the heat of her gaze. Despite himself, despite all his worldliness, he felt a shiver of sudden desire.

Then she turned and walked away, leaving the room even gloomier than before she'd entered.

*

After that, the visit to Menestheus in Athens was all but meaningless, though the new king did make a concession.

"I'll talk to Agamemnon," he promised. "I can't say I'm happy at the way this has dragged on. Women are abducted all the time, of course; we kings couldn't stop that even if we tried. Too many pirates. But Hesione comes from an old lineage, and that matters."

Too many of the pirates were Greek kings, with cloths tied over their faces so they could deny having been there. This wasn't the time to mention that. "Will Agamemnon listen?"

"Probably not," Menestheus conceded. He stroked his dark goatee beard. "But we might be able to work something out. Perhaps if I traded something to Telamon, in exchange for Hesione... I might be able to persuade him, if the High King helps. A couple of servant girls and some Attican wine... or better yet an engraved shield from Egypt. Something he can show off to visitors."

"How would this help?"

"Well, because I could then hand Hesione back to Troy." Menestheus looked faintly surprised that Antenor hadn't understood at once. "It wouldn't hurt *my* pride... and I could use lower tariffs on the Trojan Road."

Antenor was amazed. This was the first time a reasonable suggestion had been made by an Argive, any Argive, in nearly twenty years of constant talk. More, it sounded as though it might actually work. If Telamon had a shield or some such he could boast about how he'd extracted it as a price for the woman he gave up, and so his pride would be assuaged. He'd have two pretty bed girls as well, assuming he was still capable of doing anything with them, fat and old as he was.

"If you could do this," he said, "Attican merchants would reap the benefits, I can promise you that."

He meant it, and he was sure Priam would agree. The king longed for his sister's return so badly, he wouldn't hesitate to award a lower duty on the goods of the country which had delivered her. Not that Attica was doing badly. There was a huge mural painted in the *megaron* of men leaping a bull, the famous sport of Minoan Crete painted in the style of that people; the bull brown and white, the dancers tanned golden against the white sand. One each side of the scene stood a man wearing a strange headdress, set against a crimson background that didn't match the bull scene at all.

Perhaps the standing men were not part of the main image. Antenor didn't know enough about Minoan art to say. It seemed that Attica was as modern as Nestor had promised though.

But in truth, Antenor struggled to keep his mind on business, even that of Hesione, all through the two days he spent in Menestheus' palace in Athens. Or on art. He couldn't keep it on anything, except for the memory of a woman with violet eyes and a voice that might have come from Aphrodite herself.

Helen.

*

"Will it work?" Menestheus asked.

The small man next to him at the window shrugged, a motion which looked strange on him. "Who can say?"

"No riddles," the king said. He felt very tired. "I took a risk there. Answer my question, Thersites."

The bard fingered his lyre. "I'm a storyteller, not a seer."

"Give my body to the dogs!" Menestheus cursed. "Will you give me a straight answer?"

"I'd say it should work." Thersites didn't seem to notice the king's outburst of temper. "The Trojans will grasp at any straw if it holds out hope for the return of their princess. Whether Agamemnon will approve is another matter."

"Yes," Menestheus said heavily. He stared out across the sea, where the Trojan's ship was dwindling in the distance. "Whether Agamemnon approves is always another matter."

Chapter Seven

The Black Ants

There were watchmen posted in the tower on the headland, where they had a view out over miles of the Greensea. At first sight of an approaching they would ring the tocsin, a bronze bell with a high, clear note, and everyone would hurry for the sanctuary of Teos and its wooden walls.

The attack came over land, from the north, almost as though the raiders knew the weakness in the town's defences. Nobody knew until it was too late.

*

Hiram was trying to push past, eager to join the fight at the town gate. All of thirteen, and he wanted to kill raiders. Balzer shoved him back with one arm, hard enough to send him sprawling on the wooden floor.

"You will stay here," Balzer said. "No argument! You have a sister and brother to protect. Do your duty to them."

"But the Greeks –"

"Must I tell you again?"

The street outside was full of shouts and running feet. Someone screamed, a sound of pure terror that brought Balzer's heart into his mouth. It had sounded like his wife; half the cries he heard made him think she was dying out there. He took a step towards Hiram. Behind the boy Paltal and Išbardia stood by the door, their eyes wide. "Must I?"

Hiram dropped his gaze. "No, Papa."

"Then stay here. Get into the pantry and bolt the door. If the first man in is a Greek, then kill him." Gods, let that not happen. *Tarhun guard them, Arinna smile on their souls.* He forced himself to go on. "I will fight for all of you."

"Mother's out there," Hiram said.

"I know that. She'll know how to take care of herself." He hoped she would. "Go now. Go!"

Hiram scrambled up. He was turning to his siblings when the door flew open behind Balzer, who yelled and spun around with his sword already rising for the strike. It was too late, far too late: one of the black-armoured warriors would have killed him already. But instead it was Didia, streaks of dirt on her face and a rip in her dress, and his heart leapt to see her.

"Husband!" she shouted. "We must –"

She stopped speaking. One hand reached out to rest against the door jamb, taking her weight. It was only then that Balzer noticed the blood running from her mouth, saw the bronze blade projecting from her chest. He screamed and sprang forward just as her body fell, rattling the door against the wall. Behind her stood a large man in a sable cuirass and helmet, hiding everything of his face except jaw and eyes.

Balzer screamed and struck at him, his chipped sword slashing down at the raider's shoulder. The blow was taken on the man's shield, and a return cut knocked the blade from Balzer's grip and sent it skittering across the floor. He jumped back and fell over his dead wife's body, crashing down on his back. Behind him Hiram scuttled for the sword.

"Leave it!" Balzer shouted, and the boy froze.

"Good advice," the Greek said, in accented Luwian. He stepped through the door, a muscular man made bulkier by the tough leather cuirass he wore. "We would rather have slaves than corpses. Do you yield?"

Slaves. Balzer longed to seize his sword again and cut this man down, hack at him until there was nothing left but shredded flesh and broken bones beneath. But he would never reach the blade – and if he did, then what? The raider would almost certainly kill him first, and even if not there were more in the streets. Hundreds more. Balzer swallowed hard.

Slavery. For his children.

"We yield," he said.

"Medon!" the man shouted, over his shoulder. A second Greek appeared in the doorway, as large as the first and spattered with blood down his left side. "Bind them for me. You have rope?"

"Of course I do." The newcomer rested a spear against the wall and pulled cord from his belt. "You make us all carry it, Eudorus."

Balzer didn't resist as his hands were tied behind him. He was careful not to look at his wife though, certain he'd weep if he did. Didia had been his first love, his only; he'd known her since they were both small. There had never been any question but that they would marry, when they were old enough. Their families had never considered anyone else. She had been killed with such suddenness that he still hadn't taken it in. He would cry when he did, he knew that, but he hoped it would not be in front of the Greeks.

"This one's older than I thought," Medon said. He'd tied the two boys and was now hauling Išbardia to her feet. "What are you girl, sixteen?"

"Leave her alone!" Balzer shouted. A moment later something hammered into the side of his head and he fell sideways, his skull bouncing off the floor. For a moment he couldn't see, and heard only his daughter's scream. He spat blood, feeling a loose tooth.

"The next one will be harder," the man called Eudorus said. His tone was quite pleasant. "The third time I'll take the horsewhip to you. You're a slave now, Mysian. Start behaving like one."

Balzer spat again, still feeling woozy.

"Seventeen," he heard Išbardia whisper. The other man must have asked her age again. Balzer knew why they wanted to know. There was only one outcome when a pretty young girl was taken captive.

He managed not to weep, but he thought that was mostly because he was too appalled for tears.

*

They were taken outside. The street was full of captives, most of them tied together in lines of five or ten people, many injured. Bodies were scattered along the road, and formed a largish heap at the far end, where it ran through the wall. Many of the dead were young, hardly more than children, though all of those were boys. A different fate awaited the girls.

Men in black armour moved among the corpses, checking them. Now and then one stabbed down with spear or sword and an arm twitched once, then was still. Some of those bodies must belong to men Balzer had known, and worked alongside: or women they had married, who had looked after his children when he and Didia needed time to themselves. He did his best not to look at them but sometimes his eyes fell on a face he knew, however he tried.

The prisoners were led to the town square. Stalls from the day's market still stood in the *agora,* though most had ripped canvas or overturned tables, and wares smashed on the ground. Other townsfolk were there already, filling the small plaza almost completely. They'd been tied in lines like cattle for sale. Balzer supposed that's what they were, now. He looked for familiar faces and found some. Not many. Not enough.

It had been so quick. One moment the town was quiet, its normal sedentary self, and the next black-garbed warriors were thundering up the road. Anyone unlucky enough to be in the fields had been cut down, except a few of the fastest runners. They'd come hurtling over the ditch barely ahead of the raiders, and by then it was too late to close the gate.

Balzer had seen that much, and known at once there was no hope. There were too many of the attackers – Argives, they had to be, nobody else made raids like this – and too few defenders. Only some forty townsfolk had reached the gate by the time the raiders crashed came crashing in. Balzer should have been one of them. He'd stopped to make sure his children were hidden, and found there wasn't even enough time for that.

"Balzer," a man in the next line said. It was Chilbu, a carpenter from one street over. "How did they do it? I never heard the tocsin."

"It didn't ring," Balzer said tiredly. He felt empty, hollowed out. The words tore his throat as they emerged from it. "They came overland. I saw them come out of the wood beyond the north fields."

"Papa," Išbardia said, her voice very small.

He couldn't look at her. There was nothing he could say, no comfort he could offer her. He'd have scrambled for his sword and let Eudorus spit him like a dog if it would save his children, any of them, but he knew it wouldn't have done. The tears were close now and he fought them, taking deep breaths of the warm air and blinking at the sky.

"Here he is," Eudorus said, not far behind him.

There was something in the Greek's voice that made Balzer turn around to see. A note of excitement, even in the midst of this carnage and despair. He looked down the street towards the gate.

A man was coming towards them, bigger than Eudorus but seeming almost dainty, stepping like a dancer between the bodies. Where the other raiders wore black armour his shone like gold, and his hair was scarcely less bright. He was very big, tall and broad as well, which made his light-footed movement seem strange, like an auroch skipping.

"Achilles," Eudorus said.

Balzer felt a fool. He should have realised who led the raiders from the moment he saw the black armour. Achilles and the Myrmidons were known across the Greensea, pirates who struck and struck again and never lost, no matter where they appeared. They had raided Samos, and seemed to strike along the Thracian coast every summer more or less at will: the Thracians had no ships and little organisation, and were easy prey. Two or three years ago the Myrmidons had attacked the coast of Egypt itself, smashing their way into a town outside Rosetta and making off with a fortune in worked gold.

They even attacked Argives. Under Achilles the Myrmidons played no favourites, except perhaps that they didn't raid the Greek mainland itself. But they had raided Rhodes, at least twice that Blazer had heard of, and were accused of the same in Crete, whose long coastline made it especially vulnerable to seaborne raids. King Idomeneus had supposedly threatened to feed Achilles' body to the dogs if he ever caught him. Because Achilles was at the heart of it all, the reason the Myrmidons still devastated coasts and sailed away laden with plunder, when the rest of the Argives hardly did so anymore. Greek kings had begun to protect their own lands rather than raiding against others'. The world was not what it had been.

Except for the warriors in black. And everywhere they went, they took prisoners and sold them into slavery, earning even more wealth as they did.

"Numbers?" Achilles asked. His voice was surprisingly soft.

"We could take six hundred captives if we wanted to," Eudorus said. "Not that we have room for them all."

"Or could sell them all," a new voice said. It came from a man almost as tall as Achilles, striding to join them across the *agora*. Balzer thought he looked almost feminine, with his blond hair and a chin that looked as though it had never needed a shave. "We'd have to sail the Greensea for weeks to be rid of them all, unless we sold them for coppers."

These are lives! Balzer wanted to shout. *We are people, with our own plans and our own loves. Not things, to be bought and sold.* But the world was cruel, it had always been cruel, and the Fates wouldn't listen to one mortal's pleas. He felt one of the boys' hand slip into his and gripped it hard.

"Pick out two hundred," Achilles ordered. "Choose the best, Patroclus. We'll leave the others here."

"Just leave them?" the androgynous man asked.

"Sacking a town is good," Achilles said. "Burning it to nothing isn't. If we let them rebuild there will still be something here for us to raid again, twenty years from now. Start checking the houses for treasures and send word to the ships; it's time they moved around to the strand here. I want everything loaded and the hulls back out at sea before –""

He broke off. For the second time Balzer felt that brittle something in the air, and again he couldn't help but look.

Achilles was staring at Išbardia. Goggling at her, in fact, as though he'd been struck to the heart and couldn't tear himself away. Balzer turned his head and saw his daughter staring back, with the same intent expression on her face. Something inside him plunged queasily.

"In the name of Aphrodite," Achilles said at last. "The Shining One sends us fair wind and calm seas, when we voyage. I did not expect her to also send such beauty as yours. What are you called?"

"Išbardia," she said. The small, shocked tone was gone, replaced by a strength Balzer hadn't expected, or heard from her before.

"Išbardia," the golden man repeated. He smiled brilliantly. "Išbardia. A lovely name. I am Achilles."

"I know who you are," she said.

He nodded. "Of course you do. Everyone on the shores of the sea knows the name of Achilles."

There was unmistakeable pride in his tone, but Išbardia stood very straight and looked him in the eye, without a hint of fear. "As a plunderer. As a stealer of lives and a wrecker of towns. Only that."

"What else should a warrior be known for?" He seemed genuinely bemused. "Men know my name. I can ask no more."

Išbardia said nothing to that, merely studied him, but she still carried the earlier flush in her cheeks. Balzer didn't like that, but he couldn't see what he could do about it. Everyone in the *agora* had fallen silent to listen. Behind Achilles his two captains, Eudorus and Patroclus, exchanged glances of what Balzer thought was weary resignation. He didn't understand that at all.

"Will you come with me?" Achilles asked.

She didn't blink. "As what? Your slave?"

"My companion," Achilles said.

Balzer took a small step forward, all the ropes allowed him without dragging others in his wake. He stopped even before Eudorus and Patroclus cut their eyes towards him, at precisely the same instant. There was nothing he could do to stop this, and anyway it would be better than any other possibility open to Išbardia now. She'd know that, of course. She had never been a fool, any more than her mother had been.

"My family goes free?" she asked.

Achilles gestured to his men. Patroclus came forward and cut the ropes at Balzer's wrists, then his sons'. He smiled slightly as he stepped away. "The gods are with you today, townsman."

He supposed they were. His wife murdered in front of him, his daughter lost to an outland barbarian, and it was his lucky day. He still had two sons, and they were free. He could feel the envy of the other captives as they glared at him. "But you're not happy."

For a moment Patroclus looked startled, and then the smile returned. He lowered his voice. "Achilles has his fancies. They blow hot for a month, or half a year, and then his passion turns elsewhere and the darling is forgotten. But she'll not be left helpless, townsman. My word on it."

The word of a raider and killer: that was not at all comforting. Balzer was suddenly sure, looking into Patroclus' blue eyes, that he himself was one of the fancies who had been forgotten. It was hardly unknown for men to share love together, after all. For an instant they stared at each other, and then Patroclus turned and went back to the lines of Myrmidons.

Balzer turned to his daughter. She was already looking at him, her head held high. Achilles had come closer and stood a few paces away.

"I'm sorry," Balzer said. It wasn't enough. How could it be? It was his task to keep her safe, and yet she was about to leave everything she'd known to be the companion of a pirate. His bed girl, in short. Balzer tried to speak again and no words came out.

"You have no reason to be sorry," Išbardia said. "You don't control the world. If you did, Papa, I know I would have always been safe."

"Let us know if you need us," he said. She wouldn't, of course. A woman on one side of the Aegean couldn't send a message to the other, unless she was high born. And Išbardia couldn't even write. Few people could.

"I will," she promised. She came to him and held him tight, though only for a brief moment. Then she stepped back, and kneeling she held her arms out so her two brothers could go to her. They were both crying, even Hiram, who thought himself so strong. Balzer was glad to see it. They had lost their mother today, and now their sister, and the consolation of their own freedom and safety seemed a small return for that.

At length Išbardia eased the boys away and stood up. Achilles came and took her arm, and then led her away down the body-strewn street, his hand gripping her just above the elbow. It reminded Balzer of the way a groom will lead a horse, his hand proprietorial and controlling. He watched her until she was out of sight, and when she vanished breath left him in a soft gasp.

"Papa?" Paltal asked.

He shook his head, not answering, and took the boys' hands. Together they started towards the home now being looted by Myrmidons.

"Papa?" Paltal said again.

"Hush," Balzer said. He was already thinking about what to take. There wasn't much, really. Clothes would be most of it. Balzer could take his pack, and the boys could tie their cloaks into makeshift bundles, perhaps fastened to the end of a pole. They could manage.

"Papa?"

They'd need food, of course. There was a good bit in the pantry, assuming the Myrmidons didn't take it all. Even if they did there would be fruit and berries in the high woods, and game to hunt besides. Balzer might not be any use with a sword, but he could use a sling.

"We're leaving," he told Paltal. The younger boy's eyes were huge and terrified. "As soon as we can. You heard what the warrior said. They want us to rebuild just so they can raid us again, on another day."

The Argives had raided half the world, but not the coast of Asia. Not since Miletos fifteen years ago, when the Hittites came and slaughtered every Greek they could find, a few years after the city had been taken in a raid. That had left the Argives afraid to try again. Now, it seemed, they were recovering their nerve. At least, Achilles was. That was enough.

"Where will we go?" Paltal asked tremblingly.

"Somewhere not even an Argive will raid," Balzer said.

"Yes, but where?"

"Isn't that obvious?" Hiram took his hand from his father's and strode on ahead, turning to call back to his brother. "We're going to Troy."

Chapter Eight

Built on Riches

"*Tarhun's Hand* is late."

"Only by a day."

"I don't care if it's by an hour, or a minute," Crescas said crossly. "She's late, when the other ships have all made good time. My own, and the vessels of my rivals too. Why should the *Hand* be dawdling?"

They both knew the possible reasons, of course. *Tarhun's Hand* was making her way home from Naxos, or should be, unless something had gone wrong on the outward leg. But it was a long run, the sort of journey Crescas' ships only made once a summer, because time-consuming trips to smallish settlements weren't very profitable. It was risky too. There was a section with no land for miles, making the ship vulnerable to sudden storms, and Poseidon Earth-Shaker's bad temper could whip up waves at any time. In another place the route jumped from island to island, perfect water for pirates, who seemed to reappear as soon as they were cleared away. Either could have snatched *Tarhun's Hand* as she voyaged.

Sometimes ships vanished without anyone knowing why. Crescas loathed that. A ship being late at all made him edgy and irritable.

"What about *Nereid Borne?*" he asked. "Will she be unloaded before dark?"

Eteon consulted his slate. "She should be."

"I don't want to hear *should,*" Crescas grumbled. "Make sure those amphorae are packed into wagons and stored in the warehouse by sundown. And tell the men to be careful. Greek olive oil is the best, we'll get a good price for it in Colchis or Sarmatia."

"Right," Eteon said. He made a note on the slate.

The warehouse they stood in was mostly empty, with five of Crescas' six ships away. Several were due in over the next few days though. One was *Tarhun's Hand,* assuming she hadn't been smashed on rocks or looted by pirates; *Scaean Sail* was returning from Egypt, hopefully with a cargo of cut glass and ivory; and *Troas* was coming home from Phoenicia laden with faience and lapis lazuli from far India. The stockroom would be packed to bursting then, until the wagons could pick the goods up or they could be shipped on to another destination. But you couldn't send the ships out again right away. The sailors needed time to waste their pay on wine and whores, and Crescas liked to have the hulls checked too, whenever possible. He lost fewer ships when he took a little extra care, which was better for profits and better for the crews too.

Best to get the olive oil jars on their way immediately, then. They could go east along the Trojan Road tomorrow morning, following the coast north-east to Dardanos and Arisbe, then on to Priapos and transfer to other ships. Crescas didn't concern himself beyond that point; he had no ships on the Euxine Sea, nor any plans to buy some. It was the Aegean and the Greensea he knew, and had sailed in his day. At times he still missed those days. Salt in his hair, and arrows of sun darting off the waves into his eyes... a man couldn't ask for much more.

Except a good wife and children, he reminded himself, and a life of moderate wealth in a fine city. Yes. That was what he was glad of now.

"Excuse?" someone said from the doors.

Crescas turned, but he couldn't make out anything about the visitor while he stood there, outlined by the sun. "Yes?"

"I am look for," the man paused, glancing at a paper in his hand, "Crescas the Argive?"

He'd lived in Troy for fifteen years now, and still they called him 'the Argive'. He supposed they always would.

Crescas had been born in Argolis, across the sea in the south of Greece. A land of nested valleys with sharp ridges between, rocks protruding from them like broken claws. There long ago had lived Argus the Hundred-Eyed, a Titan who never slept and who defied Zeus and the Twelve Olympians. He'd even defied them in battle, refusing to be beaten. Finally clever Hermes lulled him to sleep by playing on his flute, and while the giant slumbered cut off his head. Hera then placed the eyes in the tail of a peacock so they should not be lost.

Crescas had been born in the south, on the coast where young boys learned the sea from their fathers, generation after generation. He'd never seen a Titan. Or a peacock, for that matter.

He'd seen ships, and loved them, from an early age. By the time he was thirteen he was sailing the Greensea, or more usually hauling at an oar because the wind was too soft or blew in the wrong direction. By twenty he was captain of his own ship. Three years later he owned two vessels and had become a merchant, spending steadily more and more time ashore while other men did the sailing. He regretted that often, though he told himself it was silly. There were dangers on the sea, and beneath it. A man would have to be a complete fool to want to face them just to feel that salt in his hair.

Most of the time on land was spent in Troy, and just before he turned thirty he married and settled in the city. He had a daughter now, two years old and toddling, and already trying to speak. Althea's first words would probably be Luwian, not Greek.

He supposed she was Trojan, in fact. And still people called him 'the Argive', even while he worshipped at Trojan shrines and knelt to the Trojan king when Priam passed in the street.

"I'm Crescas," he said. "What can I do for you?"

The man came into the warehouse, which meant he wasn't silhouetted by the sunlight anymore and Crescas could see him clearly. He turned out to be a little fellow with brown skin, probably from somewhere in the interior of Anatolia. Perhaps a Phrygian or Hurrian, it was very hard to tell. He was new to the city though, to judge by his halting command of the language.

"Am Mursili," the man said. "You sell iron?"

"No," Crescas answered. "It's not worth bringing by sea. It's too heavy and takes up too much space. You need to speak to merchants who run wagon caravans to the south."

The man shrugged. "Too slow. Need iron quick."

"I can't help you," Crescas said. He'd begun to turn away when something connected in his brain and he twisted back to stare at the little fellow. "You're the Hittite. The ironsmith."

"Work iron," Mursili said. "Yes."

There had been talk about this man. Hattusa had never allowed the secrets of iron working to leave the capital, but now Hector had brought an expert west with him, apparently as thanks for his heroics in the battle against Assyria. Crescas, made sensitive to changing political realities by the nature of his work, had pricked up his ears at that. It sounded as though the Hittite Empire was in trouble, despite the victory at Emar. Sole access to iron weapons had been a major reason for their power over the past hundred years, perhaps *the* major reason. They wouldn't let the secrets or ironwork go if there was any way they could prevent it, and that could only mean their strength was fading.

But Crescas didn't trade with Hattusa, at least not directly, so he'd forgotten the story until the Hittite walked into his stockroom. Not that it made any difference.

"I still can't help," he said. "Iron is just too expensive to transport by sea. The weight means a ship can't carry anything else, which makes the voyage unprofitable. You need the caravan masters, as I said."

"Need you," Mursili said in his halting Luwian. "For speed. Hittites won't sell. Must come from Cyprus mines. By sea."

"You're not listening," Crescas said. He wondered if the man understood him, actually. "It can't be done, all right?"

The little man handed over a second piece of parchment, this one still rolled up. "Look."

The parchment was sealed with wax. Only the very wealthiest bothered to do that, and Crescas frowned as he broke the seal and opened the letter. A token fell out and he caught it automatically as he read.

The Royal Treasury will pay the merchant Crescas the Argive in silver for any iron he ships to Mursili, weight for weight, until summer's end.

Crescas looked at the token. It was an engraving of a stylised horse, just a few curving lines to convey the impression of an animal at the gallop, more speed than shape. He knew it, of course; the symbol of the city. Only Priam used it; not even Hector was allowed. This permission had come from the king.

He handed the letter to Eteon, who read quickly.

"Weight for weight?" the factor said. His voice had gone slightly hoarse. "In silver, in return for iron?"

"So it seems." Crescas managed a fairly normal tone. "We give Mursili here a pound of iron, the treasury gives us a pound of silver."

"But must be soon," the Hittite said.

Soon. Yes. Crescas closed his eyes, rearranging schedules and plans in his mind. It could be done. "Eteon."

The other man waited, chalk poised over his slate.

"Get *Nereid Borne* unloaded tonight," Crescas said. "Have the men work in the dark if you must, ask permission to keep one of the gates to the city open, whatever it takes. Stack the amphorae in the moat, if you must, but get that ship unloaded. I want her ready to sail at dawn."

"Captain Bienor won't like that."

"I'll speak to Bienor." The man wouldn't like it at all, that was true, and his crew would like it even less. Men just back from one voyage wanted a few days before they set out on another. But this contract would make Crescas' fortune, turn him from a reasonably wealthy man into a rich one indeed. He might one day watch his little girl marry a prince, perhaps not of Troy itself, but of one of the lesser cities: Pedasos maybe, or lovely little Lyrnos. He didn't mind sharing a little of that good fortune around. Perhaps the crew could be paid double wages when they went to Cyprus for iron.

Crescas' mind was racing. Three more ships were due back within days, and all could be sent to Cyprus. The king's seal hadn't set any limit on the amount of iron he'd pay for. Each ship might be able to bring back half a ton. More, possibly, but even with the prospect of such riches something in Crescas rebelled at the idea of taking *too* big a risk. Four ships' worth meant two tons. For which Priam would pay two whole tons of silver.

Two whole tons. Crescas felt his palms begin to sweat as he wondered just how rich the king of Troy actually was.

*

When Crescas was new to Troas, he'd lived in a single room in Bunarbi, three miles north of Troy itself. It was a fisherman's hut, really, and at that nearly more than he could afford. Later he took a little house in the main city, just inside the Scaean Gate in the south, on the site of what had once been a tannery. The old buildings had been demolished, and new ones built, but residents all said that when the summer heat was high and the wind still, the tanner's smell still rose out of the ground. Crescas hadn't believed the story. The next summer it had been impossible to doubt it.

Two years ago, when he married, Crescas bought a house at the other end of the city, below the wall of the Pergamos. The best houses in Troy were there, places where royal cousins and master horse breeders lived. Crescas' home was small compared to those, modest even, but it had seven rooms on two floors and a tiny garden on the roof. He'd never have said, back in Bunarbi, that he'd ever own such a home as that.

It was a mark of the changes in his life that he hadn't even chosen it.

Thaïs was waiting just inside the door, at the top of the steps down to the street. She usually was; she liked the receiving room, the *andron* as it was called in Greece. She'd picked up the habit of using the term, but kept the tradition of women in the east, that they were an equal partner in any marriage. Which meant she was allowed in the *andron*. Thaïs insisted she was willing to learn from how things were done in Greece, but that didn't extend to Crescas being allowed a room his wife couldn't enter.

And come to that, Thaïs might say they were equal partners, but it seemed to Crescas that he was only her equal when she let him be.

Althea was sitting on the floor, banging a carved lion against a model ship. The lion was probably bigger. Children's toys didn't seem to make much sense.

"Supper is ready," Thaïs greeted. She kissed him, and for a moment he forgot all about his daughter in the taste of her lips, and the yellow sunfall of her hair. All the years of work had brought him a respectable standard of living, with a servant of his own and plenty of good food, but the prize he treasured most was Thaïs. His hands itched for a tiller sometimes, and his eyes squinted against the glare of a sea he hadn't faced for years, but the thought of Thaïs stopped the itch and settled him heart. If only for a few days.

And then a few days more, and more, and here he still was, enjoying his life while other men faced pirates and storms for him.

He was hungry, he realised. "Good. Are we eating alone, or will we have a woman from the Dressmaker's Guild to entertain? Again?"

"Just the family," she said, still in his arms. "Though any more quips like that, husband, and you can eat downstairs – alone."

"Point taken," he said. A Greek wife wouldn't say such a thing to her husband. Crescas would be *so* bored.

Althea stopped hitting lion against ship when he crouched down beside her, and regarded him from huge blue eyes. Her mother's eyes, in fact; she had Thaïs' hair as well, but she'd inherited Crescas' nose. A bit unfortunate, that. She was beautiful anyway, and Crescas prayed every night that she grow up more beautiful still. His prayers went to Aphrodite of Greece and Arinna of Troy alike. There was no sense in choosing one and ignoring the other.

Supper was chicken in garlic, served with eggs and figs, and slabs of honeyed bread. Thaïs brought the plates herself, and they took turns feeding Althea, who loved eggs but stubbornly shut her lips against figs. She ate some chicken but then coughed it back out again, mysteriously mixed with an odd green liquid. Crescas and Thaïs were used to that sort of thing by now and just wiped the mess up before going on with the meal. If you let a baby's horrible habits put you off food you'd starve in a month.

Half an hour later Althea's eyelids were drooping, and Crescas carried her downstairs to bed while Thaïs stacked the plates for washing in the morning. Then, finally, there was time to pull his boots off and relax on the divan, a glass of heavily watered wine on the table and a dish of raisins at his elbow. Thaïs sat beside him, her eyes half-closed. She looked very tired.

"Althea was difficult today?" he asked.

Thaïs nodded. "She gets frustrated that she can't explain what she wants. It will only be a few weeks until she starts talking, I think, but until then she's going to be bad-tempered."

"You could leave her with the maid."

"I know I could leave her with the maid," she said irritably. "But I want to be there for her first word."

So did Crescas, actually, but that wasn't likely unless he was very lucky. He was away most days, either down at the Bay checking over a ship, or overseeing the arrival or departure of a caravan from the Trojan Road. When he managed to find time away from those things, the warehouse needed to be watched over, and there were always Notaries to consult. Once they'd loaned him money to finance his plans: now he kept his money with them, and they fawned over him in gratitude. He didn't trust them fully, though. There was a bag of gold rings buried under the ground floor, just in case they cheated him.

"I heard a story in the market this morning," Thaïs began, but she never got to tell Crescas what it was. Someone knocked on the door three times, quite hard, and she sighed.

"That's Eteon," she said. "I recognise the way he raps."

Crescas doubted that, but his short marriage had already taught him there were some things a wise husband just didn't say. He pushed himself up from the divan and went to open the door, and found Eteon standing there in the dark. He didn't need to turn around to know his wife was looking satisfied.

"Trouble, boss," Eteon said.

Domestic concerns vanished. "What trouble? Is the ship all right?"

"Nereid Borne is fine," the factor said. "But there's trouble in the palace. Can I come in for a moment?"

Crescas stood aside to let him pass. Eteon stopped just inside, so he didn't track dust and whatever else might be on the streets of Troy at this late hour through the house. He bowed slightly. "Lady Thaïs."

She nodded her head. "Eteon. I'd like you better if you didn't interrupt my husband quite so often."

"I apologise," he smiled. Eteon knew her well enough to realise she wasn't really complaining. "But this is important. Crescas, there's word from the palace. Priam is going to increase duties on the Trojan Road for all Argive goods and merchants. It will be announced tomorrow."

"All of them?" He frowned. "By how much?"

"By half," Eteon said.

Crescas nearly yelped. A fifty per cent increase would be impossible for most Greek traders, they couldn't pay that and still maintain enough profit. It would shut Greek goods out of the Euxine market completely as well; they wouldn't be able to reach that huge, rich market. Sales of their wine and olive oil would fall, their pottery and bronze work, emery and marble figurines. They wouldn't be able to buy Colchian grain or salt fish. Prices of Indian lapis lazuli would soar, and of pepper and faience too. Greece was going to be *hurt* by this.

So might he be, too. Any merchant who didn't adapt fast enough was going to suffer.

"Does it include Greeks living in Troy?" he asked.

"I don't know. It might." Eteon shrugged.

"Diomedes is king of Argolis," Crescas muttered, annoyed, "but he isn't *my* king. I've been here ten years and people still call me an Argive."

"They always will," Eteon said.

"This is all because of Hesione, isn't it?" he asked, exasperated. "It always comes back to her, and that bad crow Telamon."

"I expect so," Eteon said. "Does it matter?"

He supposed it didn't. Not to him, at any rate. This was going to *ruin* his profits; roughly half of the business he did involved the Trojan Road, one way or the other. Except, he realised, that he might not be included in the new tax. He was an Argive by birth, but a Trojan by choice. He'd even married a woman from the city, had a Trojan daughter with her. It should be possible to argue that the new duty didn't apply to him.

Then he remembered the Hittite in his warehouse earlier, and the offer from the royal treasury to pay weight for weight in silver, in return for iron. He dug a hand in the pocket of his shirt and pulled out the token of the stylised horse. Priam would have to give him some leeway, surely.

"I'm sorry," he said to Thaïs, "but I think I have to go to the palace, before they all go to sleep up there."

"Of course you do," she said. "Take Eteon. I don't want you walking the streets alone at night."

He didn't want to walk the streets in the dark at all, but there was no help for it. He snagged his cloak from behind the door and swung it around his shoulders. The bitter north wind had faded for the moment, but it could return quickly. Crescas tugged his boots on and went back to the door.

"I'll leave a light on," Thaïs promised.

He would have kissed her, except that Eteon was there. Instead Crescas just nodded, and went out into the Trojan dark.

Chapter Nine

Three-Eyed Rats

Sometimes his mind went back, all the way to his adolescence, when he'd been too young a youth to be allowed to join the hunt in Thessaly. He'd seen hunts before that, of course, even taken part in some, though never with so dangerous a foe as the great boar in the woods that day. Never so far from home, either. His father had wanted him to go so he could meet the other young lordlings of Greece, the men who would lead and shape it in years to come.

"Ithaca is small," Laertes had said. "Alone we will be overwhelmed, or at best forgotten, by the rising flood that is Greece. You'll need friends if you're to help this kingdom flourish, my son."

Well, Odysseus had friends, though not as many as his father would have liked, and perhaps not the right ones. Nestor was a man he trusted, but the king of Messenia was approaching sixty now, and hardly an ally for the future. He liked Menestheus in Attica too; Theseus' successor was a clever man, behind the square jaw and goatee beard. He seemed like a typical Greek warrior until he spoke, in that slow thoughtful way he had, but he was a good deal more.

So, few friends, but at least Odysseus had avoided making enemies. He'd become quite good at sitting in some grim hall and smiling in the midst of stupidity or outright boorishness. Most of the Greek kings were one of those things, or both, at least some of the time. Schedius, Agapenor, Leonteus; they were all guilty. But the worst by far were Telamon and the Atreide brothers, Agamemnon and Menelaus, men who understood nothing but pride and sheer force. Odysseus hated spending time with them, but he had to. That was just the reality of life as the king of a small island.

The truth was that Odysseus was more comfortable in the east, in one of the cities that dotted the coast. He didn't like to go too far inland: Ithacans were coastal folk, born with the sea in their bones. That still left plenty of choices. Ephesus in Caria, with the pillared library facing the sea; or Miletos, rich with Minoan reliefs and murals brought by the refugees from that poor, broken culture. He might go to one of those before he turned for home, or to both, if time and weather allowed. It had been a long time since they did.

For now he would settle for Halicarnassus.

It was three years since he'd sailed into the harbour here too, a deep bay protected by arching breakwaters of stone filled with sand. Since then an island had been added at the end of one pier, with a fortress built on top, two tiers of high walls studded with towers. Anyone trying to raid into Halicarnassus would pay a high price now. Odysseus wondered how much it had cost, and why the king had bothered. Piracy was always a problem on the Greensea, but reavers never struck at a city this big. That castle could only be aimed at stopping fleets of raiders, and that must mean the Greeks.

He pondered that as his ship eased deeper into the bay. It was unsettling, to see how great the fear of Greek attack had become, even as far away as Halicarnassus. The whole Aegean lay between here and Greece. And if Halicarnassus had done this, what had others done?

What might they do in the future?

The thought brought his mind back to Thessaly, to the boar hunt. To Antenor asking for the return of Hesione to Troy, and Telamon's furious, blustering refusal to even consider it. That had been Odysseus' first taste of the greed in the nature of the Greeks. They took what they were strong enough to seize – women, wealth, land – simply because they could. They had never wanted to learn to live alongside equals. To them a man dominated, or he failed.

They gave nothing back. Nothing. Not unless it was wrenched from their hands.

Once ashore, he and Eliade made their way into the streets, leaving the crew to unload and find buyers for the cargo. Wool and carpets this time, as so often, since it was mostly what Ithaca had. But it was *good* wool and carpets, as good as those from Troy Odysseus thought, and much less expensive. There were some who would buy Trojan anyway, just for the name, but many more bought Ithacan. He'd learned to be happy with that.

Halicarnassus was built on a steep hillside behind the bay. There was flatter land just to the side, but it was marshy and prone to flooding, and anyway wet ground meant disease in summer heat. As it was, the marsh served as a defence for the city, a flea-infested moat two hundred yards wide. On the other sides of the city the wall was taller and towers more frequent, and another fortress sat at the top of the hill, guarding the approaches. That one wasn't new, but squinting up at it Odysseus thought it had been extended, and the walls built higher. Halicarnassus was being very careful.

Houses in the city were built in rows along the line of the hill, with streets zigzagging their way between them in tight switchbacks. Almost all were built of fired bricks and painted in pastel colours, pale blues and yellows and greens, bright in the sunshine. Window boxes were filled with herbs, rooftops planted with them or else home to clucking chickens. Once Odysseus saw a beehive up there and shook his head in admiration. Ithaca was too windy to try the same thing, its rooftops too exposed to storms, but he had to like the ingenuity.

"Where first?" Eliade asked.

Odysseus had thought about that, as he thought about everything, and had his answer ready. "The *agora*. I want to get a feel for the situation here before we start talking to people."

The marketplace of Halicarnassus was unique, as far as he knew. Because of the steepness of the hillside it was built in a series of tiers, each one more than a yard above the next and reached by means of wide steps. Sometimes there was only room for a single row of stalls before the ground fell away again. That made it hard for wagons to reach there, and servants or debt slaves had to carry goods in and out by hand, trying not to drop or break anything as they did. It made the place crowded too, shoppers forced together in tight streams at the steps, so Odysseus tied his money bag on the thong around his neck and tucked it into his chiton before he reached the first stall.

The *agora* was full, of course. It always was, at a major city like Halicarnassus, with the Greensea on one side and the roads into Anatolia on the other. Most of the merchants sold everyday goods; grain from the interior or from overseas, figs and olives, raisins and wine and wool. All things which could be found almost anywhere, though not always of a good quality. He wasn't much interested in that, honestly. If Ithaca needed imports she could find them on her own side of the sea, and for less money too.

Odysseus was looking for goods from inland, even from far India, brought on wagon trains from the east.

He found it scattered among the stalls, some here and some across the market. Ivory at a ridiculous price, one he could beat with ease if he voyaged to Egypt, and at that cost he would. A ragtag little stall near the bottom edge of the *agora* offered faience pottery, beautifully glazed, even better than the clear finish the Trojans used. If he could figure out how that glaze was made Odysseus would make Ithaca rich at a stroke. But nobody knew, and so the prices were extortionate, though no worse today than he'd expected. He did like the intricate paintwork of eastern faience though, and had once bought a set of plates for Penelope. She'd exclaimed over them, and love for the next few nights had been as good as it ever was, but then she wrapped the plates in linen and Odysseus had never seen them since, even when they had guests.

Women were odd. People said Odysseus was clever, but he was never going to understand females.

On another side of the market he found two stalls next to each other, one selling lapis lazuli jewellery at quite reasonable prices. Decent quality too, as far as Odysseus could judge. He haggled with the merchant for a while, trying to see how far he could argue him down. Adjacent to that was a trader selling carved figurines, none more than two inches high, allegedly made by holy men in far Persia and imbibed with mysterious eastern magics. Throw them on the soil of a fresh grave, the seller claimed, and any curse you invoke or prayer you make will be answered favourably, guaranteed.

"Are you really doing this?" Eliade asked, as Odysseus argued prices with the Carian merchant.

"I seem to be," he answered. "Why?"

"They don't work," Eliade said, as though talking to an idiot.

Odysseus broke off the haggling to frown at him. "I know they don't work. Other people believe they do work, and will buy them. Besides, I'm not really interested in the figurines, as such."

"Then why are you bickering with him?"

"Because I'm interested that the figures are *here,*" Odysseus replied, "and I want to know what it cost to bring them."

He went back to arguing with the seller, who eventually grew so angry that he threw a figure at Odysseus and stalked off to the other end of his stall, where another customer had been watching the discussion with increasing amusement. Eliade snatched the model out of the air and pocketed it, unseen.

"I thought you don't believe they work," Odysseus said.

Eliade grinned. "Other people believe they do, and will pay for it."

He had to laugh.

They spent half the afternoon crossing to and fro across the market, checking prices on every product they could think of. Even Trojan wool, and Egyptian animal hides, not that there was much of either. The hides in particular were ruinously expensive. Odysseus' father had owned a leopard hide rug once, complete with head, taken on a raid when Laertes was young, but it had worn out long ago. Odysseus had never replaced it. Wool was what Ithaca made; it looked bad if even the king didn't use it on his floor.

"I think I see," Eliade said finally. They were standing by a stall selling herbs and spices from the east, including tiny pots of pepper for a silver ring each. Odysseus knew it was no good haggling over that price: pepper was, literally, worth its weight in gold. "You're working out trade routes, aren't you? What travels which roads, and what it costs."

"Yes," Odysseus said.

"We came here from Ithaca just to study mercantile methods? Why?"

"Troy," Odysseus told him.

*

It was obvious to anyone with eyes what Priam was going to do.

He had been asking for his sister's return for over twenty years. First politely, directly, as that day in Thessaly while the boar roasted over a fire. Then with subtle threats of stronger action, if nothing was done. Agents from Troy came to talk with kings alone, rather than at a gathering; to Nestor in Pylos, or Menestheus in Athens, Diomedes in Argos. Usually the agent was Antenor, though he didn't seem to enjoy the duty very much.

None of it had worked. Hesione had borne a son to Telamon early in her captivity, proof for the whole world that she was not merely a trophy captive but was brought to his bed when the mood took him. Dragged to it, Odysseus had heard, though he didn't know if the information was reliable. He could believe it easily enough. Telamon was that sort of man.

There had been no children since, but nothing either to indicate that anything had changed. She might still be forced to Telamon's bed, for all that Priam knew. The knowledge must have burned in his veins like acid, all these years. And slowly the threats had grown less veiled, the language used blunter, as Priam's patience finally ran thin.

Now he was going to do what the threats had suggested he would, and raise duties on the Trojan Road. For all the Greeks, probably, even those kings who'd shown a degree of empathy for Hesione's plight. Odysseus, watching events from his eyrie on Ithaca, had become almost sure of it by spring. A conversation with Nestor had revealed the old man thinking the same thing, and for Odysseus that removed the last doubts. He knew his own mind, and trusted it, but Nestor had been clever for longer than Odysseus had been alive. When he formed an opinion, it was wise to listen to him.

If trade through Troy was about to become impossible, then Greece needed other sources of supply. Odysseus couldn't arrange that – but he could make provision for Ithaca.

"I'm interested principally in wheat," he said.

The merchant across the table nodded. "I have good contacts in Lycia. I can get you wheat."

"Three hundred amphorae a month," Odysseus said. "Paid for by myself, and by Nestor of Messenia."

"Not by traders?"

"We *are* traders," he said. "Have it brought to the harbour here, in Halicarnassus. Either Ithacan or Messenian ships will collect it in the first week after each new moon."

The two men were sitting in a roof garden, at a table in the shade of a citron tree. A tree, for Artemis' sake, on a rooftop. The easterners certainly knew what luxury was. They had a bowl of raisins between them, and jugs of wine and water. Both men had used more of the water than the wine. You needed a clear head when you were trying to make deals.

The merchant, whose name was Nashuja, leaned back in his chair. "And your price?"

"That depends on you. We can pay in wool, wholly or in part, if you prefer. Nestor could offer goat's cheese, or perhaps olives."

"I'd like payment in coin."

Odysseus nodded. "Very well. Nestor and I believe a price of two silvers per amphora is fair."

"Two?" Nashuja guffawed. "Please don't waste my time. You make that offer knowing it's much too low."

"I never expect the first offer to be accepted," he said, smiling.

"If you habitually make it such a poor one, I am not surprised," the Lycian replied. "Come, now. Two silvers covers the transport costs from inland, but only just. It's a derisory offer."

Odysseus sighed. "My friend, the transport costs are minimal. All you have to do is maintain a wagon, feed the ox that pulls it and pay a driver and a guard. The total expense is between two and three silvers for a trip from the interior to the coast here. There are eighteen amphorae in each cart. That means, simply, that the cost of transport is one silver for six amphorae."

"There are hidden costs," the merchant began.

"No, there are not," Odysseus broke in. "My friend Eliade has factored in the risks of broken wheels and outlaws. We do transport goods by road in Greece, you know. We're aware of the perils."

"You're a tough bargainer," Nashuja grumbled.

"I'm from Ithaca. We don't have much coin, so we like to know it will be worth it before we spend."

Nashuja knew that, of course. He and Odysseus had dealt with each other before, though never on an agreement as large as this one. He was a good businessman, a good fellow overall, though not half as canny as he thought he was. What passed for guile in Halicarnassus would mark a man as foolish in Troy. The hagglers in that city could take your money, goods and clothes, and still make you grateful to be naked. When negotiating with *them* Odysseus never drank any wine at all.

It was the same on Naxos, the little island in the Aegean dominated by marble quarries that had chewed holes in the hillsides. It sat roughly in the middle of a triangle formed by Greece to the west, Anatolia in the east and Crete to the south, so trading ships stopped there whichever way they were sailing. Sometimes the captains decided to sell their cargoes on Naxos rather than carry them the extra distance. When they did they took a slightly lower price, setting that off against the time saved, which could then be used to ship more goods. It was the gift of Naxos middlemen that they could talk those captains into selling at just a *little* less than they wanted to, again and again.

"Two silvers and six coppers," Odysseus said after a moment. "For the full three hundred amphorae, that totals seven hundred and fifty in silver. It's a lot of money, Nashuja."

The merchant grimaced. "Ithacan pig-shagger. Two and six isn't enough. Three silvers."

"No. Too much."

"Why do you want the grain, anyway?" Nashuja asked. "Ithaca never needed it before. Or Messenia, either."

"Rats," Odysseus said, straight-faced. If he told the truth, that the Trojan supply route might become untenable, Nashuja would push up the price without stopping to think. "We have a terrible rat problem in Greece. They've eaten through most of our stores."

"Rats?"

"Great big ones. With three eyes, and teeth that can chew through stone."

"Hmm," Nashuja said. "Life on Ithaca must be harder than I thought. Either that, or you're stringing me along."

"Only a little," Odysseus said. "All right. Two silver and nine copper, but that's as high as I'll go, Nashuja. If you can't meet me on that price I'll look for someone else who will."

"Agreed," Nashuja said. "I'll send one of my aides to discuss the details. Should he talk to your man Eliade?"

"That would be best."

"Pleasure doing business with you," Nashuja said.

Halicarnassus was not a dangerous city, and Odysseus walked back to the rented house alone. He wasn't surprised to find Eliade absent. The younger man had a taste for outland women that he usually satisfied when he was overseas, by charming a woman into bed if he could, or paying a girl when he had to. He claimed Anatolian women were the best lovers of all. Odysseus couldn't see why that should be true, but if Eliade was happy it wasn't really anyone else's business.

Odysseus poured himself a cup of wine, with less water this time, and went to drink it on the balcony. He sat and watched the sun set over the bay, thinking as he drank.

His next stop was Egypt, to secure a second source of grain if he could. Wheat there was more expensive than here, and it had to be brought from further away, which made it worse. But Halicarnassus was close to Troy, politically. If Priam's trade sanctions led to something more serious, the Lycians might side with him against Greece, and the supply Odysseus had just arranged would be lost. Egypt, further away and more powerful, didn't care two figs for policy in Troy. A supply from there would be safer.

Odysseus couldn't rid himself of the fear that it would be needed. He felt as though there was a chasm in front of his feet, and soon enough he'd find himself sliding helplessly into it, with all the rest of the Greeks tumbling down beside him.

Chapter Ten

Words of an Owl

Troy raised duties on all Argive goods on its roads, eleven days after Odysseus signed a trade agreement in Egypt.

The higher transit tax came into effect immediately. Ship captains sailing into the Bay of Troy found themselves faced with a price they hadn't expected, or planned for. Turning around wasn't an option; they had bought their goods with Troy in mind, and would make less money elsewhere. Besides, they would only be wasting time. Those who could pay, did so. Others were forced to hand over a tenth of their cargoes in lieu of payment.

Wagon masters reaching Troy had even less choice. Confronted with extortionate fees at the toll posts, it was inevitable that some of the traders would turn violent. They were Argives, after all. Priam had expected that though, and placed soldiers there to enforce the law; Scamandrians in lacquered red and black, Palladians in cuirasses of bright yellow. The trouble didn't last long. A few people were bound and carried away, a few more had an arm or hand broken by the haft of a spear to encourage civility. One brawl left three men dead, and buried in small cairns beside the Road.

Crescas heard the news in his warehouse and shared a tight smile with Eteon. They'd managed to secure a meeting with Ucalegon in the Pergamos, and been assured that the new duties did not apply to an Argive who had left his home for Troy. Not one who had married a Trojan woman, and especially not one who was supplying iron to the city's new Hittite smith. Crescas was well aware of the anger the fees would cause, and knew it might lead to more than a handful of deaths on the Trojan Road. But it didn't affect him. Not yet at least, and that was enough for the moment.

Mursili heard it too, though his command of Luwian was still poor enough that he wasn't sure at first what he was being told. Something about prices, he knew that, and people being attacked on the road east of the city. It wasn't until the afternoon that he could put everything together well enough to understand what had happened. Even then he didn't see what reason there was for the king to do this. In Hattusa tax hikes on a single group were a weapon of punishment. When he talked with his new friend Phereclus, in a tavern later that evening, he realised that was exactly the point.

Phereclus himself had heard the news down at the Bay, where he was supervising the construction of seven new ships. Troy had never had a navy of its own; had never needed one, in truth, with Argives and others sailing the Greensea for them. But Priam thought it was time for that to change. If Troy had her own ships she could keep prices down, and perhaps in time also train archers and spearmen to fight from the decks, the way the Argives did. Phereclus had been brought all the way from Colchis to make that possible.

He heard about the taxes and frowned, pushing a hand through hair the wind had already strewn around his head. One problem with ships was that they did go missing between ports, even when the weather was mild. Pirates, mistakes, even plain bad luck could see a ship holed, and unable to reach land in time. Rivals could sink a lone vessel in the knowledge that they couldn't be blamed for it, not with certainty… and the Argives had a lot of ships. A *lot.* If they were angry enough, this new little fleet of Phereclus' might see the bottom of the sea rather sooner than he would like.

News reached the stables down by the Scaean Gate, at the southern end of the city.

"Will the Argives attack us?" Tanith asked.

Troilus was rubbing down a newly-tamed mare. She was still skittish around new people, and would snort and stamp if any hand but Troilus' touched her. "How would I know?"

"They would break their spears on our walls and sail home weeping," Tanith said, with more confidence than she felt. The Argives frightened her. Every time word came of another raid on some far-off coast, carried out by the terrifying Myrmidons and their dread captain perhaps, she trembled inside. But Troy was too strong, its walls too high, surely. Surely.

"I expect so," Troilus said.

"You really haven't heard anything?"

"I spend more time in these stables than I do in the Pergamos," he said. "Taxes and politics have never interested me."

"What does interest you?"

She struck a pose as she spoke, knowing he'd see her from the side of his eye. When she worked she wore a short, simple dress, tight-fitting at the bodice and cut lower that Trojan dresses usually were. It was rather like an Argive chiton, in fact. It showed off her figure well. Troilus turned his head slightly and grinned, but he didn't stop rubbing down the mare.

"Horses," he said.

Horses interested Tanith too. She'd grown up around them back in Phrygia, and taken the chance to come to Troy because the best animals in the world were here. Everyone knew it. She'd uprooted her life to work with these horses, but still, she wasn't as passionate as Troilus was.

Not about horses, anyway. About him… but that was not a thought she ought to be having. He was a prince, she an outland stable girl. She'd take what he gave her, and try to be happy with it.

"Say that again," she said, striving for a light tone, "and I'll upend this bucket of manure on your head, I swear I will."

He finished with the mare and left the stall, taking care to bolt the door behind him before he turned to Tanith. When he did he crossed the distance to her in a stride. He picked her up – she was small, had never really gained weight – and kissed her soundly. There was hay in his hair.

"I locked the door," she said breathlessly, when their lips parted.

"Wouldn't matter if you hadn't," he said. He carried her into an empty stall and knelt on the floor, so she could lie back onto a pile of straw. She was already pulling at his shirt. He rucked her dress up around her hips and she grabbed his head so she could kiss him, and shortly afterwards forgot all about the Argives, and taxes, and everything but her prince.

*

The prince's brother was several miles away, sitting at a campfire as afternoon faded into evening.

Three fat, red-breasted geese hung on spits over the flames. A fair return for half a day's hunting, though less than they'd hoped for. These wooded slopes in the upper Simois valley usually teemed with game, everything from boars and wild goats to leopards, but today they'd seen nothing. Only old spoor, long since dried out, and the remnants of tracks almost worn away by the summer wind. Hector had been hoping to find a leopard, if he was honest. A brush with danger would have fitted his mood perfectly.

"So what do you think?" Lycaon asked.

It was unusual for Lycaon to be home long enough to join a hunt. Most often he was off sailing somewhere, in a galley he'd bought from an Argive and crewed with men from all over. Trojans, Lydians, a couple of Phoenicians; even an Egyptian, a man with the blackest skin Hector had ever seen. All of them must have sailed to their homes since then, probably more than once. Lycaon had seen things Hector knew he never would, from the Cypriot copper mines to the strange pyramids that rose out of the sand in Egypt.

But Lycaon was married now, to a member of the Hittite royal line no less, albeit a fairly remote cousin. Marriage changed a man, changed the way he lived. Hector knew that for himself now. He loved to hunt, felt more at home outdoors than in the streets of a city, but part of him now longed to be home, where Andromache was. Where half his heart was.

"I think Father has tried everything else," he said. "The Argives deserve it. Maybe now they'll see sense."

"That's right," Pandarus said. He turned the spits and fat sputtered. The smell of the birds was driving Hector mad. "And really, what are they going to do? Attack Troy?"

He chortled, as though that was a great joke. Probably it was. Troy's mighty walls, and her position on the ridge above the plain, made it almost impossible to attack. Even so, the surrounding area might be threatened, even seized, which would be a disaster anyway. The horses would be lost the moment that happened. It had taken a hundred years to build up those herds; it would take a hundred more to replace them, if they were lost. And to what point? Once the Argives had

Trojan bloodstock they could sell it around the world, and no one would ever need to buy from Troy again.

Pandarus didn't understand that. He was lord of Zeleia, the growing city in the Scamander valley, halfway to Mount Ida. Zeleia didn't have a coastline, or a hinterland threatened by raiders. The only way into that valley was either over the peaks or through the gorge, and the routes were watched. That made Pandarus more confident than he should be. He was a good man to have around though, one of only two warriors who could stand against Hector and meet him blow for blow – more or less. Whenever Hector's spirits flagged Pandarus was there, as full of energy and spirit as ever.

And yet he was nagged by unease, over this business with Greeks and taxes. The Argives would be mad to attack Troy, but Hector couldn't shake the worry that they might.

"No Argive kingdom is strong enough to challenge us," Lycaon said. "And they can't work together anyway. I've visited enough of their halls to know. Whenever two kings meet they bicker over something. It might be trade, or borders, or women," his mouth tightened, as though he was thinking of Hesione, "or who the gods love best. But they don't work together in warfare."

"They have a High King now," Hector murmured.

"And what difference has that made?" Pandarus demanded. "How many times has their High King led all the Argives into war?"

He never had, of course. Agamemnon was a surly sort of man, by all accounts, long on intimidation but short of subtlety and tact. And the other Greek kings didn't like having an overlord, and took every opportunity to show that they were more than Agamemnon's lackeys. It didn't make for stability. Agamemnon seemed to spend most of his time trying to prevent his subject kings from smashing one another into pieces over some minor disagreement; and even then, the kings fought in a constant series of minor raids against each other. Nothing short of the end of the world seemed likely to end it.

That was the Argives for you. They knew how to fight, by the gods they did, but they didn't know how to stop. They had conquered their way across the Aegean and beyond, but when they met their match they would have no other gift to turn to, no other way to live. They would fail, and night would fill their eyes as they died, and were forgotten.

"What about you?" Hector asked the fourth man. "What do you think?"

He looked up, a tall lean man with thoughtful hazel eyes. "It doesn't matter what I think."

"How can you say that?" Hector asked, surprised. "It always matters. Father always asks you, Aeneas."

"Not this time," he said. "The decision was made without me. As is Priam's right." He hesitated. "What I think… is that this is dangerous. The Argives don't like to be challenged. It makes them angry."

"Abducting our women makes us Trojans angry," Pandarus growled. "Especially royal women."

"With reason," Aeneas murmured. "I'm not defending the Greeks, my friends. Lycaon here can journey to their halls if he likes, but I've no stomach for it myself. If I want to watch half-educated beasts fight over the table I can let my dogs into the supper hall."

Hector grinned. Aeneas was the other man who could stand toe to toe with him and not back up, and he liked him even better than he did Pandarus. There was more intelligence behind the slim man's words, more consideration than Pandarus could match. That was why Priam took him into his confidence so often. But not today, apparently. He hadn't counselled Aeneas before deciding to raise the taxes. Hector found that surprising.

When he was king, he was going to make Aeneas his main advisor. It would take him away from Dardanos of course, and that would need to be dealt with, but Hector would find a way. He'd have to. Aeneas was too clever to be allowed to dither away in that little town.

"But I wonder if this course of action is wise," Aeneas went on. "To be blunt, Hesione is one woman. What's been done to her is monstrous, it's appalling – but still, it has happened to one woman. And it has *happened,* my friends. Nothing we or the king of Troy can do will change that."

"We can bring her back," Lycaon said.

"But we cannot undo the last twenty years," Aeneas said. "What we *can* do, however, is embroil Troy in a dispute with no resolution, for the sake of a woman we can no longer save. If Hesione comes back to Troy it won't be home to her any longer. She'll hardly know the city. And Priam, for all his love for her, will hardly recognise her. She's no longer the sister he remembers."

"So you think we should abandon her?" Pandarus demanded.

Aeneas regarded him calmly. "I think she was abandoned twenty years ago. The time for direct action was then."

"You think the Argives will attack us," Hector said. The others fell silent as he spoke. "Don't you?"

"I think the Argives are Argives," Aeneas answered. He stared into the fire. "Nobody knows what they'll do until they do it. Least of all them. But it will probably be mad, and dangerous, and foolish." He shook his head. "Never mind. The dice have been thrown, they're rolling now, and there's nothing we can do but wait to see how they land."

Aeneas was uneasy too. Hector thought there should have been comfort in that, of a strange kind to be sure, but still. Every man likes to know his fears are not mere creations of his own mind. In the event, hearing them spoken by Aeneas only made Hector more concerned. He didn't know what to say. The four of them sat in silence for some time, staring at the flames or the stars, each lost in his own thoughts.

"The geese are done," Pandarus said finally. They took them down from the spits and shared them onto four plates, and then sat and ate as the stars wheeled, and owls began to talk above them.

*

Word reached Nestor too, in his palace in Pylos. He had expected it, even planned for it with Odysseus, and made what preparations he could. He didn't know if they would be enough. The new taxes on the Trojan Road wouldn't merely hurt, they'd make it all but impossible for Greeks to trade with the nations of the Euxine Sea at all. Merchants would lose their businesses, shops and traders their supplies. Nestor had already set aside a fifth of his treasury to help support small tradesmen through the troubles, through a variety of tax reductions and specially funded market fairs. But he knew all that, the work had been done a long time ago. He didn't need to dwell on it now.

The news made him restless, though. Nestor went out into the gardens, then back inside to prowl around the kitchens for a while. He nibbled at a plate of figs, but left a cup of *kykeon* untouched; he didn't need wine now, even honeyed. Not in this mood. The servants, as familiar with the king's temperament as anyone, kept out of his way. He wandered back outside again and finally, as the maids and butlers had known he would, he found himself upstairs in his bed chamber, the room he'd shared with his wife through so very many years.

There was nobody there. Of course not; the servants would have been advised to find something else to do. Nestor put it out of his mind and went to the balcony, looking out over the sea while a breeze filled the air with spray and the tang of salt.

"It's happened, Eurydice," he said. "As we thought it would."

His dead wife made no reply, unsurprisingly. Though there were times when Nestor would swear on his own soul that he heard her, just a whisper in wind or in the rustle of a bed sheet. Usually at night, when the world was sleeping and the air hung quiet and heavy. Still, when he talked to her it was only ever his own voice Nestor heard. He supposed he did so because he always had, when they were married, and that had been for a long time. Thirty years. He hadn't been ready to let her go.

Strange, the things people did, to deal with grief. Nestor's mind tugged on that thought and then followed it, and was led to Tyndareus of Laconia, Helen's father, dead these five years.

Tyndareus hadn't coped well when Castor died. Grief had broken him, in truth. Until then he'd been a typical Greek king, all swagger and the threat of force, convinced he could bend even the Fates to his will. *He's a fighter, that boy of mine,* he'd said in Thessaly, after the boar had snapped Castor's leg like a toothpick. As though by bravado, by sheer strength of will, he could browbeat destiny into letting his son live.

He'd failed, and after the loss Tyndareus withdrew, shrivelled into himself, becoming wrinkled and worn in the space of one winter. He clung to life for a long time after that, but Nestor had never been quite sure why the Fates didn't take him too. Tyndareus had decided he had nothing to live for. Every morning he awoke without his son was torment.

Castor's death made Helen a prize for the princes of Greece to fight over. Her only brother was dead, her only sister already married to Agamemnon in Mycenae. Helen was now heir to Laconia, to the rivers and hills of that pleasant land, its wealth and the red-cloaked warriors who guarded it. Nobles and heroes began to circle like wolves around a lamb.

Nestor and Tyndareus had never been close. But they had fought together, two proud young men riding their chariots into war, throwing their spears at the same enemy. Some of the time, anyway. Over the years Nestor had come to respect the other king. Tyndareus might have been an old-style Greek, still caught up in the pride and brag of the warrior culture, but he wasn't a fool. Or he hadn't been, until his son died and he fell into self-willed decay, while the wolves crept closer around him. His hand had loosened around his spear haft then, and he hadn't the will to close his fingers again.

Helen must have been wounded too, though she didn't show it. Her brother lost, her sister gone away, and her father shrunken and silent. How could that not affect her? But she carried her scars inside, if scars she bore. All Nestor could say was that she seemed content enough with Menelaus; and a good thing, too, because there was no way for her to leave that marriage. Not when she had chosen it herself, so publicly. Still, he wondered sometimes what her griefs were, and how she coped with them.

"Listen to me," he told Eurydice. "Worrying about another woman's feelings. You'd have words for me, I know, if you were here. I don't even know why I'm thinking about her."

He knew how he coped with grief though. He worried for Thrasymedes now more than he had since his son was a small boy, toddling through the world with wide eyes and a perpetual smile. Mostly there wasn't much he could do: young men liked to test their strength, and Thrasymedes was going to hunt and spar no matter what Nestor might say to him. And he'd have to, since a king who couldn't command the respect of warriors wouldn't hold his throne for long.

Nestor could work to hand Thrasymedes a wealthy kingdom to rule, though. One stable and at peace. But he couldn't help feeling that this news from Troy, expected or not, made that a lot less likely.

He shook himself and left the room, pausing only to touch his fingers to the headboard of the bed where his wife had lain so often.

Book Two   The Doves That Speak

Caesura

A year, those taxes remained high. A year, while Greek merchants struggled under the burden and granaries ran low – or else treasuries did, as kings spent their wealth on wheat to feed the people.

Prices rose. Farmers liked the extra coin, but then spent it on other goods as everything began to cost more. The bulk of the populace suffered poverty from the start. There were stories of wagons standing abandoned on the Trojan Road, left by owners who couldn't afford the new duties at the toll posts. Some were still laden with merchandise. Ships that had once plied the Aegean back and forth to Troy now lay at rest on the beaches of Euboea, or Pieria, drawn up out of the waves they were built to ride.

I travelled from town to town in that time, as a storyteller must. Sometimes I told my tales to small audiences, crowded into what passed for a meeting hall; once it was just a large *andron* in a private home. Other evenings I was in a city, even a capital, and I recited and played for kings. Menestheus in Athens, then Leitus in Boeotia; later Schedius in Phocis and Agamemnon himself, glowering from his throne in Mycenae. In the summer I took a ship to Crete and played there for Idomeneus, at his request. Bards and storytellers didn't often make the journey to the Hundred Towns without an invitation, and the promise of enough silver to make it worthwhile.

Everywhere I went, there were grumblings about the new taxes. But nobody blamed Telamon: that struck me even then, listening. The Greeks muttered and cursed, but their curses were for Priam and Troy. Once I recited a tale I'd written myself, of a foreign princess pining for her home in Greek captivity, and I thought my audience would tear me apart. I switched to an old favourite about Perseus before that could happen, and never dared again. The people had seen their ease taken away by taxes on the Trojan Road, and it was Troy they accused, and Priam. What had been meant to divide the Greek princes instead united the common men, against the city which grew fat as their own bellies grew emptier.

Priam intended the hardship to put pressure on Telamon in Salamis. He envisioned princes going to the island to plead with Hesione's captor. It worked, in a way. More than one king sent requests for Telamon to consider their difficulties. What could one woman matter, they asked, against the welfare of all Greece?

Telamon never answered, as far as I know. When Menestheus went to visit him, and later Agapenor, he made sure to be out hunting in the hills, though by then he was so monstrous fat that running was impossible and there was no chariot that could hold him.

Early the next summer, a Magnesian galley tried to pass the Hellespont going east, to Propontis and the Euxine Sea beyond. It was caught in the *Meltemi* and driven onto the waiting reefs, its crew killed or left far from home and helpless. Three more ships tried a few weeks later, after their captains worked out the cycles of the Moon and took several auguries, seeking the blessing of the gods before they set their sails.

All were wrecked before they reached the midpoint of the Strait. The Trojans sent a few survivors back to Greece, full of terrible tales of the crashing rocks, and currents that snapped vessels like old bones. No one else tried, after that. Jason had taken the *Argo* through, but he'd had Hera on his side, and Heracles pulling at an oar. There was no Heracles today.

I remember the *agora* in Athens that summer, full of angry citizens and shouting merchants. Every day it was the same. Every day soldiers were sent to restore order, while Menestheus fumed in his palace and his treasury shrank. Such times are made for the fall of kings. And they know it; a lord who cannot read the mood of his people doesn't last long.

Then the message came from Troy.

*

Tyche is a daughter of Zeus, one of the many. It is her joy to decide on which mortals to bestow good fortune, heaping gifts from a cornucopia: her joy, too, to deprive others of everything good they have. Oft-times she changes her favourites, casting a lucky man into misery and raising an unfortunate to heights undreamed-of. She juggles a ball as she works, sometimes tossing it high, sometimes dropping it to the floor.

When that message came to Athens we thought Tyche had turned her random mood on us. Whether our fortunes were to rise or fall we did not know. But we knew chance was in the room at our side.

The missive invited Menestheus to Troy, to discuss the matters of high taxes and the abducted sister. Similar overtures had been sent to Nestor in Pylos and Menelaus in Sparta, we were told. The message fell on us like a stone into clear water. We could barely credit it. Priam had Greece groaning for relief and now he offered it. Menestheus saw a chance to end the discord and he snatched at it, of course.

How was he to know it was a trap?

Clever Priam, to play so on our hopes. And clever Paris, whose scheme it was, though we didn't know it then. Clever, but foolish too. The Greeks had borne hunger. Their princes would not bear humiliation.

Chapter Eleven

Wild and Fierce

Cape Sigeum thrust out into the sea pointing north, a finger made of mud and sandy dunes. The three galleys rounded it together, oarsmen straining against a moderate northerly wind.

The Bay of Troy opened up before them, filled with ships coming and going from the strand at the southern end, a mile or more away. Those heading in had their sails raised, those emerging did not, and men worked hard at their oars as they struggled against the wind. Nestor counted thirty vessels and then stopped. There were a lot, as always. Troy had not suffered as Greece had, this past year.

The rowers pulled in their oars as the sail was raised. The wind was behind the ships now, as they turned south into the Bay. It freed men to stare in awe at the sight before them.

To the left was a town with a wooden palisade, set back from the shore of the Bay. That was Bunarbi, Nestor remembered, though it had doubled in size since he was last in these waters. Behind it hills rose, carpeted with bushes and trees, a blaze of fertility unmatched in Greece. Southward, his ageing eyes could just make out the gorge from which the Scamander emerged to water the Plain of Troy, there beyond the beached ships.

He looked across to the ship which carried Menelaus, to see the king of Sparta staring with his mouth open. He wasn't looking at the river or the hills, but at the city which waited before them.

Troy.

It was still a mile distant, just to the east of the strand where ships unloaded their cargoes. But it towered over everything. The base of its walls stood a hundred feet above the ships, and its towers reached fifty feet above that. Mighty Mycenae's walls only rose twenty feet, and like all Greeks Menelaus had been raised to think that was awesome, a feat achieved by an army of Cyclops in the days before Men came to live there. It might even be true.

Troy made Mycenae look like a cave, cut into a cliff by generations of men with stone hammers. It was a palace alongside a hut, an ocean shining beside a pond choked with weeds.

Nestor thought it had grown, actually. The west wall looked to have been extended, so it reached a little further down the slope of the ridge on which the city was built. Nestor hadn't heard about that. He knew Troy's outlying towns were expanding though; Leris. Zeleia, Bunarbi to the north. The kingdom was doing well, gaining in numbers and wealth, and so too in power. Given another generation it might be able to found an empire.

There were rumours coming out of the Hittite kingdom these days, whispers of woe and looming disaster. It might be that Troy found herself able to build an empire just when a gap opened up for one. In fifty years the whole coast of Anatolia might be under Trojan rule, one great homogenous realm blocking access to the riches of the interior.

That wasn't a comfortable thought. Troy had sent half of Greece into penury by closing a single road. A coastal Trojan empire might be able to destroy cities from Sparta to Meliboea just by raising prices.

He made a mental note of that thought, storing it away for reference against what Priam might say when the three kings reached the city. The invitation had implied an effort to resolve the problems of Hesione and high taxes, mentioning them together in an effort to link them in the minds of the Greek kings. Nothing had been made explicit, though. For all Nestor knew, he and his peers had been brought here for a tongue-lashing.

And something didn't feel right. On the surface Priam's offer seemed fair: more than generous, in fact. But still… why these three kings? He'd invited Nestor, Menelaus and Menestheus, but why them, and not others? Agamemnon would not have come, of course. But Diomedes of Argolis would, or Thalpius of Elis. Agapenor, Peleus, Leonteus, even Odysseus from western Ithaca, if they'd been asked. So why hadn't they been?

Dust had begun to rise from the road leading down from the western wall of Troy. Quite a lot of it, in fact, as though many vehicles were moving rapidly down the slope. Nestor watched it as his ship drew closer to the strand, pulling ahead of Menelaus' and Menestheus' vessels now, its sail opening to catch the steady north wind.

*

Far to the west, two days after Menelaus had set sail from Gythium, a ship nosed into the harbour.

It looked like a Phoenician vessel, with a raised stern and square-cut mast, only a little larger. Larger than any Greek ship too, come to that. Only an Argonaut would have known that the Colchians built their ships that way, and they were nearly all dead now. Certainly no one in Gythium knew. This was one of Phereclus' designs, not seen yet on the Greensea. The crew unloaded crates onto wagons, ignoring the cries of the townsfolk to be allowed to buy any food they carried. By early afternoon twenty-five men were heading north, most of them walking beside the wagons with bows in hand and swords at their belts.

The cargo crates held spears and shields, and un-lacquered armour from the workshops of Troy.

*

Menestheus jumped down from his ship, once the prow had been driven high on the beach by the oarsmen. Nestor, not young anymore, had to climb carefully down a rope ladder thrown over the side. He splashed out of the water to join the younger king, who was shading his eyes to look southwards.

"I think we have a welcoming committee," Menestheus said.

Nestor nodded. "Chariots. I saw them from the deck."

"A lot of chariots, then," Menestheus added.

He had his bard with him, the storyteller from Magnesia who'd gained such a high reputation over the past years. Thersites climbed down a rope ladder too, making heavier work of it than Nestor had. He was puffing like a bellows by the time his feet reached the water. When he limped up to join the kings Nestor was struck by how misshapen he looked: his shoulders seemed too far forward, or his chest too concave, as though something huge had struck him there and driven his ribcage back into his spine. Stringy hair hung in his eyes. He didn't look healthy enough to survive a winter, but he hobbled onto the sand and stared south with an alert enough expression.

The third galley ran its nose onto the strand a little way from them, and Menelaus leapt down almost before it stopped moving. He strode over to join them, also shading his eyes. "Bind my tongue, can you believe that city?"

"I don't have to," Nestor said. "Troy exists, whether I believe in it or not."

The red-haired man frowned at him. "Stop being clever, Nestor. You know what I meant."

"It's... remarkable," Thersites said.

Nestor eyed him for a moment. The hollow-chested man was a marvellous bard, with the sort of deep rolling voice that could make a stone hall seem someplace else: the tilting deck of a storm-wracked ship, or the mountain heights with a lion stalking somewhere among the boulders. Half-drunk, belching men on benches became a company to rival the heroes of mighty *Argo*, and felt themselves so too, for as long as Thersites spoke. But besides all that, Nestor had the sneaking suspicion that the storyteller was clever. He liked wit and guile, admired them in a man, but Nestor only liked them in a man he trusted, and he was by no means sure of Thersites.

"Perhaps it is remarkable," he said, "but it's still only one city. It would fit three times into Mycenae, or your own Athens, Menestheus."

Menelaus was craning his head back to stare at the walls. Troy was still half a mile distant, but even so it seemed to loom over them, casting a shadow as far as the sea and then beyond. "I wouldn't like to try to capture it, I'll tell you that. Any king would lose a lot of men if he tried."

That was a true Greek talking, Nestor reflected. The first thought in his head was how to fight the city, not how it had been built, or what could be learned from its people. No, Menelaus was a Greek of the old school, and what he considered important was how to destroy it if the need arose. Or simply the desire. He would have been right at home alongside the fathead Theseus, or Perseus who'd had nothing but bone between his ears.

The chariots were approaching. Several Greeks jumped down from the ships with spears in their hands, ready to form a wall around their kings, but at a word from Menestheus his soldiers fell back a few paces. The others copied them, though they remained wary. More found idle work to do near the bows of the ships, far enough away not to threaten but close enough to react quickly. Nestor was sure there would be bows hidden just out of sight, beneath the rails. They wouldn't be necessary, but he couldn't blame the men for their caution.

There were thirty chariots. *Thirty;* even Agamemnon himself couldn't put so many into the field. Each had three horses, where a Greek chariot would have only two, and just by watching them approach Nestor could see they were faster. His own kingdom of Messenia actually had some good grasslands, a rare thing in Greece, and he owned a fair herd of horses himself. But he didn't have enough, in quantity or quality, to match this.

He'd been a charioteer of note in his day, the finest in Greece some said. In honesty Nestor thought that might have been true, when he was young and strong. And he would have given half his soul to drive a chariot such as these, just once, just to feel the acceleration and see the sinews pulling in the horses ahead of the car. In the *three* horses. Zeus in his Black Cloud, he'd rick half his soul to feel that now, even aged and past his prime.

The lead chariot slowed, then drew to a halt just in front of the kings. A tall man in a kilt and patterned shirt swung down, wearing boots laced to just below the knee. Blue eyes looked out from beneath sandy hair, and Nestor guessed who this was even before he spoke.

"My lords!" the charioteer said. He bowed to each of them, a little awkward making the Greek-style obeisance but not overly so. "I cannot tell you what a pleasure it is to have you here in Troy. My father will be delighted you've come. I am Hector."

Thought so, Nestor said to himself. Watching the Trojan turn on the balls of his feet he felt a murmur of unease. He had indeed been a fighting man in his day, and he recognised a warrior when he saw one. It was something in the balance, in the poise, the same air of restrained speed and danger you sensed in a dozing leopard. Hector overflowed with it. By their sudden stillness the other two kings had noticed it as well.

"These are my friends," Hector said, indicating the next two chariots in line. "Aeneas of Dardanos, and Pandarus from Zeleia. We would be honoured if you would ride with us back to the city, one of you with each of us. We will inform your men where to bring your belongings."

"Most gracious," Nestor said. Menelaus, less comfortable with his tongue, only gave a curt nod.

"I will need my advisor Thersites, of course," Menestheus said.

"This is he?" The sight of the crippled man didn't even cause Hector to blink. "But of course! Crino, you can offer him a ride. Remember he's an honoured guest. Treat him as you would a king."

Thersites looked surprised, for a moment. Nestor wasn't sure whether that was real or faked; he was going to have to speak to that young man, to take his measure. For now he had other things to think about.

The Trojans were certainly doing them honour, but there was more to it than that. Hector was known as the greatest warrior of the Troas, perhaps of the whole of Anatolia. There were rumours that he'd won the Hittite victory against Assyria last summer almost on his own. In Greece fighting men spoke in hushed voices of Achilles, and the deeds he'd done from Thrace to Egypt, Phoenicia to Crete; in the east, they did the same for Hector. Like Achilles they said he was a charmer, a friend to all, who could make doubting men eager for the chance to fight for him. Seeing his smile, Nestor could believe it.

As for Aeneas, he was king of Dardanos, and a fine warrior in his own right. Pandarus was a name Nestor knew too, as the lord of one of the Trojan towns in the interior, and a warrior who had cleaned out the last stubborn bandits from the hills – and kept them out. That last was a great achievement, and it had meant safe roads and rapid travel between Troy and the southern cities of Lyrnos and Pedasos, and beyond to greater prizes like Pergamum and wealthy Ephesus. Safe roads meant more trade, more trade meant more coin. The passage down the Scamander valley had always been fraught with risk before. Now, thanks to hulking Pandarus, it no longer was.

Something was building here. The Trojans were spreading out, founding new towns and expanding old ones, filling up the land with bustle and business and driving the old days out. They'd reached down the coast to Leris, and up the Scamander to Thymbra and then Zeleia. Nestor had heard they had pushed east along the Simois valley and built a town on the river Granicus, fifty miles from Troy itself. Not all the people in those towns would really be Trojans, of course. But they all *called* themselves Trojans. They paid loyalty to Priam and taxes to his treasury, and in return he kept them safe and made them wealthy.

Nestor tried to work out how big Troas was. Much larger than any single Greek kingdom, that was for sure; perhaps as big as Laconia, Messenia and Arcadia all added together. More fertile, too. Wealthier by nature. Powerful enough, perhaps, to face all Greece one day.

He felt a cold finger touch his heart at the thought.

But he was thinking like Menelaus, in terms of warriors and military power. The Trojans were too, which was why they had their three best fighting men here to meet the Greek kings, but that was unusual for them. They were normally more subtle; this display of strength must be their attempt to show the visiting Greeks something they would all understand. That was unsettling, too. Troy had never felt the need to brag about her military power before.

He had to admit he was uneasy. He made sure no sign of it showed in his expression as he climbed up on Aeneas' chariot and braced his feet, but he resolved to keep himself as alert as he could manage while he was in Troy. If Menestheus did the same, and perhaps the odd bard Thersites as well, they would spy out enough to work out what was actually going on here.

Hector called an order, and the long line of trigas began to move along the dusty road to Troy.

*

The night after landing, the Trojan wagons had reached Therapne, a village five miles south of Sparta.

There they met other warriors, men who had slipped ashore in twos and threes over the previous week and made their way inland. Most of them were men from the Simois valley, or the northern slopes of Ida, well used to ghosting silently through countryside and living off the land. There had been one unfortunate incident which required the deaths of a young swain and his lover, who had chosen to hold their midnight tryst right on the track five Trojans were following in the starlight. Other than that nobody had been seen.

There were now sixty Trojan soldiers in a field outside Therapne, beside the river Evrotas. As the moon rose one of them climbed up on a wagon bed and made a speech.

He wasn't actually a warrior at all. Not someone you would expect to be leading such a daring raid as this, deep into Argive territory. This was a task that called for a Hector, an Aeneas, or at least the captain of one of the divisions, the Apollonians or Scamandrians. The speaker was none of those things. That was why the Greeks in Troy would never think to wonder where he was.

We have spoken our prayers, Paris began, *and offered our sacrifices before we set out. The gods are with us or they are not. All we can do is trust in them, and go forward with honour.*

There was a joy in him, actually, something wild and fierce that he'd never felt before. A little like the thrill of the first time with a new woman, but more intense even than that. His heart was beating hard and strong. He *felt* strong, as though every god in the east was watching him, and smiling. Tarhun of Storms was with him, Ipirru of horses, and Pallas Athena the Lady of Battle had her hand upon his shoulder. His voice swelled as he spoke.

They all knew why they were there, he reminded them. The Argives were never going to return Hesione, the aunt he had never seen. They could not be persuaded, and would not be driven to it by taxes or encroaching poverty. Their pride was more important to them than any other consideration. Either Hesione was abandoned, or the Argives were forced to hand her back.

Hesione would not be abandoned.

But he believed she would be handed back, if in exchange the Trojans could return an Argive woman they had taken in their turn. A younger woman than Hesione, more highly prized, of higher rank. A queen then, and young, and beautiful. And last summer Antenor had seen a woman he called the loveliest he had ever set eyes upon: Helen, the queen of Sparta, and sister by marriage to Agamemnon the High King in Mycenae.

This was Antenor's plan, then, fermented in his mind since that day in Laconia last year. The warriors gathered here would slip into Sparta while its king was away, lured to Troy with the offer of discussions. The best Laconian soldiers would have gone with him, while the other captains would be out patrolling the borders, making sure nobody tried to take advantage of the monarch's absence. That was what Argives did, it was how they thought. Nobody would be looking for a small party of men already inside the borders, all the way to Sparta itself.

They would slip inside, find Helen and seize her, and be gone down the road to Therapne and then Gythium, and their ship. Helen would not be touched, not harmed in any but the most minor way. They would take her home to Troy and then ransom her back for one price, and one only: the return of Hesione. No sane man could refuse that bargain.

After, the extra taxes on Argive goods could be removed. Perhaps games could be held on the Plain of Troy, thrown in honour of the Greek gods atop Mount Olympus. They would soothe raw wounds. Good wine would wash away sour moods. Troy and Mycenae would be friends again.

When he jumped down captains issued rapid orders. Six men broke away to take positions south of the ford, in case luck or planning failed and Laconians tried to hold it against the returning raiders. Six was not many, but enough to discomfit a holding force with arrows from behind. The rest of the men set out northwards, trotting along the deserted road as the moon slowly rose. They had all spoken their prayers beforehand, as Paris said, but that didn't stop them speaking more as they ran, to whichever deity they thought best.

Nothing could go wrong, as long as the gods were with them.

Chapter Twelve

A Knife at the Throat

The chariots had to go south at first, though Troy was east of the strand where the kings' ships were drawn up. Ship prows jutted onto the beach fifty yards or so apart, enough room to work the oars on the way in and to unload crates or amphorae held in great nets. Wagons were parked at various angles, some drawn by four horses, others by six. Nestor had seen it before, on previous visits, but he still found six horses a wild extravagance.

Sailors and longshoremen stopped working to watch them pass. A few top-knotted Thracians were bare chested, muscles gleaming with sweat, but most men wore shirts and either kilts or the loose trousers of southern Anatolia. Nearly all had the flattened features of lifelong dock brawlers, or the spread-footed walk of men used to swaying decks. It made no difference. They paused to gape as the chariots swept by, a long line of them rattling over the shingle, until captains or merchants yelled at them to get back to work.

Then they reached the road, a wide strip of earth tamped carefully flat, with stones and other bits of detritus cleared away. Chariots ran best on such smooth surfaces, and they picked up speed at once. On their left a channel of the Scamander whispered, flanked on both sides with willow and tamarisk, lotus and bulrushes. A similar double line of greenery stood a little way off to their right, where another of the river's braided arms flowed. The two channels drew closer and then the chariots splashed across a ford through the western arm, turned south-east and a hundred yards later crossed the joined flow, onto the eastern bank. Both times Nestor's feet were wetted but not submerged. The Scamander was low in summer, after the spring melt had passed.

They picked up speed, the horses working now for the first time. An experienced charioteer, Nestor knew the animals had plenty of speed left in them, but he realised too that it took some skill by the driver to run them at this pace. Hector and his friends were showing what they could do; and without much effort, it seemed. It had to be admired, staged or no.

Nestor's old knees had begun to ache but he was damned if he'd ask them to slow down.

They drove past a hill on the right, thick with brambles and clumped bushes, all grown through one another in a hideous tangle. Then over another ford, across the Chiblak River this time, a smaller stream but faster flowing than the Scamander. The channel had been widened, Nestor noticed, so the water ran in shallow ripples that hardly covered the rims of the wheels. And then at last they were drawing up to the city itself, mighty Troy rising above them in a mass of turrets and towers and the road switching back and forth as it climbed the slope, like the path through Minos' Labyrinth far away.

At the top, just outside the southern Scaean Gate, grew a large and gnarled oak tree. Legend claimed it was planted there by Ilos, the son of Tros who had founded the city, three hundred and fifty years before. Troy had been sacked twice in the first years, when it was still only a village huddling under the onslaught of the endless summer wind.

It had not been sacked since. The walls had been built of brick, then stone. They had risen ten feet and then twenty, then thirty-five. Nestor craned his head back to look at their distant tops and couldn't help a twinge of unease.

It wasn't just the imperiousness of Troy. That was part of it, yes; only a fool could stand in the shadow of these towering walls and not feel a degree of awe. It was unsettling, not least because it was so much greater than anything Greece had been able to do. But it wasn't that which had Nestor's senses twitching. He didn't know what it was, but he knew there was something wrong.

The chariots slowed as they neared the wall.

*

They swam the first moat and scaled the wall, using grappling hooks and ropes. There were no guards at all, amazingly. The inner moat only came up to their thighs, except for one man who walked over a deep patch and vanished for a moment with a discreet *plop*. He bobbed up again a moment later, hair plastered down, and spouted a quick dribble of water from his lips.

The inner wall was guarded, but the sentries patrolled once and then vanished for ten minutes or more, presumably so they could enjoy a chat and a cup of something to warm them. Captain Molion waited for a gap and then whispered the order, and they all went up the ropes like spiders in the dark. They were down the inner side and into the shadows of the streets before the next guard emerged from the tower.

The palace was in the west of the city, on higher ground. The raiders had entered from the south because the walls were lower there, but it left them half a mile of twisted roads to navigate before they reached their goal. They did so without incident, streaming over the cobbles with cloths wrapped over their boots so they didn't clack and clatter as they went. Less than half an hour after reaching the outer wall they were in the palace grounds, and nobody had seen them and no one knew they were there.

"Luck," Molion whispered to Paris.

"Athena watch you," the prince murmured. They clasped forearms briefly and then parted, Molion to deal with the guards at doors and windows, Paris to enter the chambers of the queen.

*

At the Scaean Gate the road turned sharply west, so it ran with the wall of Troy hard on the right hand side. From beyond the entrance itself an arm of the battlement extended to flank the road on the other side, so the chariots rolled through a canyon of stone with a parapet on each flank. Then they turned hard again, this time to the right, and passed between the bronze-bound cedar weights of the gates.

Inside, the road was made of smoothly fitted ashlar stones, similar to the walls. On the left was the long front of the stables, set back from the road so wagons had room to park when they brought straw in or night soil out. On the right were houses, and side streets that curved off between them, and all were filled with people. Some were cheering, waving their arms in the air and shouting out names. None of those names were Greek, Nestor noticed at once. The crowds called for Hector and he raised an arm in salute, at which they went crazy with excitement. They shouted for Aeneas and when he acknowledged them they roared as though cheering themselves. But not one of them yelled the name of Menelaus or Menestheus, not that Nestor heard, and none named him either.

Of course, Achaea and Troy had not been on good terms, during this past two years or so. There was no real reason for the citizens to cry in support of Greek kings. But there wasn't a reason for them not to, either, because the presence of three lords of Achaea here on the streets of Troy should mean there was a chance of better relations ahead. This universal obliviousness was... odd. His senses, already prickling, tingled anew.

He wished he'd been able to bring Odysseus. He'd invited the young Ithacan, but Penelope was with child at last and near to her time, and Odysseus hadn't wanted to leave her alone. Nestor couldn't blame him for that. But the other man's insight and dry wit would have been invaluable here, when something was niggling at the back of Nestor's mind and he couldn't for the life of him work out what it was.

He wasn't going to ask Thersites. Not until he was sure of the man, and certainly not now, in the midst of a crowd.

They drove along the High Street of Troy, through the throng that cheered only for its own and not for the visiting kings, towards the higher wall of the Pergamos, dead ahead.

*

The palace was typical Greek, all lowering walls and narrow doorways with heavy lintel stones thrown across them like barricades. A guard was standing at the one Paris found, his spear in one hand while the other scratched idly at his backside. There were twenty yards of open space between him and the shrub where Paris hid. Plenty of time for the guard to raise an alarm.

Paris took careful aim and shot him under the jaw. The man went down making a strange gobbling sound in his throat, feet scrabbling on the stones until one of the soldiers reached him and thrust a knife into his heart. The guard went still and two men dragged his body away.

"Take his armour," Paris whispered. "Stand in his place. We'll only be a few moments."

Thirty of them went inside. Antenor had given them a map of the palace so they didn't need to spread out much. They followed a corridor past silent rooms and along the back of the *megaron,* empty at this time of night except for an old servant sleeping with his head on the table, and snoring so loud it was a wonder the roof beams didn't tremble. A soldier gestured towards him and drew a finger across his own throat, but Paris shook his head. No sense taking a risk now, even such a small one.

Just after that they took the right-hand corridor when it branched, following it up a flight of half a dozen steps and around a corner. Then the warriors did fan out, surrounding the queen's chambers that they knew lay just ahead. Paris gave them a minute and then padded up to the door, eased it open, and slipped silently into Helen's rooms, one soldier at his heels.

It was obvious immediately that Helen had decorated here. The style was so different from the rest of the palace that it couldn't be missed. No battle axes hung on the walls, or armour stood in corners; that was to be expected, of course, in a woman's place. Men were not to enter here, except the lady's husband. It was an insult even to try.

This was a working room, the *gynaikon* where women did their weaving and entertained friends. But Helen had floored it with an expensive wool carpet from Egypt, to judge by the style, and hung linen draperies on the walls in streams of colours; soft yellows and greens, lilac, a splash of blue near the window. That was more Minoan than anything else. Paris wondered if Menelaus knew what his money had paid for, here. The king of Laconia was an uncultured oaf, and Antenor said he might be so dazed by his wife's beauty that he wouldn't even know what she was doing.

Paris had decided not to believe the tales of Helen's beauty until he could judge it for himself. Two doors stood in the far wall. He chose the left and pushed it open, very slowly so the hinges didn't creak. The room beyond was dark, the windows shuttered, but he could just make out the shape of a bed. He stepped forward, away from the wall.

And stopped suddenly, keeping very still, when someone laid the blade of a knife against his throat.

*

"Be welcome to Troy," Priam said. "We are honoured that you accepted our invitation. Now you are here, I am certain we can find a solution to the disagreements that bedevil us."

"I'm sure you're right," Nestor agreed.

The other two kings seemed content to let him be their spokesman. Menestheus was staring around at the blue and gold patterned throne room in obvious interest, paying more attention to that than to Priam. As for Menelaus, he bristled whenever he looked at the Trojan king, or at Hector where he stood beside the dais. Their hosts must have noticed that, but they could pretend not to, at least. That wouldn't be the case if he spoke. Probably it was better to let him smoulder in silence for the moment.

"My son Lycaon has arranged for you to be given houses in the upper city." Priam indicated another man by the dais, a blond fellow with callused hands. "Servants have also been provided, of course. I suggest you rest for a day or two. The journey must have been wearying."

Nestor barely stopped himself from frowning. A voyage across the Aegean Sea was hardly tiring at all, for a lord. The rowers worked hard for three days, perhaps four if the wind was unhelpful, but a passenger didn't have to do anything except watch the sea slide by. Nights were spent sleeping on an island shore, in a tent rather than a palace to be sure, but even so it was hardly cause for exhaustion. Priam must know that. It was an odd comment for him to make.

Unless he simply wanted to delay any talks for the day or two he'd mentioned. But that made no sense. Why invite three Greek kings to Troy and then postpone the suggested discussion?

"That would be pleasant," Nestor said. He kept his unease hidden behind a bland smile. More than one could play at secrets.

*

"Who are you?" a voice said in Paris' ear. A woman's voice, very low and smoky. He knew at once whose it must be.

"My name is Paris," he said carefully. The blade she held pressed against his larynx. "I am the son of Priam of Troy."

"Liar."

He nearly shook his head before he remembered that might be fatal. "No. I swear it."

"Princes don't usually pay visits by sneaking into a queen's bedroom at night. Why should I believe you?"

"Light a lamp," he said, mouth dry. "You'll see by my dress that I'm Trojan, and wealthy too."

She hesitated. "You light it. On the table behind you. And be slow, prince. Move a beat too fast, even once, and I'll slit your throat."

He edged backwards, taking his time, and fumbled on the table until his hands encountered a lamp and taper. It was hard, not being able to look down to see what his hands were doing because of the knife. But he found a box with a hot coal in it, lit the taper and then the candle, and a pool of light widened around them. Paris turned his head to look at her.

His breath stopped. He'd decided not to believe in her beauty until he saw it for himself. It was hard to remember why.

Helen of Sparta was utterly gorgeous, with tawny hair over a heart-shaped face, and full lips slightly parted as she studied him. But it was her eyes which held Paris, darker than the sea and brighter than the sun which lit it. He knew he was staring and couldn't stop. All his life he'd been entranced by women; he thought he'd made love with forty, perhaps fifty, some of them just for a single night, others like Oenone returned to time and again. But he'd never seen one like this. Never thought he might.

Antenor was right, his mind decided distantly. *The Argives will make any trade for this woman.*

"You dress like a prince," Helen said. "But you have the look of a stunned sheep."

He blinked, surprised, but years of smooth talk with women came to his rescue. "I *am* stunned, my lady. I hadn't believed the tales of your beauty could actually fall short of the truth."

"Empty words," she said disdainfully. "Which tell me nothing of why you are here. Were you so overcome by the stories of me that you couldn't resist sneaking in here to ravish me?"

"Never that," he promised. He held up a hand, palm skywards. "By mighty Tarhun I swear it, and Athena who guards Troy's walls. And by Aphrodite who surely gave you her own beauty. Not to ravish."

"Then what?"

"To take you away," he said. The knife was still at his throat, and he had the sense of this woman that she would smell a lie if he spoke one. "To bring you to Troy, safely and in honour, so we can exchange you for my own aunt Hesione, still held in Salamis."

He saw those captivating eyes widen. "You're here to *abduct* me? I will use this knife, prince of Troy."

"Then do so," he shrugged. "Or come with me. I promise you'll not be harmed. You'll get to see Troy, and you will help right an old wrong. How else could you ever do such things?"

She was silent. Her gaze remained on his though, and Paris swore he could feel the crackle of her thoughts, like lightning in nearby trees. Or perhaps that was just her, the sensuality he'd felt in her the moment she spoke. He wanted to reach out and touch her, run his fingers over her skin. It was madness, to want to hold her hand while she held a blade at his throat. But he did. He thought she was aware of it, too. Helen's beauty was such that she must always have been accustomed to men longing for her.

"I've heard that Anatolian women have rights denied in Greece," she said finally. "Is that true?"

"Quite true," Paris agreed. "My mother chooses who her children will marry, not my father. It's her decision which cities to tie to Troy by marriage, and which to spurn. And it's she who deals with all the spiritual affairs of the city."

There was movement in the doorway. From the side of his vision Paris saw a pair of Trojan soldiers advance into the room, and he put out a hand to stop them without looking away from Helen. "Wait. Do nothing."

"You really are a prince of Troy," she breathed. Her violet eyes had never left him.

He nodded, as much as the knife would let him. "I am."

"Do you know what I am?" she asked. She didn't wait for a reply. "I am nothing. A bauble, perhaps, to be displayed by my husband when he has guests, men he wants to impress or make jealous. No more than that. I spend my days weaving, or bathing, or having my hair put up and woven into a braid, and none of it matters. None of it. Not since I was married."

Paris said nothing. Their gazes were still locked together.

"Once I chose my husband," Helen said. "I want to feel power like that again. Here is my offer, prince of Troy. I will go to the Topless Towers with you, but not to be bargained away, not as a piece on another man's game board. I will go as your betrothed, and in Troy your mother or her priests will set aside my marriage to Menelaus and we will be wed, you and I."

He stared at her.

"Swear it," she insisted. "Swear it on every god of Troy and of Greece, or by their names I promise I will cut your throat from ear to ear where you now stand."

Her eyes really were extraordinary. Again he felt that urge to reach out and tangle his hands in her hair, cup her face, touch the flesh of her body. His tongue seemed to act on its own. "I swear it."

"Name the gods," she pressed.

He smiled. "In Tarhun's name, by Arianna of the sun and Ipirru of horses, by Athena, I swear to marry you and stand by you, Helen. Let Zeus hear, and Hera lady of marriages witness my words. By Apollo and Aphrodite, Artemis and Poseidon Earth-Shaker, I give you my word."

A moment passed, and then she took the knife from his neck. He could still feel the line where it had rested for so long. He reached out though, and finding her hand he twined his fingers through hers. She was very warm, her skin flushed with heat. Paris smiled at her.

"I must fetch my jewellery," she said.

*

Half an hour later they were outside Sparta and hurrying south. Helen had used her authority to acquire a chariot from the stables, pulled by a pair of horses so poor they would have been killed and turned into glue and stew meat, if this was Troy. But they would do. Paris drove with Helen beside him, while the sixty raiders ran on either side. Surprisingly no alarm had been raised. It might not be until morning, now, but there was no sense in waiting to find out.

Some miles down the road Paris called a warrior up to drive and swung down, to run beside Molion. He explained the situation to the captain as quickly as he could. The soldier glanced at the thin white mark on Paris' throat and grunted. "She really had a knife on you? Quite a woman."

"You don't know the half," Paris said feelingly.

"You will keep your oath?"

"I will," he said. "I invoked too many gods to risk breaking it. There would be no place in the world for me to hide from them all."

Molion nodded. He was running quite easily, even in armour and with miles of road already behind him. "Antenor won't like it. You've ruined his carefully designed plan, Prince Paris."

"The gods ruined it," Paris disagreed. "Helen had no way of knowing intruders were in the palace, or that I was in her chamber. But she was awake and standing by the door with a knife in her hand. More than mere mortals were at work in this, Molion."

"Perhaps they were," the big soldier said. "But whose gods, then? Troy's, or the Argives'?"

He hadn't thought of that. "I suppose we'll find out."

The chariot rattled on, and the men ran with it.

Chapter Thirteen

An Emerald in Silver

"Three days," Nestor said, "and not a sign of Priam since the day we got here."

He liked this trip less with every hour that passed. Troy was a fabulous city, colourful and exciting, filled with people dressed in strange clothes and speaking strange tongues. There seemed to be a stall selling exotic food on every second street corner – when there were corners. The sinuous streets meant that often there weren't. But alluring scents still wafted through the air: roasting meats, boiling vegetables, or just spices and perfumes even Nestor had never smelled before. He thought he could spend a happy week just hunting those scents down and sampling them, whatever they were.

"They say Priam's ill," Menestheus said.

Nestor snorted. "Then why haven't I seen a physician enter his palace? I have watched for one, you know. But not a sign. When a king is ill you either send for the priests or for the doctor. Priam has seen neither."

"Maybe it's a kidney stone, or something it doesn't take a doctor to diagnose. Especially if he's suffered it before."

"Possible," Nestor conceded. "What do you think, Thersites?"

The skinny man looked up from his lyre. "Me? Yes, it's possible. But the coincidence is very large."

"Exactly. Something else is going on here."

He'd learned to trust his instincts, and right now they were telling him that something was wrong.

They had been from the start, in truth. Nothing had changed since. On the first evening the three kings had been invited to a banquet hosted by Hector. The food had been excellent, and there were tumblers and dancers the equal of any Nestor had ever seen. Especially one of the women, who danced with lithe grace to a single eastern pipe and reduced the conversation to a trickle, and then to silence. If Nestor had been twenty years younger – Hades, ten – he might have asked her to join him on his divan, so he could feed her grapes and maybe talk her into something more intimate later on.

The next day Pandarus took them hunting in the Simois valley, sending his men into the reeds beside the river to scare up ducks and geese. It was an enjoyable way to spend the day, especially since the north wind had eased off and the afternoon was pleasantly warm. Then Aeneas had hosted a banquet that night, with different entertainers. Not quite as good as Hector's, perhaps, though Aeneas did ask Thersites to perform. The storyteller had recited a poem of the dawn of the Olympians, his own composition but done in the epic style, his lyre thrumming in tempo with the cadences of his voice.

Doves and Sparrows fly
Between water and land
Where the sea foams
On the shore of Cythera
Aphrodite rises, skin
Pure and glowing in the sun.

Doves represented gods, and immortality. Sparrows stood for the death of mortal men, and so for mortality itself. Aphrodite was shown rising from the latter state to the former, becoming a goddess just as she crossed the boundary between water and land. It was very subtly done, so much so that it took Nestor some moments to catch the nuances. When he did he studied Thersites over the rim of his wine cup, trying to gauge him.

You may, he thought in the privacy of his mind, *be too clever to be a storyteller. So what else might you be, crippled man? An agent for another king? Perhaps even a killer?*

"Wonderful," Aeneas had said, when lyre and voice fell silent at last. "Truly wonderful. I've never heard an Argive *aoidos* perform in Troy before, but I shall have to hear one again."

Thersites bowed, a peculiar-looking motion from a man so strangely formed. "You're most kind, my lord Aeneas."

He was most kind, everyone in Troy was most kind... but they were not helpful. The Greek kings were meant to be distracted by all this pomp and pleasure, and Nestor couldn't help wondering what it was their attention was being diverted *from.*

Menelaus didn't seem to have noticed anything. In fact Nestor was almost sure he hadn't. He was the most important of the three visiting lords, brother to the High King and ruler of fertile Laconia, but also the least perceptive, and the least interested in puzzles. He preferred to glower at the Trojans and say very little, or else nothing. Both Atreus' sons hated Troy, and that was all right. They weren't the only ones. But when the loathing became so strong that Menelaus spent most of his time in the house he'd been given, drinking too much and brooding, it turned into a problem.

Well, the Atreides were not known for their conciliation, or their patience. Best to work around it, if you could.

This third day, Nestor had spent tracking down the principal figures of Troy, without being too obvious about it. Priam was shut in his palace, Hector training with the regiments: Aeneas was often there too, and sometimes Pandarus. That was all the main battle leaders accounted for. Ucalegon was running the palaces and Antenor was busy with a dozen things, hurrying from task to task from sunup to dusk without a sign of weariness. One thing that had piqued Nestor's interest was a man Antenor visited, a Hittite he thought, ensconced in a converted house near the wall that seemed to be some kind of forge. He'd have to look into that, once he could speak to the merchants who visited here, and who would be willing to ask a few questions. For a small fee.

But what mattered now was that Antenor was in Troy, all the movers and shakers of the city were here, even the younger princes Lycaon and Troilus. Nobody had slipped away to conduct some clandestine business out of sight of the kings. Nestor simply could not understand what it was that he and his comrades were being kept from seeing.

"It doesn't make any sense," he growled, half to himself.

"I did hear a story," Thersites said. He was still bent over his lyre, tuning it Nestor thought. "Someone at the palace told me there's an emissary from Egypt in Troy. Urgent business regarding Phoenicia, he said."

Nestor frowned. "I hadn't heard that."

"People talk to ordinary folk," Thersites said, "when they wouldn't talk to a king. I hear things."

"I expect you do," Nestor said. *And if you count as 'ordinary folk', my hollow-chested friend, I'll eat my boots with a spoon.* "That doesn't add up, though. Troy is an ally of Hattusa, they fight against the Egyptians, not for them. If the pharaoh has something to discuss he'd send to Hattusa, surely? Unless," he added, struck by a thought, "the Hittites are weaker than we thought, since the Battle of Emar. Maybe Egypt thinks they're finished."

"If that was true, Troy wouldn't be… playing us like this," Menestheus said, in his patient way. He fingered his short goatee beard. "You don't risk angering enemies when your strongest friend is failing."

"Are we Troy's enemies?" Nestor asked.

The king of Athens shrugged. "Perhaps they think we are. Or why treat us this way?"

That did make sense, unfortunately. And Troy's behaviour over the past year had been that of a city which no longer cared very much for the consequences of its actions. The punitive new taxes on the Trojan Road had ruined a lot of Greek merchants, emptied a lot of royal treasuries, and left a lot of empty bellies. Priam must have known that would create widespread anti-Trojan sentiment, but he'd gone ahead anyway. Now Greece was full of angry men, shouting in the streets for their kings to do something, which was the sort of thing that made kings angry too. Troy didn't seem to notice.

"I asked around," Thersites put in. "Subtly, while I was juggling balls for some of the servants, and at a tavern down in the town. Everyone I spoke to agreed. No Egyptian emissary has been in Troy for at least two years."

Nestor nodded. "Then someone is lying to us."

"And if they lie about that," Menestheus agreed, still fingering his beard, "what else do they lie about?"

The three men looked at each other in silence.

*

The Greek kings were called to see Priam the next day, an hour after a ship ran ashore a little way up the Simois River.

Nestor thought immediately that the deceit must be about to end. He became certain of it when the three men entered

Priam's diamond-patterned throne room to find the walls lined with soldiers in full battle dress. They were Apollonians, their cuirasses lacquered in white and gold, spears upright in one hand and swords belted at their hips. The best Troy had to offer, their elites. Nestor felt his muscles tighten even as he observed Menelaus' chin come up, and his eyes flare in anger. This was not going to be a pleasant meeting. The presence of those fighting men made that obvious.

Hector was armoured too, standing to one side of the dais with his silver helmet gleaming under one arm. On the other side stood Antenor, his lined face impassive, and beside him the very tall figure of Laocoon, the seer.

Nestor was expecting trouble, but not the shock that awaited them.

"I wonder," Priam said to Menelaus, with no introduction at all, "whether you recognise this."

A servant came forward to pass something to the Spartan king. It was too small for Nestor to see what it was, until Menelaus gasped in disbelief and opened his fingers. There on his palm rested an emerald cut into twenty faces, set into a sheath of filigreed silver. It meant nothing to Nestor, but Menelaus had lost all colour and his hand was shaking.

"What is this?" Nestor asked.

Priam smiled. "Tell him, lord of Laconia."

"It's... Helen's," Menelaus stammered. "My wife's. I gave it to her when we married. It came all the way from India." He looked up at the throne. "How did you come by it?"

"Helen gave it to my son Paris," Priam said. "When he took her from Sparta five days ago. A ship brought the news this morning."

Menelaus' hand tightened convulsively around the gemstone. "You will hand her back. At once."

"Strange," Priam mused, "how often I have said that about my sister, with no result. Tell me, king of Sparta. How hard did you try to see Hesione returned to me, through all these years?"

There was a deadly silence.

"You *will* return her," Menelaus repeated.

"There is no need for this," Menestheus began, but Priam stopped him with a raised hand. "Antenor."

A door opened, somewhere Nestor couldn't see. A moment later three people emerged from behind a statue in one corner, of the Trojans' father-god Tarhun throwing a thunderbolt. A man and two boys, the elder approaching the age where he would be called a man himself. Nestor thought they were family, a father and his sons most likely.

"This is Balzer," Antenor said. "Until recently, he and his family lived in a town called Teos, on the coast of Mysia. You may have heard of it."

Menelaus only glared, but Menestheus shook his head. Nestor tried to watch them and Priam as well, with a little bit of attention left for Antenor and the three newcomers. He moved only his eyes, giving nothing away, his thoughts shut behind his mask.

"Balzer is going to tell you a story," Antenor said. He nodded to the Mysian.

"I was a carpenter," the southerner said. "I had a good business, a good life in Teos. Then we were raided. Men in black armour. They killed my wife and ravaged the town."

"You must have had sentries," Menestheus began. He broke off when Hector tapped fingernails against his silver helmet.

"I heard the names they called each other," Balzer went on. "Achilles. Eudorus. Patroclus. They were Myrmidons, and they would have sold my sons into slavery except that Achilles released us, on condition that my daughter Išbardia went with him as his bed mate."

"Thank you," Antenor said. "You may go."

Balzer put hands on his sons' shoulders and guided them away. There was silence until the hidden door closed behind them.

"You see," Antenor said then, "the Argives are still abducting women from the Anatolian shore. Hesione was not an isolated incident, and these takings are not a thing of the past. Greeks have not raided here for a generation, and you've told my emissaries that stealing our women is a thing of the past, not to be concerned over anymore. And now this."

"That was not me," Menelaus began.

Antenor spoke right over him, a shocking insult to a king. "My own thought is that the Argives have avoided our shores out of fear of Hittite retaliation. But now you've forgotten that lesson, or else you think Hattusa is no longer able to protect us. Or that Troy cannot protect herself. Whichever is true, Greece thinks, once again, that she can plunder and steal with impunity."

"You cannot," Hector said, speaking for the first time. "Troy will not allow it. If women are things of no value, to be taken at will and used, or abused, then that truth works for us as well as for you. Since Argives see women as trophies, as plunder, why should not Troy?"

"This is why you invited us," Nestor said. It was the first time he'd spoken, too. "It was all a pretence, just to get Menelaus out of Sparta so Paris could sneak in behind. No more than that."

"Precisely," Priam said.

"I will take Helen back," Menelaus grated. "Whatever it takes, I will find her and take her back."

Hector smiled thinly. "You won't need to find her. She'll be right here in Troy."

"And here she will stay," Priam said, "until the Argives show they are willing to negotiate in good faith. You have never cared a fig for the concerns of Troy. Now you must."

"I demand to see my wife," Menelaus snapped.

"Demand?" Priam repeated.

He gave no signal that Nestor saw, but the guards around the perimeter of the room took a single step forward, all as one. Menelaus opened his mouth and then closed it again. He'd never been an especially forceful man; Agamemnon was the dominant brother in that respect. Menelaus looked at the soldiers and let himself be overawed.

"Your wife isn't here," Antenor said. "She and Prince Paris will make their way to Troy at a different time. But if she was, my lord, we would still not let you see her. Go home, all of you. Go and tell your people that the women and towns of Troas are no longer yours to despoil as you please. And then, if you wish to talk, you will be welcome back in Troy."

"This is an outrage!" Menelaus shouted. But the Apollonians were moving forward again, pushing the three Argive kings towards the ornate doors. On his throne Priam smiled and seemed not to hear. Nestor watched him as he backed away, but he didn't see any emotion at all on that ageing face before the doors swung shut.

*

The Argive kings were barely out of the room before Priam swung towards Antenor, fury distorting his words. "Where is he?"

"The message didn't say," Antenor answered. "At a guess, I'd say perhaps Egypt or Cyprus, somewhere far away from Greece. Unless Paris decided it was safer to come back to Anatolia before Argive ships begin searching, in which case he might be in Halicarnassus, possibly Miletos."

"So you don't know," Priam snapped. "What use is an advisor who has no useful advice?"

Hector spoke from across the dais. "That isn't fair, Father. Paris has changed the plan Antenor made, but that's my brother's fault. Rage at him when he does come home. Don't abuse Antenor for it."

Priam glared at him, and then shook his head. "You're right, of course. I'm sorry, Antenor. The lad has betrayed you as much as me. What can have possessed him to do this made thing?"

"Aphrodite, perhaps," the advisor said, straight-faced.

"Paris has always been a fool for women," Hector said. "And they for him, just as much. The sight of a pretty girl turns Paris' head and makes him forget all sense. It might have been better to send Troilus on this mission, or Lycaon. Pandarus, even. But it's too late now."

Hector had never had any time for Paris. Until now Priam had dismissed that as the natural behaviour of an eldest son towards the youngest: the duty-bound heir's envy of the sibling free to idle, or to indulge himself. It was an uncomfortable thought, that Hector might have seen Paris clearly while their parents could not, but it had to be faced.

Because what Paris had done in this went beyond madness. It *was* a betrayal, exactly as Priam had named it. The lad had been sent as a representative of Troy – a covert one, to be sure, but still bearing the welfare of the city like a mantle on his shoulders. And he had abused it. He had abandoned the plans made with such care, thrown them aside for a smile and the glimmer of a woman's eye. Priam had never seen that weakness in his youngest son.

"We couldn't have sent others anyway," Antenor said, disagreeing with Hector. "Troilus because he's even more of a fool than Paris, but for horses instead of women. The other two because Nestor was sure to be suspicious from the moment he was invited here, and we could only allay those doubts by having all the important men of Troy here, where he could see them."

"Then we should have given Molion the duty," Hector said. "Or another captain. Anyone but Paris. It was asking for trouble to send him on a mission that involved a beautiful woman."

"If this is true," Priam snapped, still angry, "then you ought to have mentioned it before."

"I did mention it," Hector said. His tone was calm, not challenging at all. "Once, and then I let it go. Because you don't listen to criticism of Paris, Father. You never have. I would have wasted my words."

Unfortunately that was probably true. But Paris had seemed an ideal choice for the task. The soldiers would follow him, as they would any prince of Troy; but the Argives thought he was a fool when they bothered to think of him at all, and his absence would likely go unnoticed. All that had worked out just as Antenor had planned it. The three Argives had come, and their suspicions had been allayed by feasts and hunting, and the visible presence in the city of everyone who could be a danger to them, in any way.

Then Paris had gone and wrecked everything by making an insane, ludicrous promise to the Spartan queen, and thrown the whole scheme into disarray.

"Can we rescue this?" he asked Antenor abruptly. "Even after the noose Paris has put around our necks?"

"Perhaps," Antenor said. "It's hard to say, because it depends how the Argives react. They might decide to bargain with us, in which case we'll get Hesione in return for Helen. Just as planned."

"Paris says he swore a mighty oath to marry her."

"Oaths can always be broken," Laocoon said carefully. "If the gods are properly propitiated."

"And if the two of them become lovers, before they reach Troy?"

"That, too, can be overcome," Antenor said. "If the Argives decide to negotiate with us."

"You talk," a new voice said, "but none of your words matters."

They turned, all of them, to see Cassandra emerge from behind the statue of Tarhun with his stone hand upraised. Priam couldn't remember the last time she'd come to the throne room, let alone without being ordered to. Since she was a child, probably. She was neat enough too, for a wonder; often Cassandra looked dishevelled, almost wild, as though her hair had never known a comb nor her skin a cloth. Today her white priestess's robe was unwrinkled, and her face glowed with healthy colour.

"Words always matter, my lady," Antenor said.

"Not these." She stepped closer, then halted five paces away. Coming closer than that to anyone, man or woman, would have been unusual in the extreme. "You don't understand, not yet. You will."

"Understand?" Hector asked.

"That this Helen is a brand of fire that will bring the blaze down upon Troy," she said. "She will start a burning that will ravage us. If she steps within the walls, Troy will be destroyed."

Priam stared at her. She was a Bride of Ipirru, given to the god, and sometimes the immortal spoke through the women who served him. That was the point, really; it was why a royal daughter was placed in the temples, if at all possible. Cassandra had never been capable in that way, of course – or in any way, really. She'd been sworn to service because there wasn't anything else she could do. But prophecies did happen, coming sometimes from the unlikeliest of sources, so he hesitated and glanced at Laocoon.

"I have seen nothing in the auguries to suggest the fall of Troy," the Seer of Athena said at once. "The first thing I did when I heard what Prince Paris had done was to consult the goddess, and while the carved bones showed me danger, they didn't show me disaster."

"Pallas Athena is an Argive goddess," Cassandra pointed out. "Do you think she would warn us, against her own people? Are you a fool?"

"Show respect!" Laocoon spat at her. "Royal blood or no, you're still only a simple priestess!"

"Enough. We will not squabble amongst ourselves." Priam watched Laocoon until he nodded, visibly calming himself, and then turned back to Cassandra. "Thank you for the warning, my daughter. We will not forget it. Perhaps you should go and lie down now, somewhere quiet."

"You mean to do nothing," she said. She shook her head, pale curls falling in her eyes. "Well, I cannot give advice to those who will not listen. But remember I told you. If Helen of Sparta once sets foot inside the walls of Troy, the city will be doomed."

She wheeled and was gone, her robe swishing until she vanished behind the statue and the hidden door clicked shut behind her.

"That was strange," Laocoon said. "I apologise, my lord. I shouldn't have lost my temper."

"She's right," Hector said.

They stared at him, all of them surprised, and Hector shrugged his muscular shoulders. "Not about the fall of Troy, I'm sure. But the taking of Helen will bring a blaze down upon Troy. I am certain of that, as well. Because the Argives will *not* decide to negotiate with us. They will regard this as an insult to their manhood, and that leaves them only one option."

The other two men looked at him, and then both nodded slowly. They both knew what that option was. The Argives always did the same thing when they felt they had been insulted.

They would go to war.

Chapter Fourteen

What Happens in Miletos

He found Andromache deep in discussion with two priests of Athena, in her temple right at the back of the Pergamos.

It was a surprise, actually, how fast Hecuba had begun to transfer her power to Hector's wife. Or at the least to share it with her, equal to equal. Andromache was clever and capable, and she'd shown a deft touch in dealing with the sensitivities of the various priesthoods. That had impressed Hecuba and the priests. Thebe-under-Plakos was a small city, with none of Troy's urban sophistication; for Andromache to prove so capable so soon was a surprise.

Which was all Hector knew, even as the husband of one woman and son of the other. It wasn't done for a man to inquire into the dealings of a queen and the clerics. Perhaps when he was king. His parents shared their duties, so he and Andromache might too.

But he wasn't king yet, so Hector didn't ask what his wife and the two white-robes were debating, or even approach close enough to hear. He simply stood by the doorway and waited for them to notice him.

At the far end of the long hall, half in shadow now, stood the Palladium. It was a wooden image of Athena herself, carved twelve feet tall in the midst of a stride, with a spear in one hand and her *aegis*, a hide-bound shield, in the other. Legend claimed the goddess herself had given it to Ilos, mighty son of the founder of Troy, as recognition of his warrior prowess. It was said Troy could never fall while the statue stood inside her walls.

Her wooden face was hidden in darkness, but Hector stared at it anyway. Was it a true representation of how Athena looked? He didn't know. Nymphs seemed to appear almost daily, surprising a shepherd or traveller at the side of the road, often with no cairn or altar to mark their presence. But the gods and goddesses of the world, whether Greek or Anatolian, didn't show themselves to just anyone. They appeared rarely, and in isolated places, seen by only one or two mortals in a generation. The most worthy, the finest of their times.

Athena had shown herself to Ilos, at a time when the Trojans worshipped no Argive deities, and made herself preeminent in the city. Now the people cried that Hector was Ilos reborn, the great warrior clothed once more in flesh... yet she had not shown herself to him. He had to wonder why. What was missing in him, that she hid herself from his eyes?

And did she hide from Achilles?

It was a name the artisan from Teos had spoken, and one Hector had heard before. Everyone close to the Greensea knew it, just as they knew the word *Myrmidon*. The Ants of Thessaly had been raiding coasts for a century, men in black carapaces swarming ashore from black-hulled boats. But they'd become something more under Achilles, a deadly force that eschewed the easy targets of villages and farms and struck instead at towns, and then overwhelmed them. Settlements all along the coast had begun building higher walls, wider moats, anything to keep the terror of the Myrmidons at bay.

Achilles himself wore golden armour in battle, shining amidst the black armour of his men. There were stories of arrows sent at him that never seemed to hit, spears that simply bounced off the cuirass. The man seemed invulnerable, and he swatted warriors like leaves in the wind.

Even so, the raid at Teos was the first time the Myrmidons had attacked the Anatolian coast for years. Fifteen at least, Hector thought, since the Argive catastrophe at Miletos. They'd contented themselves with attacks on the Aegean islands, or in the south against Egypt; even against their own people, in Cyprus and Crete. That they had come to Anatolia again was more than unsettling. It was a threat, clouds in a sky that had been clear before.

And now came this lunacy, this utter insanity of Paris, taking Helen not as a bargaining piece but as a prize.

"Husband?" Andromache said by his elbow, and Hector blinked in surprise. He'd been so deep in contemplation that he hadn't even noticed her there. "I thought you were with the king."

"I was," he said. "Can you spare a moment?"

"Of course," she said. She held up a hand to the priests, one finger raised to indicate she'd only be a minute. They bowed politely and retreated. "What is it, Hector?"

"Not here," he said. He was struggling to hold in his anger. "Upstairs. I need wind in my hair."

A narrow flight of steps was hidden behind one wall of the temple, reached by a door set in the corner. It was so small that Hector could only pass through by turning sideways with his head and shoulder bowed. But at the top was the roof, all but hanging over the northern wall of the Pergamos and then the city wall below, and the almost-sheer fall under that down to the Plain of Troy. If you lifted your eyes a little you could see the Bay to the north and the Hellespont beyond, and the Simois River, with Bunarbi town sitting beyond it at the edge of the sea. Horses grazed everywhere you looked, forming small clumps according to some unknown bonds of friendship or dislike that not even the wranglers had ever been able to work out. Sheep grazed on the pastures of the hillsides, on poorer grass than the horses. Between the two, on the slopes, was a narrow strip of cropland, yellow now with ripening wheat. Men moved there and in the fields, tending this and nurturing that, tiny specks at this distance.

Andromache took his hand. "Now, then. Tell me what's got you so frustrated. Or have you tired of me already, and you brought me up here to throw me over the wall so you could marry another outland wench?"

"What?" he said, startled. "No, I'm not –"

He stopped then, because Andromache was laughing at him. Hector began to tell her it wasn't funny, there was some real trouble here, and then realised that his rage was gone. Well, not gone entirely, but it had faded away to a hot whine somewhere deep inside him, rather than the rampaging red thing he'd hardly been able to bottle up. He grinned at her, a little sheepishly.

"That's better," she said. "Tell me, then."

He did so, pouring the words out like Myrmidons flooding across a helpless village. Antenor's plan, though she knew about that of course, because he'd told her when it was first proposed. The arrival of the Argive kings, and the amusement of seeing Nestor grow more and more suspicious, sure he was being tricked but unable to see how, or why. And then the sudden, devastating news from Paris, brought only hours earlier by the ship beached on the bank of the Simois below them – if she looked, Andromache would be able to see it. That part she didn't know, because there hadn't been time.

"Paris swore to marry her," Hector finished. "By every god he could remember to name, it seems. His message says that he intends to keep that vow, whether my father supports him or not."

She'd folded his hand into both of hers. "You don't think he should?"

"Support him? No. We should keep to the original plan. Treat Helen with all courtesy, and give her no reason for complaint. Don't abuse her or ravish her. And then exchange her for Hesione and remove the higher tolls Argives face on the Trojan Road. Some of the Greeks might still argue for revenge against us, but most won't. They need the goods of the Euxine Sea too badly."

"You'd abandon Paris," she said, nodding. "Have you suggested this to your father?"

"He knows what I think," Hector said. "Paris is a wastrel, a man whose interests stop with his own desires. He doesn't care about anything but his own gratification, and when it's satisfied he moves on to the next thing, and the next, and he never spares a thought for the consequences. But this time there *will* be consequences, and he should be the one to face them. Not Troy."

"I see," she said. "Paris has taken the choice away, hasn't he? By not returning to Troy at once he's made the decision his own. Priam can't promise that Helen will be left unmolested."

"This is Paris," he said. "Of *course* she won't be unmolested. His lust has got the better of him, and now he'll take her in ten different ways before he even comes home. And the Argives know what he's like anyway. Even if he does leave her untouched, by some miracle, they will never believe it."

"And what do you fear the Argives will do?"

"Something," he said darkly. He wasn't sure exactly, but he knew the Argives would never let this insult go by without riposte. Even Antenor's plan had been a huge risk, taken only because all else had failed and Priam so badly wanted to see his sister home in Troy again, before one of them died. But an exchange of women was one thing: the outright abduction of a queen was quite another. That wasn't a risk, it was madness.

"Something," he said again, and felt Andromache's fingers tighten about his own.

*

She was in Miletos.

It had been two days now, and still Helen was overwhelmed by it. She had come to believe, before the sudden appearance of salvation in the unlikely shape of Trojan raiders, that she would never leave Greece in her life. Probably she'd only leave Sparta once or twice, when Menelaus wanted to show her off to his fellow kings in Mycenae or Argos. Even then she'd be driven through the streets and then left inside a castle much like her own in Sparta, to maunder away her days with nothing to do and no hopes to fulfil.

Choosing Menelaus as her husband had been a mistake.

The gods knew, there had been other options. She'd just judged them wrong, that was all. She'd thought Diomedes of Argolis too flashy, too concerned with his appearance to other lords. Ajax of Salamis was handsome but intimidatingly huge, and his voice was more a bear's growl than anything human. Menestheus had seemed to preoccupied, Agapenor too tempestuous, and marrying Idomeneus would have put Helen in Crete, far from all she knew and wanted to be part of. There had seemed to be something to dislike in all of them – except Menelaus. He'd struck her as just right, not too arrogant or too quiet, handsome enough but not a preening peacock.

She knew now that he was simply ordinary. Boring, even. A good hunter, but not a great one; a fair but not exceptional warrior; a reasonable administrator who never saw the nuances. Helen did, she'd learned it from her father, and she knew – she *knew* – she would make a better ruler than Menelaus. But she wouldn't be given the chance. He didn't ask her advice, wasn't interested in what she thought or knew about Laconia. She was never wanted.

And then she'd been awake at night, as she so often was now, when Paris came stealing into her rooms.

It was easy to believe the gods were watching over you, when a life changed so abruptly. She'd been sitting in the dark, alone and sorrowful; ten minutes later she had a bag of jewellery in her hand and was slipping through the corridors of what had been her father's palace, surrounded by Trojans in cuirasses with spears ready, on her way to a new life. Now a week later she was in Miletos, a city she'd never thought to see before she died.

She knew of it, though. Every Greek knew of Miletos, since what had happened here when she was a child.

It had always been a city that attracted foreigners. A little like Troy itself, she supposed, though she'd have to judge that for herself when she was there. At first a Phoenician outpost, Miletos had slowly been transformed by the Leleges, a local people who learned their culture from more advanced neighbours. Lydians had moved in, and then later Minoans came in numbers, establishing themselves as the dominant force in the city. Later still the Hittites had made Miletos capital of a client province, again much as Troy was, and an influx of their own people had changed the city again.

Then the Greeks appeared, first raiders from Locris and Boeotia in search of easy plunder. They found the land plentiful and the defenders weak. Twenty years ago they returned in numbers, fifty ships loaded with warriors who burst into the city and took it for their own. In their wake came families, artisans, all the people who made a city work. Local people were driven out of their shops and off their land. More simply left, migrating to other cities north or south: Halicarnassus, Sardis, Ephesus. Some of them warned that vengeance would come. None of the Greeks listened.

Then the Hittites appeared.

Their army was vast, a hundred thousand men some said, though Helen's father had thought less than half that. It was too many, in any case; too many by far. The defenders were swept aside. And then the Hittites killed every Greek they could find, warriors and farmers, women and priests, children and babies alike. All. They slew and butchered until the city streets were wet with blood, and gave no quarter to any Greek, for any reason. Helen could still see the scars of those days: chips in the corners of buildings were swords had struck, new cobbles where the old had been smashed by thrusting spears, and homes rebuilt in the wake of fire.

The Hittites had nominated a new king, and rebuilt the walls of the city in stone. And then they'd gone away. They had bigger concerns than a minor Greek incursion, greater enemies in the shape of Assyria and Egypt. They hadn't bothered to make any demands, or send any warnings to Greece. Probably they considered the slaughter at Miletos warning enough, and it had worked. In the years since there had been an occasional raid, small in scale and quick, but nothing more. No town had been attacked at all.

Greeks needed land as badly now as they had twenty years ago. Greece itself had too many people and too little land, and food was always a little scarce. Not urgently so, most of the time; the harvests were reliable, at least. But even a small upset in the weather could cause a serious shortage of grain, for example. Greece needed new supplies, and secure ones, before a really bad year spread famine through the land.

Today they found their new fields in the west, on Sicily and the coasts beyond, where there was no empire to rebuff them.

But Helen was had come east, to walk the streets of storied Miletos with four soldiers as her guard. She hardly noticed anymore when people stopped to stare at her, mouths slightly agape and eyes wide. Her beauty was something she lived with, and the reactions of men not worth her attention. She looked instead at the Harbour of Mermaids, and the island fortress of Lade beyond it, shining white in the sunlight. She crossed the Meander River by a bridge made of bronze, a thing she'd never even heard of before and wondered at, amazed by its beauty. In the south of the city she roamed the great stadium, a semi-circle cut into a hillside and lined with tiers of seats, and she gawked at pillared halls and red-tiled houses, and ate slivers of spiced duck from a street vendor until juices ran down her chin and she laughed as she wiped them away.

In the market she sold some of the jewels Menelaus had given her. A set of pearls from Egypt, and lapis from far India. Probably she took less than they were worth, but that didn't matter. It was important to be rid of them, those reminders of her time as little more than a pampered slave, or a captive. If her life was beginning anew then let it be so, with no baggage from her former existence left to weigh her down as she walked.

She used some of the coin to buy diaphanous silk scarves, and some simple silver bracelets. At a sweet-smelling stall she stopped for a hair lotion scented with jasmine, and lotus-blossom soap. She was aware of her guards watching her, no doubt imagining how she would look wearing only those scarves and her perfume, but she ignored them. None of this was for their benefit.

She went to Paris' rooms that night, for the first time, and when he looked up she slipped off her robe to reveal her body clad only in the scarves, her jasmine-smelling hair a tawny cascade down her back.

In the next hour she learned that Menelaus was an ordinary lover too. He'd been her first, and until tonight her only; that was the reality of life for noble women in Greece. A princess who took lovers would never be marriageable, and once wed there was no opportunity. Helen had always been trailed by guards and handmaidens, alone only when she slept. Because of that she'd never known whether Menelaus was delicate or clumsy, compared to other men.

As Paris touched her, and kissed her skin, she learned. Her husband was simply inept in bed, at least compared to Paris. Twice Helen found herself gasping under Paris' dextrous touch, before he'd even entered her. When finally he did she clawed at his back and cried out, calling Aphrodite's name.

It was a long time before she felt able to speak, after. She lay in a welter of sheets with Paris' head on her stomach, stroking his hair and looking at the red weals on his shoulder blades. *I made those,* she thought wonderingly. She'd never done anything like that before.

"We're married now," she said at last. "Even before the priests speak the words. We're married."

His head moved slightly. "I promised we would be."

"In Troy?"

"Right now, if we can find a priest to set aside your vows to Menelaus," he said. "I little coin should make that possible."

"Then now," she said. "But, Paris. Don't ever mention his name in our bed again. I don't want even his memory here with us."

He sat up, a sheet tangled around his waist. He was a smaller man than Menelaus, perhaps equal in height but more trimly built. "All right. I'll take you to places where he never went, and they'll be just for us, Helen. Memories only we share."

"Take me where?"

"Egypt," he said. "My brother Lycaon has been there. He still talks about the great pyramids west of the river, shining white in the sun. They're thousands of years old, and no one remembers now who built them, or why. I'll show you Tyre, in Phoenicia, a city built on an island off the coast. I'll take you to Hattusa, the City of the Lion; and to the Euxine Sea and all the lands around it, even Colchis itself. We'll drink the forest wines and watch men draw sheepskins out of the rivers with gold heavy on the fleece."

"I'd like to see Crete," she said.

Paris shook his head. "That's too dangerous. The Argives will be looking for you. I don't think you should go near the Greensea again, at least until all this settles down again."

"Ephesus?"

"We'll go home that way," he promised. "Overland, so we avoid Argive pirates. The road runs through Ephesus and Cyme, and if there's time I'll take you to the carpet bazaar in Sardis. They have a glass roof there, each pane coloured so the light dances on the floor.

"And in each place," he went on, before she could speak, "I'll show you another pleasure of the bedroom." He drew her closer. "And you'll forget *him* a little more each time."

She opened her mouth to his kiss, and was already reaching for him as he laid her back down on the bed.

Chapter Fifteen

Women and Bulls

After the summons came, the king went up the hill to his palace alone. He used one of the servants' doors, as he often did, slipping in unnoticed except for a single maid carrying laundry to the washroom out back. She nodded to him and carried on with her business: this had never been a formal palace. The king went upstairs, into the nursery, and stood staring down at his son for a long time. His wife found him there, late in the afternoon.

"Was it what you expected?" she asked.

He nodded without turning around. "Yes."

"The kings will gather in Mycenae?"

"Yes."

She came closer, putting a long-fingered hand on his shoulder. "That will not commit you to anything. Why do you fear it so?"

"Because of the High King," he replied. "Because of what he is, and longs for. Agamemnon wants to be the man who breaks the cage which holds Greece. The cage of too little land, too few farms. He dreams of seizing territory across the sea, a land greater than Crete was, as rich as the delta of Egypt. He and Menelaus used to talk about a conquest there, did you know that?"

"I expect it was Agamemnon who talked of it," she said, "and Menelaus who listened, and followed along."

He laughed, a short hard sound. "Yes. I expect it was, at that. But the Greek kings would never follow him there, and he knows it. So he must look elsewhere, and there aren't many places around the Greensea that are large and productive enough for his dream."

"And one of those is Troy."

"One is Troy," Odysseus agreed. "Priam has given Agamemnon a perfect excuse. I would never have thought he'd be so stupid. Troy is mightier now than she was thirty years ago, or even ten. In another generation she'll be a power to rival Hattusa, or Thebes itself, if she has peace to grow. Now, with one act of folly, she has put all that at risk."

He could feel her thinking, and then she said what he'd thought she would. "But why do you fear this?"

"Because Ithaca will be dragged in. A war against Troy will be too large a thing for any Greek king to stand aside." He drew a breath, nodded at the cradle. "And because of him."

The baby boy slept on, oblivious to the conversation. Telemachus wasn't even a month old yet, and was still at the stage where he looked like any generic baby. To someone else's eyes it would likely be hard to tell if he was a boy or a girl. But Odysseus thought he knew every crease of the boy's flesh already, every fold of skin and crinkle of eye. He drank the sight of his son the way a bird drinks from a pool in a hot summer.

He and Penelope had been married a long time now, years in which she had three times carried a baby and three times lost it, always to tears and bitter grief. Odysseus had done his best to comfort her, hiding his own keening sorrow; when he wept it was alone, out on the hills as he watched over flocks, or in the cold hours of the night when he cried in empty rooms before going back to bed. Penelope almost certainly knew some of that. Wives picked up their husbands' moods, and she more than most.

Then she had fallen pregnant again, and the weeks had turned into months without disaster, with no return of the familiar pain. They had begun to see the faint light of hope in one another's eyes as Penelope's belly swelled. And Telemachus had been born, a little small perhaps but healthy, a pink crying thing that changed the world forever.

Had changed Odysseus's part of the world, at least. Other things remained the same, among them the endless hunger of Agamemnon for glory, for a name to ring down the ages.

And this war wasn't even necessary. There were Greek colony towns in the west now, small as yet but growing rapidly. Several had appeared on Sicily, using soil made fertile by the looming volcano, Etna. Further north there were more on the mainland, in Locri and Hesperia, built in narrow valleys much like those in Greece itself. Odysseus had been there, seen the black earth for himself; he knew how productive those towns would one day become.

Beyond that were more lands, long coasts washed by the gentle Greensea and fed by great rivers. Hardly anyone lived there, except a small band of tribesmen now and then. The land was *free,* or as near as mattered. All the Greeks needed to do was sail there and claim it. Instead the Atreides thirsted for a ruinous war in the east, against an enemy stronger than any other on the Greensea except Egypt itself. And if Troy was thrown down, Odysseus wouldn't bet against Agamemnon's eyes turning south to the pyramids before many years had passed.

"If I must go to war," he said at length, "I cannot be here to protect him. I've made the trade agreements we needed. There's no reason for me to go sailing again, or to leave Ithaca at all. I had planned to be here, to watch him take his first steps, and to grow."

"Then persuade the kings not to go to war."

"Persuade them," he said, and gave that bark of a laugh again. "You know what they call me, love. The shepherd king. They tolerate me when they must, but they don't listen to me."

"That's not all they call you," Penelope said. She could be harsh sometimes, when she thought he was being self-indulgent. "They call you *chorikos,* the peasant. They say you spend your time with your arm up an oxen's arse helping it give birth, or rolling in the manure of your sheep. And you do, when it's needed. It never bothered you before."

"We didn't have him before," Odysseus said, with a gesture toward the sleeping child.

"Then speak better than you have before, for his sake," Penelope said implacably. "Find the winged words that will sway them, pour Olympian doubts into their hearts. Sow the dragon's teeth that gnaw at their heart for war. Find a way to turn this evil aside."

He was silent for some time then. His fear threatened to swallow him, but her words had brought him back to at least a semblance of normality now, and he could think. Nestor would help him, of course: it was the old king of Messenia who had warned Odysseus about events at Troy, three weeks ago now. Menestheus might join them too, though that depended on what he thought Attica could gain from war. His was a crowded country even by the standards of Greece. And then there was Diomedes, the warrior lord of Argolis. If he argued against war there might be a chance to prevent it.

But the kings who would vote for war were more numerous. Agamemnon and Menelaus certainly would, the two sons of Atreus; there was no doubt of that. Telamon of Salamis would join them, angered by Priam's constant demands for the return of Hesione. Agapenor did whatever Agamemnon asked of him, like a trained and faithful hound. Thalpius of Elis just liked to fight, as so many others did, including Schedius and Prothous – neither of them popular men, and both would be loath to defy Agamemnon because of that. They didn't have enough friends to risk the anger of the High King.

"It's going to depend on Diomedes," he said. "If he decides on war I don't think it can be stopped."

"Then go to Argolis and talk to him," Penelope said. She took his hand and lifted it to her lips. "You're a good man, husband. Whatever happens, Telemachus will grow up knowing he has a father who loves him."

"If he grows up knowing his father at all," Odysseus said. He shook himself though, refusing to let the dark mood take him again. Penelope was right. The struggle was not yet lost.

*

The message was simple, the wording blunt. *Just like the Atreides,* Peleus thought as he read.

King of Thessaly

The High King has called a gathering of all the Greek monarchs at Mycenae, two days after the next full moon. Your presence is required. Be sure to bring your son.

On behalf of Agamemnon, Lion of Achaea

"Lion of Achaea," Thetis said mockingly. She was reading the missive over his shoulder. "He calls himself that because there are lions carved into the gates of his citadel. It's not as though he earned the name."

"Hush," he said. "You never know who might hear."

"In your own palace?" she asked, even more scornfully. "Well, if there are spies here, then let them hear me say Agamemnon is more the Great Bull men call him, than the Lion he calls himself."

"He hates that name."

"With his broad nose, so he might," Thetis laughed.

She had never really understood the way kingship worked. Thetis had been raised on Scyros, among coastal folk who spent as much time in the water as they did on land. She'd told him once that she was born in a boat, out of sight of land. Later she became a priestess of Dionysius on the island, giving herself over to a life of joy and abandon, spending as much time playing in the water as she did at the temple.

Peleus had met her on the beach on summer night, during one of the festivals of wine and fertility. Priestesses often took men to their beds on such nights – or to a bed of sea-grass in the dunes, if that was closer – but it wasn't compulsory. Peleus had been surprised when a lovely girl with dark hair took his hand and drew him into the darkness. He'd been even more astonished when he returned three months later to find she was pregnant with his child. Priestesses were supposed to have ways to stop that happening.

She'd left the priesthood behind, and the island too, to become his wife. Peleus hadn't even thought about rejecting her. There was a streak of white in her hair now, running back from above her right eye, but she was still beautiful. Like a sea-nymph whose veins were filled with brine, and who didn't feel the passing years as mortal men did.

He had felt too many, himself. Peleus was well past forty now, and every winter seemed to have added another ache to his body. In his knees, his shoulder from throwing a spear, in his hips. He didn't want to go to war again. Raiding was one thing, but a struggle against a committed foe quite another. He sighed and rubbed his eyes.

"Send to Achilles," he said. "A letter from you will reach him quicker than one from me, on that island."

"And tell him what?" she asked.

"You read the letter. You know what to say," he replied evenly. "Tell him I wish to meet him in Mycenae, no later than a day after the full moon. Greece is going to war. He won't want to miss it."

*

"He summons me," Idomeneus said. "Like calling a dog to heel! I tell you I will not have it!"

He threw the parchment down on the floor, which didn't really work. The sheet fluttered gently to the tiles, impervious to his anger. Servants around the room cringed and sidled backwards if they could, putting an extra few inches between them and their king. Idomeneus' temper was well known. Servants had been injured before, by fists or flying crockery.

He wheeled and strode out onto the roof terrace, just to get away from the cringing, and all the eyes that wouldn't look at him. Being there calmed his anger, at least a little. Sometimes it did. This was one of the buildings which had survived the earthquake twenty years ago more or less intact, and Idomeneus liked to look over the city below and remember that Minos had once stood at this parapet, with the crimson pillars of the upper storey behind him.

There was a double-headed axe at each corner of the terrace, the *labrys* that had been the symbol of Crete in the days of its glory. It still was, really: the Greeks called Idomeneus *Lord of the House of Axes,* among other names. The palace was different, too – an *anaktora,* it was called here. The Minoans had built in an open style, fearing no attack while their navies ruled the seas. As the palace stepped down the hillside and became the city, Idomeneus eyes were drawn to wide stairways, rectangular pools of cool water, and rooftop platforms exposed to the sun. Knossos was a beautiful city, if one liked that sort of thing. Idomeneus didn't, not really, but he did prefer this airy palace to the cramped castles of the mainland, where he always felt the walls were pressing in on him.

"I am not his subordinate," he growled, to no one in particular. "That *kopros* eater mistakes me for one of the whining curs of Greece."

"So stop whining," Meriones said behind him.

Idomeneus glowered at his cousin, not that it did any good. The other man had suffered worse setbacks in his life than a glare from his king. He would look rather like Idomeneus, tall and angular, were it not for the hideous scar on the left side of his head, which in truth was more of a crater than a wound. The earthquake two decades earlier had trapped him under falling rubble, some of which had caved in his skull and really ought to have killed him. Somehow Meriones had emerged rasping with thirst and smeared in dust, but otherwise perfectly healthy. He was the only man brave enough to follow Idomeneus onto the terrace in one of his rages, or to tell him the truth when that was unpleasant.

He still looked appalling, though.

"I am not whining," Idomeneus snapped. "I am complaining, and give my body to the dogs if I don't have a right to. That tyrant in Mycenae is getting far too self-important. Atreus was the same in his day, and a bad egg comes from a bad crow, they say."

"Whining, complaining," Meriones said, "it's the same thing in the end. You know very well that Agamemnon can be as arrogant as he wants, but he still can't force you to attend this meeting. What's it about, anyway? Helen?"

"Of course Helen," he said, still angry. "There's no other reason to summon the kings, is there?"

A shrug. "I don't know of one. But Agamemnon would find a reason if he needed one, for whatever scheme he's hatching this time. You're right about him, cousin. He isn't to be trusted."

"That's what I've been saying," Idomeneus said, aggrieved. Meriones gave another shrug, as though to say he knew that, and the king wheeled away again and stalked to the stone balustrade, fighting to control his temper.

Damn Agamemnon to Hades for his pride. Damn him and damn him.

Crete could be as powerful as any of the kingdoms of the mainland. More so than any, in fact, as it had been before. Even today the island boasted cities to rival any in Greece – Phaestus, Kato Zakros, Knossos itself – and innumerable smaller settlements: it was known as the Land of a Hundred Towns. It contained some of the richest plains, the lushest mountain slopes. Yet still, it was only a shadow of what it had been when Minos ruled here, before Zeus turned the sky black and Poseidon threw a wall of water against the land. You could still see the line, where the sea had reached. Idomeneus had stood on that high-water mark and shuddered at his distance from the shore.

In the end Crete was a maritime nation. The sea could be an enemy, but it was also the island's best friend, a provider of food and protection from attack. And Crete lay halfway between Greece and Egypt, between Greece and Phoenicia too, a natural place for galleys to stop as they journeyed across the Greensea. It should benefit from passing trade just as Troy did. Again, once it had, when Minos ruled in Knossos. But to do so it needed control of the seas, and when Minos fell it was the Greeks who built ships to replace the ones smashed to matchwood on the north coast of Crete. It was they who dominated the waves now.

His hands gripped the balustrade.

On the wall behind him, at the top of the crimson pillars, a carved bull's head glowered over the terrace. It was huge, many times life size, black with blood red eyes that sometimes seemed to gleam in sunlight, as though alive. Idomeneus had often felt it was watching him, or the spirits of the dead Minoan kings were, with contempt in their shrivelled souls.

He was half what Minos had been. A quarter as much. But he could be more, if the Fates were kind.

"I don't want to go to war," he said. "Certainly not in Troy. Those walls would stand against a hundred Cyclops."

"So don't go," Meriones said. "Don't answer the summons."

"Agamemnon would go insane. He'd likely bring his fleet here on the way to Troy, just so he could burn the harbour of Knossos to teach me a lesson." His knuckles whitened where they clutched the stone. "It grieves me to say it, but we're not strong enough to stop him."

Meriones said nothing to that. He knew it was true better than anyone, being captain of Idomeneus' armies, including the ships. The Cretan navy could inflict terrible losses on Agamemnon's fleet, but not enough to stop them. Knossos would still burn, which meant Idomeneus couldn't simply refuse the High King's summons, though that admission gnawed at his innards like wormwood. He had to find another way.

Temper fading, his mind began to work.

"The loss of trade from the Trojan Road has hurt us," he said finally. "Caused unrest in the villages and towns."

"Not much of it," Meriones began. Idomeneus cut him off with a raised hand before he could go further.

"Enough that I have to decline the High King's invitation," he said. "With regret. Matters here require my attention, though of course I have as much desire to see the Trojans whipped as any king. Instead I'll send you, cousin. You can make my excuses, and listen to the discussion in my place. I doubt they'll protest too much, at least not to your face."

Meriones lifted a hand to touch the caved-in part of his skull. "Because few men can stand to look at me for long, yes."

"But Agamemnon will talk to you," Idomeneus went on, thinking it through. "He'll want Cretan aid, if he's going for Troy. Hades, he'll *need* it, especially in terms of ships. We can't match the rest of Greece together, but we've a larger fleet than any single nation except Egypt.

"So he'll ask for our aid. And you, cousin, will tell him Crete stands ready to supply ships – fifty of them at least. No! Tell him a hundred. Perhaps not enough men to fill them all, if I have to keep some back to quell trouble in the villages, but promise the ships. At a price."

Meriones waited, and then asked quietly, "What price?"

"A wife," Idomeneus said. "Helen refused me, two years ago. I wasn't really surprised, given the number of rivals for her hand, though I couldn't believe she chose that hairy fool Menelaus. But anyway, she was a chance to bind Crete more tightly to the Greeks of the mainland, through marriage into the great kingdoms. To Laconia through Helen herself, and to Achaea by means of her sister Clytemnestra. And to Ithaca, I suppose," he added as an afterthought, "if we count their cousin, Penelope. And how the peasant king of *that* arse-spawned island won her, I don't understand at all."

"What wife?" Meriones asked.

Idomeneus turned to face him. It was an effort to unclench his fingers from the balustrade, actually, and more difficult not to let it show. "Iphigenia. Agamemnon's eldest child." The maimed man's expression said he'd already guessed as much. "She can't be more than fifteen."

"Old enough." Idomeneus waved a hand. "Ideal, in fact. Neither you now I have children, cousin. Our line will die out unless we act, and we both lack wives. You because you never wed, and me because she died. I need heirs. Iphigenia is the perfect age."

"She is twenty-five years younger than you are," Meriones said deliberately. "She will hate being your wife and she'll tell her father so. Agamemnon will never forget what you made him do. Or forgive you for it."

Idomeneus nodded. That was the risk, right enough, but it was worth taking. Any king worth the name tried to make his country stronger, and there would always be danger in that. But he thought in this case it could be dealt with. His mind worked, foreseeing possibilities.

"He won't be able to spare the men to do anything about it, if he's going after Troy," he told Meriones. "And if he isn't he'll just refuse, and I'll smile and say I understand, so nothing will be lost. But if he agrees... I get children, Meriones, and I gain allies so strong nobody will dare move against me. With that shelter I can begin to make Crete strong again, while the Greeks and Trojans smash each other into pieces."

"Risky," Meriones said. A smile was growing on his lopsided face though. "But I like it."

There would be details to work out, of course. Meriones couldn't simply demand that Agamemnon hand over his daughter for marriage: the High King would just knife him in rage. Delicacy was the key, and Idomeneus had never been very good at the soft approach. Well, he'd think of something. The new moon was a week away yet, plenty of time to hatch a plot.

The Greek settlers on Crete, newcomers here really, told a tale of a dolphin woman named Amphitrite, who like all her kind was a shape-shifter. One day she was sunbathing with her friends on the beach, in human form, when Poseidon saw her and fell hopelessly in love. But she refused him, and in sorrow and loneliness he stirred up the seas and wrecked ships on all the shores of the Greensea, until at last the god persuaded her father Nereus to go to her. He found her hiding high on Mount Juktas, south of Knossos, and spoke so eloquently that Amphitrite relented, and she married Poseidon in a sea cave at the eastern end of Crete in the summertime. No sooner had the ceremony been held than the Earth-Shaker's angst subsided, and the sea grew calm and tranquil once more.

The indigenous Cretans, descendants of the old Minoans, told a different story. They said the seas had churned because a stone god rose to challenge the sky, only to be smashed into pieces which fell into the Greensea and threw up enormous waves. One of those fragments struck Crete and was transformed into a black bull with crimson eyes, which lurked beneath the earth until Theseus came from Attica and slew it.

It was time for Crete to become the land of bulls again, and perhaps the marriage of Amphitrite could serve as a prophecy. The seas around the island would become tranquil again, and safe. And Idomeneus would be the new Minos, rising from the ruin of the old.

Chapter Sixteen

At the Ships

Soldiers were working along much of the road from Troy down to the beach. Mursili thought they were Idaians, the ones usually in armour lacquered green and blue, though today they wore only shirts and kilts with swords belted at their waists. Short swords, he noticed, barely a foot and a half from hilt to point, with fullers half an inch thick to give the weapon strength. Bronze cracked easily when struck. Iron did not. Mursili would make much finer swords, now the promised supplies had begun to arrive.

He thought the soldiers were surveying the eastern channel of the Scamander River. The shallower parts could be dredged, and the earth and stones piled on the eastern bank to make it higher, a more formidable barrier. Or to provide shelter for archers, he supposed. Mursili wasn't a warrior, had never been in a battle in his life, but you couldn't live in Hattusa and not pick up the basics of war and how it was fought. The Hittites had built their empire on military power. There was hardly a family in the land without at least one son in the army.

Troy had not constructed its power from warfare, but the signs were unmistakable. The city was preparing for war.

It wasn't just the men at the river. Other soldiers had spent several days clearing undergrowth from the slopes of the ridge on which Troy sat, stripping it right down to the rock-strewn soil. To keep spotters from coming too close to the walls, of course. More were at work in Bunarbi; Mursili had seen them walking out, not long after dawn two days running. Probably they were strengthening the village's wooden walls, and digging the moat deeper or wider or both.

Fletchers and bowyers had suddenly begun to scour the eastern hills, looking for good wood to make arrows and bows. Mursili had wondered why they didn't cut the willow and tamarisk along the Scamander's banks, since the trees there were closer and grew straight.

"That river wanders across the Plain as it is," Phereclus had told him when he asked. "Take away the trees, and the

Scamander might break into twenty channels when the spring floods come, instead of the two it has now. That would be bad for the horses, do you see?"

Mursili saw. He saw it would be bad for defence as well, if instead of two deep braids the river formed two dozen shallow ones. Attacking Greeks wouldn't have much trouble forcing a way across those. He didn't think Phereclus realised that. The Colchian was clever, and becoming a good friend, but he thought of everything in terms of the sea.

Mursili stood aside as three wagons creaked slowly up the road, each one drawn by four oxen. They didn't move fast – a man could walk more quickly – but once oxen were moving, they just kept plodding on. They'd trample right over Mursili if he didn't get out of the way. The wheels were wet from the ford, but they still raised clouds of dust behind them, and he tied a cloth over his mouth and nose before he went on.

The Bay of Troy was as busy as always. Mursili estimated there were about thirty ships in view, all but a handful drawn up on the gritty beach. Some of those were unloading cargo or taking it on: others just lay there like seals on rocks, waiting for their crews to return from wasting their wages in the taverns and reed houses of Troy. A few were heading north, out to the Hellespont and the Greensea beyond it, taking advantage of the *Meltemi's* absence. The north wind hadn't blown for several days now. Mursili wondered if he should see an omen in that, and if so whether it was a good sign or bad.

Not far from where the road ended, right where the three Argive kings had beached their ships, another vessel now sat. It rested on logs for rolling, but ropes held it in place for now. Some two hundred men stood in a wide semi-circle around the prow, talking among themselves. White and gold armour flashed brightly in the crowd, the colours of the Apollonians, and Mursili realised that Hector himself must be here.

He was looking for a different man though, and when he found it Mursili skirted around the crowd towards him. They were alike, in a way. Both foreigners, both here at Troy as the summer waned. Their reasons might be different, but then, reasons usually were.

"Have you been aboard?" he asked.

Crescas nodded. "Until Phereclus told me to get off his deck before he had me thrown over the side."

"You like it, then."

"It makes the ships I grew up with look like children's toys," the Argive said. "I'm going to have to take a look at Phereclus' shipyard, see the hulls before they're finished. That boat has a *keel.*" He pronounced the word carefully, as though unused to it. "Apparently it's how the ships in Colchis hold together in waves that would break a Greek vessel apart."

Mursili couldn't see the keel, whatever that was. Or if he could, he didn't recognise it. But just glancing from the new galley to the more usual Greek ones, resting on the strand, he could see differences. Phereclus' creation was longer, perhaps by six or eight yards, and the stern swept up higher than any other on the beach. Something was new about the mast as well. He had to stare at it for a long moment before he saw it was square-cut, not round as on Argive boats. Whether that mattered, he didn't know. He was even more clueless about ships than he was about warfare.

"Your Luwian has improved," Crescas said. "It was a year before I could speak the language as well as you do."

"I learn quickly," Mursili said.

He shouldn't be curt to this man. It was Crescas' ships that were bringing iron to Troy for Mursili to work. Everything Mursili hoped to do here depended on him. Success would mean an honoured place, a reasonable amount of wealth, perhaps even marriage to a distressingly tall Trojan woman. Failure led to disgrace and probably exile from the city, in which case he'd have nowhere to go. Who would take on a Hittite smith who couldn't shape metal?

The crowd was growing, as more people came down from the city or wandered along the beach from their own ships. The Apollonians gathered around the ship, forming a loose cordon, though they weren't fully armed. Mursili didn't think they'd need to be. None of the watchers showed an urge to push forward. They knew what would happen to anyone who challenged the Apollonians.

"Ah," Crescas said.

Mursili had seen it too: a pair of figures had appeared on the prow of the ship, standing by the rail. One was Phereclus:

his thinning hair looked lush from down here. The other was Hector, unmistakeable in his size and bearing, and the whole crowd sent up a spontaneous cheer. Hector asked for quiet with raised hands, smiling down on them all.

"Normally we wouldn't bother to hold a ceremony for the launch of a boat," Hector began. "But this – what is it?"

Phereclus had leaned across to murmur in the prince's ear. A moment later Hector grinned.

"It seems I've transgressed," he said. "This is a ship, not a boat. Since it's our esteemed shipbuilder from Colchis who tells me this, perhaps I ought to listen, don't you think?"

There was laughter, which Hector allowed to ride for a moment. *He really is good,* Mursili thought as he watched. Hector knew how to play a crowd, could even laugh at himself and use that to gain sympathy and support. In Hattusa the princes would never have bothered, except with the soldiers, and even then Mursili doubted any did so as easily as Hector.

"This ship is different," Hector resumed when there was silence again. "It's the first completed by that esteemed shipbuilder I mentioned, namely Phereclus here. He's been teaching our own shipwrights the tricks of Colchis. This will be the finest ship on the Greensea, my friends, and in a few short years we'll have the finest *fleet* besides.

"But the first thing to do is let a crew sail her. The men who'll do so are down among you now, waiting to roll her into the water. In a moment we'll stand aside and let them get to it, but first this vessel needs a name. I thought we should let Phereclus choose. My friend?"

"She's the *Qulha,*" Phereclus said. "An ancient name for my homeland."

"*Qulha* it is," Hector agreed. "Move away then, everyone. Phereclus, she's your ship."

The crowd didn't move back much, if at all, but the Colchian nodded to someone Mursili couldn't see and a moment later a bass voice began shouting orders. Fifty men took positions by the ropes which held the newly-named ship steady atop the wooden rollers. At another yell axes thudded down to sever the ropes, and slowly the logs creaked as *Qulha* began to move.

"Hold her!" Phereclus shouted from the deck. The sailors were already doing their best, muscles straining as they hauled on the ropes in four long lines, fighting to keep the ship straight. Beside Phereclus the prince kept his balance easily, not even holding to the rail for support. That must be what half a lifetime riding chariots did for you.

The stentorian voice snapped more orders and on Mursili's side the men let tension off the ropes, so the ship was pulled the other way. She was moving quite fast when there was a mighty splash and water sprayed up from the stern as it entered the sea. Most of the crowd cheered again.

"I wonder what will happen," Crescas said, "when the Greeks see that ship sailing the Greensea."

That was a thought Mursili had already considered. The Argives would sink her, of course, especially now their relations with Troy were so poor. Though in fact they wouldn't even need that excuse. Greek prosperity depended wholly on mastery of the seas, just as Crete had relied upon it until half a century before. Any potential challenge to that dominance needed to be crushed at once. Surely Priam and his advisors knew that.

They had still launched though. Perhaps they knew something Mursili didn't. He hoped so.

"Just as long as they don't sink the ships with my iron on board," he said. He'd thought earlier that Phereclus' mind focused entirely on the sea, but the truth was that Mursili was just as obsessed by his own work. Phereclus had said something to that effect the day they'd met, in fact.

Mursili pondered that, and then asked, "Do you think the Argives really will attack, then?"

The Greek-born merchant looked at him. "Do you really think they won't? War is what Argives do. It's how they respond to any threat or problem. Of *course* they're going to attack."

There was a sinking sensation in Mursili's stomach. He didn't want to find himself in the middle of a war, not here in windy Troy. He'd expected to find tranquillity here, when he came. "Then I'd better make my swords quickly, hadn't I?"

"Yes," Crescas said. He'd turned back to *Qulha,* now floating free in the waters of the Bay. "I think you better had."

*

"I'm surprised you made it," Nikos said. "Tore yourself away from your redhead, did you?"

"Shut up," Isander said.

The other man's grin widened. "Such a witty retort. I don't know how you think of them so quickly." Gorka smiled and, typically enough, said nothing.

In truth, Isander didn't really mind the teasing. Since he and Meliza had become lovers Nikos didn't seem quite as sophisticated as he had before. Or perhaps it was that Isander was *more* sophisticated. He supposed that was inevitable, now he'd left his little village behind and moved to Olympia instead.

It was Meliza who had changed him though, and not the city itself. She'd shown him bed games, of course: things to make a goddess blush and cover her eyes. But she'd shown him much more than that. Singing in the ceremonies of Aphrodite at her Temple, surrounded by smiles and laughter. The sterner rituals of willow-bound Artemis, the virgin goddess, whose favour Meliza asked as all reed girls did, that their bodies not betray them with pregnancy or disease.

She took him to the theatre, where her whispers in his ear meant he actually understood the play for once – though they also filled him with such heat that he all but groaned with it. She took care of that later, back at her room. There were honeyed apples eaten on the slopes of Mount Cronos, and a pigeon cooked over her own hearth stuffed with raisins and sesame seeds, and a blend of herbs she wouldn't describe.

With her he discovered markets tucked away in back streets, almost impossible to find unless you knew where they were. Instead of stalls there were small handcarts, or sometimes just bags that folded out to reveal their contents; things that could be moved swiftly away if a soldier or taxman came sniffing. The bazaar could vanish in less than a minute, its traders melting into alleys and the customers becoming no more than citizens taking the air. But while the sellers were there you could buy things at half their usual price; saffron from the east, powdered ivory from Egypt, lion's teeth and tiny clay pots of pepper. Meliza had stopped Isander buying one of those until she could check that it really was pepper inside, and not dried bat guano or something just as vile.

No taxmen meant cheaper prices, but no government checks meant more chance of being fleeced.

Meliza was working today. Isander found he didn't like that very much, but he couldn't think of a way to raise the subject without making her angry. Besides, he didn't know *why* it upset him to think of her with other men, or what he could do about it in any case. Until he could figure that out, he'd do better to keep quiet and enjoy the time he had with her.

More sophisticated, he thought, and chuckled inwardly.

"You're just in time, as it happens," Nikos said. "Let's get moving before crowds block all the gates."

They set off through the city, hurrying a little. Olympia was busy today, the streets thronged with people in from the countryside. Word had spread rapidly of Troy's shocking raid on Sparta, and the seizure of Helen from her own palace. It was plain treachery, captain Socus said, to lure a king away with promises of talks and then kidnap his wife while he was gone. Isander agreed with him, actually. When women were taken it was usually as a result of impetuousness, not this carefully planned plot.

Most people didn't seem to care very much about Menelaus and Helen. Several times Isander had heard someone say that if the king of Sparta couldn't keep hold of his wife that was his affair, and nothing to do with them. But they could work out consequences as well as anyone. Farmers were buying grain for winter planting before prices rose, and masons bought up porphyry just as eagerly. Lapis and faience were already more expensive, which had caused a fight which Isander's squad had broken up two days earlier, before anyone suffered worse than a smashed nose. And there was no pepper to be found at all, not in any of the stalls in the *agora* or the back alley markets either. *That* had led to a fight which left two men dead, just this morning.

Isander kept his precious pot wrapped in a tatty chiton, right at the bottom of his rucksack in the barracks. In a month's time he might be able to sell it for three times what he'd paid, or more, but he doubted it would last that long. He seemed to have a taste for pepper, and Meliza would live on it if she could.

The three friends went down the main street to the west gate, which as Nikos feared was already crammed with people waiting to come in or out. They joined a queue of raucously unhappy citizens and waited their turn, trying to be patient about it. After what seemed like an hour they were passed through by a guard they knew, and headed quickly down the packed earth road past fields of ripe wheat, towards the Kladeos River ahead.

There was already a good-sized mob there, centred around a trio of ships drawn up on the shallow strand at the outside of a bend in the river. Trading galleys stretched away on each side, but those three were fighting ships, from the navy of Elis. Soldiers is dusty cuirasses made a half-circle to keep the citizens at bay, while the last preparations were made to sail.

Isander looked for the king but couldn't see him. He did spot Socus though, distinctive in his boar's tusk helmet. The captain strode over to shout something to a man aboard one of the ships; even two hundred yards away his voice was audible, if not the words. The man's lungs must be made of leather.

Street vendors had appeared around the crown, pushing barrows from which they sold figs and glazed fruit, olives and raisins and herb bread. Isander thought those sellers must be related to flies, to judge by the way they were drawn to any place where sweaty men gathered in numbers. They seemed to appear out of nowhere, as though they'd flown in. Today neither he nor his friends were hungry though, so they found a fence to lean on and watched the ships preparing down at the river.

"Do you think there will be a war?" Isander asked finally.

Nikos had picked up a grass stem and was chewing it. He often did that, munching on the stalk as it grew shorter and shorter until only the seed was left, at which he'd throw it away and pick another. "Maybe."

"What do you mean?"

"I mean maybe," Nikos said. "King Thalpius has been complaining for years that the High King's laws mean he can't fight neighbouring countries, even when he has cause. But he's kept on training new soldiers – like us," he added wryly, "which doesn't seem quite such a good idea just now, does it?"

Isander didn't understand. "So?"

"So every land in Greece has a lot of soldiers," Nikos said, "and no wars to keep them busy. Can you see any problems with that?"

He could, of course. Bored soldiers were apt to take risks, do foolish things just to break the monotony of long days with nothing to do, and no one to fight. Sometimes they'd support a rebel, back a rival claimant to a throne, simply for something to do. Every king must know it. Those idle, trained killer's hands needed to be kept busy.

He looked down at the ships again, and presently said, "We're going to war in Troy, then."

"Perhaps," Nikos said. "And perhaps not. Because Troy is powerful, my friend. I'm not sure all of Greece together is strong enough to break through those walls. Not if what they say is true: that the towers touch the sky, and men can walk four abreast along the parapet. Idle soldiers is one thing. Sending them to pointless death is another."

"Well, now," a voice said from further along the fence. "I reckon you're not a bone-headed idiot after all."

The speaker was a large man with black hair, and a vivid scar on one muscular forearm. He wore a cuirass, worn with hard use but well cared-for, which would have named him a soldier even if the friends hadn't recognised him. That they did was not much comfort.

"Axylus," Nikos greeted coolly. "I see you're not going with the king. Must be a disappointment."

Isander tensed despite himself. They all knew Axylus as a bully of new recruits; Gorka had escaped the bruises because of his size, but the other two had not. Few new soldiers did. But the soldier was here alone now, which Nikos had doubtless noted before he spoke, and after a brief tightening of his mouth he relaxed again and grinned.

"I wouldn't want to go to Mycenae anyway," he said. "The soldiers who do will have to camp outside the city, and I prefer sleeping in a pallet in the barracks to making do with a mat in the open air. Better to stay here, I reckon."

Gorka spoke before Nikos could throw another barb. "What did you mean, about him not being an idiot?"

"What he said about Troy," Axylus replied. "There's not going to be a war there. I've seen that city, which I bet none of you young 'uns can say. And only a god-cursed fool would send men against the walls. You'd leave a lot of men cold on the plain with their mouths full of dust, and for nothing."

Isander couldn't help a shiver at those words. He'd joined the army because he wanted to fight, and thought he could make a success of life as a soldier. Besides, there were few ways for a poor villager to rise in the world, apart from fighting. The temples, maybe, but Isander didn't have the patience for that. He preferred to be out doing, using his own hands, rather than praying for a god to do it for him.

But he had expected his battles to come against bandits in the mountains, or at worst against neighbouring kings. Familiar foes, on familiar land. The thought of going into combat on a plain across the sea terrified him. Death wasn't something a true man should fear, but the prospect of dying far from Greece and the gods made him cold inside and out.

No one said anything for a long time. Axylus went away after a moment, probably to find his friends and then a recruit to harass, but the three friends stayed where they were. Nearly an hour later the king appeared, a stocky man dressed in a soldier's gear, though with a flowing cloak over the top. He boarded the central ship and then crewmen began to work the oars, sending up sheets of spray over the labourers who shoved at the prows. The vessels groaned and then slid into the river, turning as the current caught them.

Isander saw Socus' tusked helmet once more, but then the sails came down and hid the deck from view. He still watched though, until the ships were out of sight and the crowd dispersed, the vendors going in search of a new gathering where they might sell.

Chapter Seventeen

The Gathering of Kings

There was a square-cut gateway, overlooked on both sides by flanking walls made of huge, irregular stones, and cut through another just the same. The builders had used none of the Naxos white marble, no porphyry from the distant east. Every stone was grey and unpolished, seeming coated in dull dust. It was a wall designed not for beauty, not for style, but to overawe.

Two lions were carved above the gateway, facing each other with their paws on the base of a fluted pillar. In grey, of course. Anyone raised near the Greensea would know what that meant, even if they'd somehow been brought to the gate without the first idea where they were.

This was Mycenae.

Inside the city teemed, a crowded mass of people thrust together in a collision of huddled houses. Many of them looked as though one of the Cyclops said to have built the wall had picked them up and smashed them back down, so they stayed upright only by leaning together. Other buildings were mostly wood and cheap clay bricks, patched and lashed together in the gaps between stone dwellings. In places whole streets had been swamped by the rising flood of people, and the shacks they built.

But the main avenues were was still clear. The king's men kept them so, sweeping away any detritus which spilled out from the alleys. Shacks were tolerated if they were out of sight, but build near the main roads, and the walls would soon be broken by axes and the hafts of soldiers' spears. Up the slope the avenue ran, once passing through a gate set into a smaller wall, this one made of rammed earth faced with stones. That was the old city wall, back when Mycenae was just a small town with a warlord dreaming of greater power. Well, all the warlords had wanted greater power, in those days. The kings of Greece today owed their lineages to the warriors who had seized it first and held it tightest.

Up the road went, through a more affluent city now, until a mile from the first gate it reached the Citadel.

The lions appeared again here, at least twice as large as before. It was this portal that was famous, the Lion Gate of Mycenae, entrance to the fortress of the inner city. Towers overlooked the road on both sides, and spikes protruded from between the stones so attackers couldn't flatten themselves against the walls. Only welcome visitors could pass under the lintel and into the Citadel beyond.

There the road ran on to the crown of the hill, with guard houses on one side and a circular tomb structure on the other. Further along, the right hand side was lined with residences for visiting nobles. For kings, in effect, and the buildings were small palaces, each a miniature copy of a ruler's hall. Across the roadway from them trees grew in neatly trimmed stands, on a steeper hillside cut by flights of stone steps. Beyond that, looming over the whole site, was the Palace. It was designed to mimic an Egyptian pyramid, though with many different buildings: small ones around the outside, then higher, and the tallest at the centre. Right in the middle a square tower rose, supported by black pillars, from which the king could look out over his city and the lands around it, like a god atop his mountain.

There were those who said Agamemnon thought of himself that way, a deity peering down from his eyrie at mortal men. But he was High King, and dislike or no, at his summons the lesser rulers had come. They filled up the guest residences built by Atreus, Agamemnon's father, to accommodate them, billeting their servants and entourages where they could. Even then there were too few guest halls, and that caused problems.

Pheidippus of Calymne flew into a rage within minutes of his arrival, when he was told he would have to camp among the trees. He took it as a personal insult: other kings are housed, so why should he not be? Finally Talthybius, the High King's herald and advisor, ejected some priests from quarters on the far side of the Palace, which gave Pheidippus a proper house – though it was rather small, and isolated from the others.

Later that day two of the other kings arrived at the same time. Schedius and Ialmenus had never been friends, as their predecessors as kings of Phocis and Locris had never got on. Even the High King's authority was hardly enough to keep them from clawing at one another every summer, sending their armies to battle over some minor transgression or imagined slight. Beetle-eyed Schedius was a warrior of the old sort, tough and uncompromising: Ialmenus was even grimmer, if anything, since his son had been killed hunting lions early in the year. Which made it inexplicable that Talthybius had placed them in residences side by side, like two strange and hostile dogs sharing a single small yard.

It was Carystus who sorted it out, the king of Euboea giving up his own guest palace close to the wall so Schedius could take it, and instead accepting the offer of a marquee from a harried-looking Talthybius. It meant he had to camp among the trees, but he had hardly less room than his fellow kings, and they already knew he'd made a sacrifice. If another was needed during the discussion he would not be expected to offer again.

The full moon passed. The last kings trickled in, and it was time for the Gathering.

*

"As the High King summoned, so have you come," Talthybius said. He stood in the centre of the *megaron,* a silver-worked sceptre in his hand. "Only two kings are missing. Telamon of Salamis has sent his son Ajax to represent him. Do we accept him in his father's place?"

Seated in two long lines on either side of the hearth, the rulers murmured assent. They knew why Telamon was absent: he was simply too fat to travel now. There was no need to say so aloud. Such disrespect was unseemly – and besides, Ajax was *very* large.

"Idomeneus of Crete is unable to attend," Talthybius said, due to unrest in his homeland. His cousin Meriones is here in his stead. Do we accept him as his king's voice in council?"

There was another murmur, less certain this time. Several kings crossed their arms over their chests and didn't speak at all. The crater-headed man gave no sign of noticing. Neither did Talthybius, perhaps as much from choice as convenient blindness.

"Then we are assembled," the Herald said. "I declare this Gathering of Kings open. Let none speak except that he carries the sceptre," he raised it above his head, "and then briefly, and with respect to gods and men."

He turned to Agamemnon, bowed deeply, and placed the silver-inlaid rod in his hand. Then he withdrew, back towards the doors where the priests had gone after performing their auspices, moments before. Talthybius stopped short of them though, lurking in the shadows at the edge of the hall, ready to answer if his master called.

Seated at the very foot of the line, Odysseus watched these events with a carefully bland expression. He'd tried to judge the mood of the other kings over the past two days, with limited success. Some were easy to read, like Menelaus with rage and humiliation burning in him every moment, though often it was subsumed by sorrowful maundering. Or Leitus of Boeotia, bursting as always with a fury his small frame seemed hardly able to contain. Leitus was extremely short. Odysseus suspected his endless antagonism towards everything must have something to do with that.

But a few exceptions aside, the kings had kept their thoughts private, hidden behind meaningless smiles and empty words. Even Nestor hadn't been able to divine anything. The aged king of Messenia sat near the head of the twin lines, only a few seats from Agamemnon himself, as befitted a king of his power. Odysseus wished he and his friend were close enough to whisper.

But the High King was standing, and there was no time to waste on wishful thinking.

"You know the insult that has been done to us," Agamemnon said. He was wearing a chiton patterned in rainbow stripes, and a gold circlet decorated with oak leaves. *Peacock,* Odysseus thought, keeping the contempt well away from his lips and expression. "Paris of Troy slipped into Sparta like a thief, and like a thief made off with my brother's wife, Helen. We are told she will be returned in exchange for Hesione, as though we are merchants haggling over prices or trades. Trojans may be merchants, but we are not. After their betrayal, I am not of a mind to indulge them in this.

"Hesione is Telamon's wife, in any case," he went on. "The mother of his son, Teucer, brother to great Ajax there. Sending her to Troy would break up a family. I'm not of a mind to do that, either."

That was a weak argument. Troy had been asking for Hesione's return for more than twenty years, almost since the day she was taken from the Plain by Heracles and Telamon. If the only reason to refuse was to keep the family together, then why had she not been sent back before Teucer was born? Before Telamon raped her, to put it bluntly?

"None of that matters," Agamemnon said. Odysseus' eyebrows lifted in surprise before he could control himself. "What matters is the insult to Greece. The Greensea isn't a place where weaklings flourish, and if we allow this to stand we will be seen as weak indeed. What, the whole of Greece, united, did not dare defy a single city? We must force Troy to hand Helen back, by any means required. What my brother does with her then is his decision," he nodded to Menelaus, "though I, for one, would not blame him if he had her whipped through the streets and then given to his men for sport."

He looked down the two lines of lords, and then said, "My belief is that we, all the Greeks, should assemble an army to break Troy and fetch Helen back. Before others around the Greensea decide we are weak."

He sat down. *That was brief,* Odysseus thought. Brief and to the point, with little time wasted on irrelevancies. The High King held out the sceptre and a servant came to take it, by which time Diomedes of Argolis had already risen to his feet. There was a susurrus of surprise as he was given the sceptre. Diomedes was not normally so forward, at least not in councils.

"Break Troy?" the golden-haired man repeated. "You've never been there, High King. I have. So have others here today. And I'm sure they will tell you what I do: Troy cannot be broken. Her armies are strong, especially in chariots, with those magnificent horses to pull them. Did you know," he asked the kings, "that they use three horses to a chariot? They have horses to spare, and every one of them is Olympian-born.

"Troy's spearmen are hardly less formidable, and she draws them from all over Troas. Break Troy?" Diomedes snorted. "We would likely break our own teeth trying, and for nothing."

Agamemnon began to stand up, face tight with anger, but Leonteus was on his feet ahead of him. A servant conveyed the sceptre across the gap between kings, then withdrew in silence.

"What I hear is that Paris took Helen from Sparta without a single life lost," the king of Pieria said. Legend claimed there was a spring of clear water in that country which bestowed wisdom to any man who drank from it. Odysseus supposed it might be true, but if so then the kings of the land didn't know where it was. They hardly ever had a full set of wits.

"If that's true," Leonteus said, "where were the Spartan guards? Who did Menelaus set to watch his wife? Did he assign no one to keep her safe? Or are Laconia's soldiers now so inept that they cannot protect a single woman?" He shook his head. "My country sits at the border of Greece, my lords. I deal with the threat of bandits every day, and I know this: one *never* leaves a treasure, or a woman, unguarded. I wonder why I am being asked to fight, far from my home and against an enemy who may be as powerful as we are, because one man couldn't take care of his wife."

Odysseus winced as the hall erupted in shouts. The white-robed priests came gliding back in, but they'd have a hard time restoring order after that little barb. *Couldn't take care of his wife;* there was a phrase which could mean more than one thing. People would already have wondered why Helen wanted to leave anyway, as she apparently had. What had made her unhappy? Was Menelaus simply not enough man for her?

If someone said that bluntly, there might be blood on the tiles of the *megaron* before the day was done. There might have been already, if the insult had been at the other son of Atreus. Agamemnon would have responded with violence: Menelaus only glowered, his broad face flushed.

The angrier kings were still on their feet, refusing to be calmed. Odysseus tried to catch Nestor's eye and couldn't. He signalled for wine as Leitus was finally cajoled into his chair, still fuming over something that had been said to him in the middle of the yelling. Odysseus hadn't heard what it was.

Peleus had the sceptre when the room was quiet again. He'd grown fat with age, if not as grossly as Telamon had, and hadn't risen when so many others had done. "Leonteus makes a fair point, *but,*" he added hastily before the shouting resumed, "it doesn't affect the central issue. Troy has stolen our most beautiful woman, a queen famed across the Greensea for her beauty. If we do nothing, who else will think they can goad us?"

"Exactly what I was saying," Agamemnon muttered. He didn't have the speaker's rod, but he was High King, so nobody challenged him over it. Besides, he'd always been surly. His peers had learned to let him grumble at times, to forestall a larger explosion later.

Now Nireus of Rhodes had the sceptre. "What does it matter if Helen is beautiful? I never saw her before in my life."

Ajax bounded to his feet and snatched the sceptre from his hands. It was impressive to see Ajax bound: the palace seemed to shake with the weight of the man. "It matters that she's Greek! I will not accept sitting here listening to a *kopros*-faced weasel while a Greek queen is despoiled by a Trojan!"

"What will you do?" Menestheus asked mildly, though also without the sceptre. "Storm Troy on your own?"

"If I must!" Ajax bellowed.

The gods save us from men who think with their muscles. Ajax was a decent man, actually, much easier company than his overbearing brute of a father, but he wasn't the longest spear in any fight. The probability was that Leonteus was right, and all the Greek armies together would have a Titan's task trying to overthrow the power of Troy.

"What happens if outsiders think Greece is weak?" Agamemnon had the sceptre again. "Leonteus, your land is on the northern edge of Greece. Those raiders you spoke of are Keltoi, or else Thracians sneaking in to steal. How long will it take them to decide your armies are not to be feared anymore? Troy deals with both peoples. Word will spread."

Curse him, Odysseus thought, *that's actually a good point.* To judge by his frown, Leonteus knew it too.

"As for beauty," Agamemnon continued, "The Trojans will parade Helen around the Greensea if they can, and beyond. To Hattusa, or Colchis. And people will say, 'There goes a queen the Greeks couldn't keep, for all their armies and their swagger.' Our trade will suffer because others don't believe we have the strength to protect shipments."

Nestor stood up. He was far from the largest man present – though he was among the oldest – but the mutters and catcalls died as he held out his hand for the sceptre. Agamemnon moved to hand it to him, not bothering to wait for a servant. That was real respect, the kind of thing earned only by wisdom and long life. The hall was quiet.

"The High King makes a good point," Nestor said. That caused more murmuring, but the old man wasn't finished. "Especially in mentioning Hattusa. The Hittites are still a power to consider. We mustn't forget what happened in Miletos."

There was silence. All of them remembered Miletos, though Odysseus didn't think any of the kings had ever laid eyes on the city, except himself. They knew the story, though. Greeks had taken the city, made themselves its lords, and then been smashed into the dirt when the Hittites came to avenge their vassals. There had been no survivors, not even women or children taken as slaves. Every single Greek in or near the city had been killed. Today Miletos was an Anatolian city again, filled with disparate peoples from all over the Greensea... but not from Greece. The memory of so much spilled blood was too fresh for that.

As though thinking of stories had summoned him, Thersites moved in the shadows at the far end of the hall, pen in hand. Odysseus wouldn't have recognised a normal man, but Thersites' deformed shape meant it could be no one else. The man did manage to put himself about. One day Odysseus might wake up to find the bard standing by his bed, a quill in his hand as he prepared to take notes for a song or a poem he had in mind.

"We mustn't be intimidated by it either," Agamemnon said. He didn't sound very certain though.

"Well," Nestor said, "if you're not intimidated by power, High King, perhaps you should sail your fleet to Egypt and set flames in the streets of Thebes. Or better yet, climb Olympus itself and throw down Zeus with your spears. No? I thought not. Power is to be respected. As you know, since you realise what will happen if Greece is thought to be weak."

"We have to do *something!*" Ajax bellowed, making the walls shudder.

"I would be very interested in knowing what Menelaus thinks," Nestor said, "since he has not spoken a word so far."

He didn't raise his voice, but the hall fell silent once more at his words. Every head turned towards Menelaus, sitting slouched in his chair to Agamemnon's right. When the big man looked up Odysseus; first thought was that he'd been drinking, but then he changed his mind. Menelaus looked like a man who hadn't enjoyed a good night's sleep in a week, or eaten a filling meal. A man tormented by Furies every night and Harpies by day.

Menelaus stood up, looming over the kings with shoulders lowered like a bull. He was still flushed, either with wine or rage, or perhaps both.

"I want her back." His voice was thick with barely-suppressed rage. "I want her back and on her knees before me. I want that Gorgon-faced prince of Troy to spend years screaming for mercy in my dungeon. And I want to world to know it, every man and child around the Greensea; I want them to know what it means to anger Menelaus of Sparta, And all the Greeks."

"We did not come here for *you,*" Nireus said caustically.

Menelaus launched himself at the man, and Nireus threw himself forward in reply. It was always that way; a Greek king who failed to meet a challenge would be bullied for the rest of his life. He was much the smaller man, but still fought furiously against the other kings and Agamemnon's servants as they struggled to keep the two men apart. Menelaus almost managed to reach Nireus before Ajax caught his arm and hauled him away, with no apparent effort.

Nireus had been one of those who sought Helen's hand. He'd never had much chance, perhaps, coming from far-off Rhodes as he did. But the memory of rejection might lie beneath his reluctance to help Menelaus now, and the speed with which he'd leapt at him. One woman had already caused a great deal of division among the Greeks.

She might cause much worse yet.

"This will stop," Agamemnon said. His voice carried even over the uproar. "I will not accept this behaviour in my hall – no, not even from you, brother! Can none of you see? This is a gift from the gods. We stand at the moment of decision for all Greece. Do we rise, and grow? Take the farmland and wealth we so badly need? Or do we cower and sidle away, unwilling to deal with thieves and liars as they deserve, and condemn ourselves to a slow and slinking decline as Troy and Egypt grow great around us?

"Troy is mighty." He looked around at the kings. "But Greece is mightier yet. And I would gamble my fortune and my life on our fighting men against any in the world, whether Trojan or Hittite, or Assyrian from the far lands of the sunrise. Who tells me I am wrong?"

A moment, and then Odysseus stood up. He heard the disparaging mutters as the sceptre was carried to him, and ignored them. He was the peasant king, the shepherd, but he could make them listen. He had to.

"If this is the moment of decision," he said, "when we Greeks decide on war against one of the powers of the world, then we need our greatest men here to help us make that choice. Our High King is present, and the wronged husband. The warriors Diomedes and Ajax stand with us. But with respect to them, the greatest warrior in Greece is not here."

He let the murmur pass again. It was more approving this time. "Where is Achilles? Was he not summoned?"

Eyes turned to Peleus, who shifted on his chair. "He was."

"Then where is he?"

"He didn't reply," Peleus said uncomfortably. "Or come, as I told him to. His mother's doing, I think. She wrote the letter to him."

"Then he may not have known he was needed," Odysseus said. "My lord kings, I have two suggestions to make. First, that we send for Achilles, at once, and bring him here to ask his opinion. If Troy can be taken it's he who will know how. Who else has fought so often in Anatolia?"

Heads nodded around the room, and then Agamemnon said, "And the other thing?"

"Ask the advice of the Oracle at Delphi," Odysseus said.

The nods were firmer this time. He could see the kings thinking: before they risked their fortunes and lives in war against Troy, they wanted to be sure the gods were on their side. Without Olympus' help there was no chance Troy would fall, none whatever. It was a reasonable request, one Agamemnon could not possibly deny without losing the support of half the room. The High King's jaw was clenched in frustration.

"Let me add to that," Nestor said. "Send five kings to Delphi. The High King must go, of course, and Menelaus as the wronged party. Ajax should go, since his father's taking of Hesione has led to this. No, my friend, I lay no blame," he added when Ajax seemed about to erupt. "And deeds of decades ago should not be offered as an excuse for insult today, in any case. But I should go to Delphi, as one who doubts the war's wisdom, with Diomedes to make the five. We will decide on behalf of all Greeks, if the other kings will permit us."

They didn't like it, but clearly not all of them could go to Delphi. The little town was used to holding the Pythian Games every two years, but the unexpected descent of twenty kings would overwhelm it. Besides, they could only ask the Pythia, the prophetess of Delphi, one question. Only the five need go. Slowly they conceded the point, heads nodding all around the *megaron*.

Odysseus was careful not to glance at Nestor as he sat down. The other kings knew they were friends, and knew too that they were probably the cleverest of all the Greek kings. They often forgot Odysseus, and forgot Ithaca, but when they were reminded they admitted that he was shrewd. Now, with the two of them having stood and spoken as they had, some of the other lords would be wondering how much of it had been planned.

All of it, was the simple answer. But quietly, back in Messenia before they came to Mycenae on separate ships. Nestor had agreed that much rested on how Diomedes decided, but there wasn't a chance to speak with him before the Gathering. What they needed was time. A few days might be enough to persuade him, or for other kings to feel the beginnings of doubt. The Trojans might even lose their nerve, and agree to hand Helen over. It was possible; no mortal man could foretell the future. A week, or a month, might change everything.

"Very well," Agamemnon said. His jaw was still tight with tension. "The five of us will go to Delphi, and ask the Pythia what will happen if Greece goes to war with Troy. But," he smiled thinly, "I want a service from you, Odysseus, in payment for the journey you force me to make."

He felt his stomach plunge. "What service?"

"A journey of your own," the High King said.

Chapter Eighteen

The Groves

Most of the islands of the Aegean were Greek now, in culture as well as politics. It had been different once, in some cases only a few decades ago. But those older peoples had been wiped out or absorbed, becoming indistinguishable from mainland Greeks in dress and speech, and the rituals they observed. There might be an occasional trace of a former culture – a ritual perhaps, or a sacred day still observed – but that was rare.

Crete was different, simply because of its size. The island had been called the Land of a Hundred Towns long before Theseus brought an end to Minoan glory, and the people had put down deep roots. That way of life survived today, especially in the mountain villages where few ethnic Greeks went. There were stories of heathen gods still worshipped, ceremonies where women dressed as water goddesses and dominated the men: even of children sacrificed on mountaintop altars. It would take generations to eradicate all that, but if there was a people in the world who could, it was the Greeks.

Scyros had kept some vestiges of its indigenous culture too, though it was a much smaller island, and had been conquered longer ago than Crete. Odysseus didn't really know why. Some cultures were resilient, that was all. Or perhaps a benevolent god was watching over the island, preserving its festivals and rites.

If so, that god was surely Dionysus, patron of wine and amusement, and outright desire.

Scyros was dotted with his temples, mostly found in secluded places in the woods that covered the northern half of the island. There were stories about what went on in those glades, tales to make men groan and reed girls blush in the dark. Some of them must be true, or the island's reputation for sensuality would have died out. Odysseus was actually quite pleased he hadn't had to tell his wife he was coming here.

A journey of your own, Agamemnon had demanded of him. It was payment for the suggestion that the High King and a few companions go to Delphi to consult the Oracle. Odysseus supposed he should have seen it coming. Agamemnon didn't like having his plans disturbed, or even delayed, and he was determinedly set on bringing down Troy. So now Odysseus was here, being rowed into the harbour of Linaria after a four-day journey from Mycenae, with a mission of his own to accomplish.

"I want you to bring Achilles here," Agamemnon had said, back on the mainland. *"Use those winged words your tongue speaks, Odysseus, and persuade him."*

"And if that doesn't work?"

"Then tell the young idiot that I'll harry him on every beach from here to Egypt unless he obeys. Do whatever you have to. Just don't fail me, Ithacan. Get him to Mycenae."

"There are rumours about this place," Eliade said, leaning on the ship's rail at Odysseus' side. "Do you suppose they're true?"

"I'm sure they are," Odysseus answered dryly. "Some of them, at least."

On the far side of the bay was a typical island town, square white houses with red-tiled roofs, sprawling on the slope of a hillside. Here and there were larger buildings; several temples, a pillared mansion that must belong to the local lord, and low structures built on stone platforms. Warehouses, Odysseus thought, raised above the level floodwater reached when it poured down the mountain after an especially heavy storm. Fields and pastures surrounded the town and invaded it, reaching into gaps between clusters of buildings to make best use of the sparse flat ground. Low down the fields were full of olive trees, while further up the hillside they were dotted with sheep and cattle. It could be any town on any island in the Aegean, except for one thing.

Ships lined the beach, drawn high up on the shingle. A few were traders, slightly broader than warships, grouped together some way north of Linaria town. But most were galleys, their hulls painted with black pitch, like long shadows in the afternoon sun.

Myrmidon ships. This was where they came to relax between raids, and this was where Achilles would be.

"Will you need me to find Achilles?" Eliade asked diffidently.

Odysseus pretended to roll his eyes. "Go and have your licentious night, my friend. I think it's best that I find Achilles on my own."

But there was no need to find him, as it turned out. They were met at the beach by an androgynous-looking man with cornflower hair, smiling with what appeared to be genuine pleasure. A closer inspection showed that his softness was an illusion, reaching no further than his face. This was a hard, fighting man, a Myrmidon for sure. The happiness might be real though. Sometimes it was.

"My lord Odysseus," the man said. He bowed briefly. "It's a delight to be able to greet you. I am Patroclus."

"I've heard of you," Odysseus said. Most people in Greece could probably say the same. Patroclus was one of the captains of the Myrmidons, serving under Achilles' command and sometimes leading a raid himself. Usually that was when Achilles was god-struck by another young beauty, and when Achilles tired of his latest inamorata it was Patroclus' bed he returned to. There were some who believed that if Patroclus should marry and abandon the raider's life, Achilles might soon follow suit, and the beach towns of Phoenicia and Egypt would breathe a collective sigh of relief.

"I assume you've come to speak with Achilles?"

Odysseus eyed the youth. "Is my coming expected, then?"

"Someone's coming was," Patroclus said. "Achilles told us Agamemnon would never let him get away with missing a Gathering of Kings, even though his father still sits on the throne of Thessaly. He's the best warrior in Greece. He'll be needed for any major war."

Ajax and Diomedes might be interested to hear that claim, Odysseus thought. Both men considered themselves a match for any soldier in Greece, and better than any except Achilles and each other. They might not claim to be Achilles' better, but they wouldn't stand for being openly named as his lesser, not for long. Especially not during wartime.

The casual way in which Patroclus made the comment was even more surprising. There wasn't any doubt in his mind who was preeminent.

Never mind that now. "Why do you mention war?"

"A full Gathering couldn't mean anything less," Patroclus said. "Especially after the news out of Troy this summer, or so Achilles said. Since he stayed away that meant someone would be sent to speak with him, and here you are." He smiled. "I knew when you passed the harbour mouth it must be you. Only Ithacan ships have those crimson prows."

"Very observant of you," Odysseus said. He meant it to carry a slight hint of sarcasm, but Patroclus just beamed as though he'd been given a wreath of oak leaves. It was no wonder Achilles found such comfort with this man, if he was so undemanding. The gods seemed to have decided that the more handsome a man was, the less he had between his ears, and Patroclus was *very* handsome. Almost pretty, in fact. He must be as dumb as an ox.

"Lead on," he suggested. A nod to Eliade brought a grin to the other man's lips, and he hurried off towards the edge of the town and the trees in search of a few Dionysian priestesses and some wine. Odysseus followed Patroclus into the streets, hoping Achilles would not be far away.

*

Quarter of an hour of walking brought them to the far side of Linaria, and a forest that marched right up to the last line of houses and overhung them, keeping them in shade. A path led away between the trunks. Patroclus started down it, motioning for Odysseus to follow.

Achilles refuses to meet me in the town, then. I've crossed half the Aegean to be here and he won't leave the groves. The Myrmidon was making it clear that he was in control here, something that happened to Odysseus quite often. The king of a small country had to swallow insults more often than most, and he gave no sign that it irritated him.

Another few minutes, climbing at first and then on smoother ground, and they came to a clearing with a temple in the middle, pillared on all four sides with white marble. A row of smaller buildings ran halfway around the edge of the glade: sleeping quarters, probably, though in Dionysian festival times precious little sleeping would be done in them. Men lay on the grass all around, some resting, others talking quietly among themselves. One group was playing draughts, taking turns to replace the beaten man. All of them carried the hard look of warriors, Myrmidons taking their ease between battles.

Achilles himself was sitting with his back against a pillar at the top of the steps, eyes closed against the sunshine that beat on the lids. At his side rested a golden battle helmet with a snow-white crest. He couldn't think to meet enemies here, in the playground of the Myrmidons, so he must carry it for show. Whether he did so normally, or had brought it just to emphasise his nature to his visitor, there was no way to tell.

Odysseus had spoken to him only once before, briefly, at a gathering of kings and merchants on Salamis two summers before. He remembered being struck by the sheer presence of the man, his ability to dominate a room while seated and silent, apparently unengaged. Odysseus had heard stories of other meetings, other men, who had said the wrong thing and been beaten for it. Or killed. Achilles was not a man to relax with.

"Ithacan," the big man said, when Odysseus and Patroclus were still yards from the bottom of the steps. He hadn't bothered to open his eyes. "Welcome. Seat yourself."

Some of the men glanced around, then went back to their idle chatter or their game. Patroclus lifted a hand to Achilles and turned away without a word, leaving Odysseus to climb the stairs alone. Either the two men had a deep understanding that required no words, or else Achilles played his dominance games even with his own men. Perhaps especially with them.

"Will you join me?" Achilles asked. Now he did open his eyes. He produced a jug of wine and two pottery cups, and poured without waiting for a reply. "It's already watered. I don't like strong wine early in the day."

Odysseus accepted with a murmur of thanks. The wine was sweet, tasting of the pine resin used to preserve it.

"So," Achilles said. "Agamemnon has decided he needs me for his war against Troy, has he?"

"If there is a war," Odysseus said. "He's gone to Delphi with some of the other kings, to seek advice from the Pythia. But yes, he knows he'll need the Myrmidons behind him."

Achilles' green eyes flashed. "Never that! Beside him, perhaps, but not behind. We don't serve him."

"All Greeks serve the High King."

"Not the Myrmidons," Achilles said sullenly.

Pride had always been the largest thing about Achilles. It might have been so anyway – perhaps it was born in him – but Odysseus thought it came from when he'd first been told the prophecy spoken in Thessaly, on the day of that boar hunt long ago. *There will be glory and sorrow unmeasured by mortals, and amidst it shall be the son of the man who slew the boar, a warrior ten times greater than his father.* Peleus had gone further; *a warrior to outshine us all,* he'd said. Once Achilles knew that, he was always going to see himself as the centre of the world, and only a small step below the gods.

Odysseus wondered what would happen when Peleus died. The king of Thessaly had been a notable warrior himself in his day, and would be still if it weren't for his expanding girth. Achilles was a greater fighting man, beyond doubt, and unlike Diomedes he defined himself by that. When he became king of Thessaly he might consider raiding with the Myrmidons more important than ruling his land; more important too than accepting the authority of the High King.

Still, that was a problem for another day, and not something Odysseus would have to deal with anyway. He'd long since given up trying to cure all the ills of the world. All he wanted now was to solve the problem in front of him.

"What will you do, then?" he asked casually. "Will the Myrmidons stand aside from this war at Troy?"

"Why shouldn't we?"

"Because Greece needs you," Odysseus said. "These past twenty years, even before you were old enough to fight, the Myrmidons have been raiding around the Greensea. Nobody else has, at least not regularly. Not since Theseus killed Minos and Crete fell."

Achilles shrugged. "We're the best at it."

"I know you are. So do all the Greeks. Knowing you and the Myrmidons are with us will give them a huge amount of belief. And it will sow doubt in Trojan minds, as well. Nestor says there was a family in Priam's palace from the Mysian town you sacked. They know what the Myrmidons can do."

"So they should," Achilles said, with more than a dash of pride. "There isn't a town on the shores of the Greensea that we couldn't take."

"So prove that," Odysseus said. "Take Troy."

Achilles fiddled with his wine cup. "Troy is... different. They have a standing army there, men trained just as well as the Myrmidons are. And they have their walls. If half what I hear about those are true, I wonder if any force in the world could breach them."

He did understand warfare, Odysseus had to admit. Almost everything else was a mystery to Achilles, but he knew war. "The walls are everything you've heard. Vast, and built on top of a ridge."

"Then Troy can't be taken," Achilles said.

"Everywhere can be taken. And you just said the Myrmidons can raze any town on the Greensea."

There was a pause, and then Achilles said, "My mother doesn't want me to join this war."

Odysseus had no reply to that. Mighty Achilles, unwilling to fight because his mother was afraid? It made no sense. He remembered Peleus had said it was Thetis who wrote the letter calling Achilles to the Gathering, but he hadn't thought anything of it at the time. He didn't know what to think of it now, but he sensed danger under his feet, an eruption of Achilles' temper if the wrong words were spoken. So Odysseus didn't speak at all, and waited to see what Achilles would say.

"She has the gift of prophecy, sometimes. It comes from her time in the temple of Aphrodite, she says, on Sarakino. Before she met my father. She had a foretelling about this war."

Odysseus hid his scepticism. If wives and mothers could see the future there would be no reason to visit the Oracle at Delphi, or any other soothsayer. "Really?"

Achilles was still playing with his wine cup. "She told me the war will last for years. Both sides will exhaust themselves as they struggle. And the greatest hero on each side will be slain, which of course means me. I will die." There was no boasting, no fear in his voice. He was simply a man stating facts. "My mother fears I will fall, if I go to Troy."

"I fear I will fall, if I go," Odysseus said. "I have an infant son at home, Achilles. We named him Telemachus. I want to spend the next two years teaching him to walk, not miss it all fighting a war I hardly care about on the other side of the sea. But I will go to Troy, if all the kings do. Some things must be done, or we abandon all honour."

"True," Achilles admitted.

"Then put your faith in the gods and go," Odysseus suggested. "It's what you do anyway, every time you go into battle. Make your offerings, purge your soul as best you can, and trust in your skill and the gods to bring you through alive. And think." He leaned forward, catching Achilles' emerald eyes. "There's not a warrior in Greece better than you. But who will men talk of, if you don't go to Troy and Ajax does, and Diomedes? If they lead the charge that surges over the walls, when Troy is torn down. What will men say then?"

Achilles jaw tightened. "They wouldn't dare. Not when I'm close enough to hear them."

"No, not then. But behind your back. When you're away. Men will say; Achilles could have been the greatest captain of them all, had he gone to Troy. But he stayed away, and Diomedes breached the walls while Ajax tore down the Topless Towers. They will say it forever."

It was said Achilles had killed men for speaking words he didn't like. Odysseus watched him carefully and sent a quick, silent prayer up to the sky.

"Damn you," Achilles said, his voice harsh. "Damn you to Hades forever, Ithacan, and your slick tongue with you."

Odysseus sighed. "I'm sorry, my friend. But all I want is for you to agree to go to Mycenae and speak with Agamemnon. What you decide after that is up to you. I'll have done my duty."

"All right," the big man said. "I will go. But only to talk, mind. I make you no promises."

"I don't ask for any," Odysseus said. He was relieved, actually: he'd thought persuading Achilles would be harder than this. Sometimes it was a relief to be proved wrong. "Do you have any more of that wine?"

*

The path wound deep into the forest, sometimes a yard wide and marked with the prints of sandals, at other times dwindling to little more than a fox run squeezing under bushes and slinking around trees. Eliade had no idea what he might find at the end of it, carnal sensuality or calm piety, but his heart was beating very fast, and he whistled as he walked.

He heard splashing water once, somewhere down the slope to his right. A little later he thought he heard a monkey screech in the trees, though that was surely impossible. He'd only ever seen one monkey, in a stout cage at the market of Tanis in the Egyptian Delta when he'd sailed there, on a trade mission for Odysseus. It had shrieked and bared wicked teeth at him when it saw him staring, and Eliade had moved on hastily. He didn't like the idea that a beast like that might be watching him from high in the trees, but that had to be a mistake. He couldn't imagine how monkeys might have come here.

Anyway, never mind worrying about simians, there was something ahead of him through the forest.

It turned out to be a small temple complex, in the usual pattern of sanctuary in the middle and sleeping quarters ranged around. Simple dresses hung on a line beside the temple, away from the shade of the trees. On the far side plots had been dug and crops now grew, mostly wheat and barley: the basic foods that kept a body alive. Two white-clad women hoeing among the stalks saw him and straightened up, exchanging glances before one came towards him. The other went into the shrine, emerging a moment later with four other women carrying cudgels and sticks. Eliade smiled to himself. Women with staves wouldn't last one minute against trained fighting men.

But here they had the Myrmidons to protect them. Eliade let the smile fade as the woman reached him.

"You're looking for some... amusement?" she asked. Her accent was odd, hard to place.

He nodded. "Am I in the right place?"

"No. We don't do such things here. Not all the priestesses of Dionysus are driven by their own desires."

"Very well, lady." He inclined his head. "Might you know where such women could be found?"

"The trail up the mountain," she said, pointing. "It's a long climb, but at the top you'll find a temple complex by a hot spring. The women there will give you wine for your thirst, and satisfy whatever other needs you might have."

He was about to thank her, and move on, when his brain understood something. "That accent. You're Mysian."

"I am," she said. "I was taken from my home and brought here, only for my captor to grow bored with me. Now I am a priestess of Dionysus. I'm content enough. As long as need not deal with the urges of men anymore."

"Who brought you?" he asked, before he could help himself.

"Achilles, of course." Her lips quirked. "As he's brought many women, through the years. Cyrilla over there was his favourite toy long before he met me."

"I'm sorry."

"And there is Deidameia," the woman went on. She indicated a girl, surely not old enough to really be called a woman... but she had a child in her arms, a boy Eliade thought. He might be a year old. "Once Achilles' favourite, now forgotten. As all of us are."

His body had forgotten its desire, for the moment. "Does Achilles know he has a son?"

"He knows. We never see him."

"I wish I could help you," Eliade said.

"I told you I am content enough," she smiled. "There is happiness here, on some days. Now go, and find your lascivious women. I don't blame you for it."

He was already walking away when something occurred to him, and he turned back. "Will you tell me your name?"

"I am Išbardia," she said. "If it matters."

"Who we are always matters," he answered. It was something Odysseus liked to say, and Eliade thought it was probably true. He gave the woman a nod and turned back to the forest, and the trail up the mountain, and a moment later was gone.

Chapter Nineteen

What will Follow

Long ago, the great god Cronus castrated his father Uranus, and seized his power. Dying, Uranus prophesied that Cronus would suffer the same fate, and be killed by his own son.

Cronus resolved to avoid this destiny. When his wife Rhea gave birth he promptly swallowed the child, a girl whose mother had named her Demeter. He did the same when Hera was born, and then Hades and Poseidon. But Rhea came to hate him, not unnaturally, and when the sixth child was born she hid it away, and gave Cronus a stone wrapped in swaddling instead. He ate the stone, and the child Zeus was saved.

When he was grown Zeus fulfilled the prophecy, of course, forcing Cronus to disgorge the contents of his stomach, including the swallowed children. Cronus was then banished to Tartarus, an abyss of darkness and endless torment, as far below Hades and Heaven is high above the Earth. He is imprisoned there still, helpless and lost.

The stone Cronus had consumed remained on Olympus for many years. Later, Zeus wished to find the centre of the world, and to locate it he released two eagles, one from the extreme west and the other from the east. They met above Delphi, in Greece, and there Zeus set down the stone. He placed it on the slope of Mount Parnassus, between two towering cliffs called the Shining Ones, on the northern side of a deep valley.

It rests there still, anointed at dusk and dawn with scented oil. Plaintiffs who visit the shrine of the Pythia attach swatches of wool, in the hope the gods will harken to their pleas.

No visitor may pass beyond the stone without the permission of the priests of Apollo, who run the Oracle there. Violence is utterly forbidden.

*

"I will tell you again," Agamemnon grated. "We will hear the Pythia's words for ourselves. You will take us to her."

"No," the priest said.

He was kneeling beside the great stone, held down by Agememnon's heavy hand on his shoulder. And kept there by the High King's sword at his neck. His breathing was ragged but that was all the sign of nerves that he gave. A man sworn to Apollo's service, and carrying that out at the most sacred site in Greece, had little reason to worry for his soul. It would wing its way to Hades when he died, but there it would walk in the Orchards of Elysium, with birdsong for company and ambrosia flowing in the streams.

"The Lord of the Black Cloud take you!" Agamemnon swore. "Put aside your cursed stubbornness!"

"It is not I who is stubborn," the priest said. His voice was still quite calm. "The laws of this place were laid down by Apollo himself. I will not break them. Neither should you. The vengeance of the gods will fall as heavily on the High King as it would on a peasant."

Nestor was actually quite sure that was true. The Twelve Olympians had never been known for their tolerance towards mortals who transgressed. Offer your sacrifices, show proper deference and respect, and the gods would smile upon you. Fail in those things and all the things you prized were placed at risk: even your life, and the lives of your loved ones. The gods spread their vengeance widely when they struck.

Menelaus was smiling tightly as his brother threatened the priest. That was no surprise; the younger Atreide brother had always followed the elder like a lamb behind its mother. There would be no help from that quarter. There would be none from Diomedes or Ajax, either; both men were standing back and looking uncomfortable, but not about to intervene. Nestor sighed to himself and moved forward.

"There's no need for this," he said.

Agamemnon turned a furious glare on him. "Be quiet, old man. I will have my way in this."

"And the gods will have theirs," Nestor said. "Assaulting a priest is not the best way to gain the answer you need from the Pythia, High King. A calmer approach might be wise."

Agamemnon glowered at him, but with Nestor to shield him Diomedes spoke as well. "Perhaps if we each swear to sacrifice a ram to Apollo before the sun goes down tonight, the god might waive the normal rules, and allow us to hear the prophetess for ourselves?"

The kneeling priest hesitated, then looked at Nestor, who shrugged and spread his hands.

"I suppose he might," the man said.

After a moment Agamemnon withdrew the sword and stepped back. "A wise decision. Do not retract it."

Nestor hoped the High King wasn't going to ruin the compromise by keeping up with his rudeness. He'd been in a foul temper since the Gathering at Mycenae, apt to snarl at anyone who came close. He'd struck his servants more than once, and while that wasn't especially unusual he'd broken one man's arm and left a maid unable to move her shoulder, and that certainly was. Agamemnon was sullen and hot-tempered by nature, but this behaviour was unlike him.

Actually, now Nestor thought of it, the High King's temper didn't date from the Gathering at all. He'd been impatient then, determined to follow the course he'd already decided on, but he hadn't been violent, or even very angry. The change in his temper had come afterwards, in the single day between the Gathering and the beginning of the journey to Delphi. Something must have happened in that time. Nestor had no idea what it could be, but he thought it would be wise to tread softly around Agamemnon until the fury passed.

"You must leave your weapons," the priest said. "No, High King, that is not open to discussion. I'm already breaking the rules for you. I will not allow you also to bear swords on the holy ground."

Agamemnon, for a wonder, only scowled. Nestor took off his sword belt and handed it to one of his followers. "Keep that for me. I don't think there's any danger for us to fear among the temples."

"Except the anger of Apollo," the man said.

"Yes," Nestor agreed. He couldn't help smiling, though it wasn't even a little bit funny. "Except that."

Once they were disarmed, the priest led the five men past the sacred stone and into the temple complex. Nestor couldn't resist touching the rock with his fingertips as he went by. He'd come here once before, to ask advice on an issue that didn't seem important now, and he'd attached his hank of wool like any other plaintiff. But he'd never walked past it, seen the stone from the uphill side. Only priests and priestesses of Apollo were allowed to walk here.

Until now, at least.

In any other god's worship such isolation might have been a source of lewd gossip; everyone knew what clerical types got up to at night, when men and women were mixed together. Or when they weren't, for that matter. There were countless stories about it and twice as many crude jokes. But Apollo's servants were sworn to celibacy, and they took the vow seriously. Nestor had never heard any plausible claim of impropriety among them, here or anywhere else.

White-robed priests stopped to gape at the little group as it made its way up the path. Nestor wondered how long it had been since ordinary folk were allowed past the Cronus-stone. A hundred years? Two hundred, or even never? To judge by the astonishment of the robed men and women, they might not know either. A few of them stopped dead when they saw the kings, their jaws dropping open in comical surprise. Most moved on quickly when Agamemnon scowled at them though. What was wrong with the man?

From the Cronus-Stone the path led up the outcrop and around it, until it crested the ridge and the temple complex was revealed. Pillared houses of worship stood atop broad marble steps, roofed with coloured tiles all mixed together, brilliant reds and greens alongside sunrise yellows. Dormitory houses stood between the temples, low-built but graceful, with herb gardens alongside and chickens picking at the ground in coops built against the walls. All the interlocking paths were lined with columns, painted red and linked with arches of white marble. The columns had been made by cutting stone into slices a foot deep and stacking them one atop the next, very precisely. There were better ways of building today.

But the temples here were old, old. The site had been ancient at the time of the earliest myths. It was here that humans had first been created, the Golden Race of antiquity who had ruled the Earth for long years, aeons of time, before the mortal Men of today came into being. The Golden Ones survived now as the spirits of pools and forests: Naiads and Dryads, Alseids and Nereids and all the others. Givers of blessings and justice, in most of the tales, and lovers of mortals in the rest. Long after they were gone early men had come here, and wondered, and had begun to build temples and pillars the best way they knew how.

The result wasn't necessarily graceful, but it did have a power to it. Something crude but vital, Nestor thought, full of primitive energy. It made his skin prickle. There was potency here, that was for certain, thrumming in the air and the rock beneath his feet. He wondered how the priests stood it, how they slept with this constant hum in their ears.

They followed the main street, right through the heart of the buildings. Presently they passed an amphitheatre on their right, cut into the hillside to form a deep artificial bowl. There were seats enough for two hundred people, perhaps more, and Nestor wondered how many priests and priestesses actually lived on this site. And how many of them performed, come to that. He could imagine them acting out a play of the birth of the Olympians, or Apollo's daily drive across the sky in the chariot of the Sun, while their fellows listened in respectful silence. Probably all the plays they acted were serious things, long on piety but short on humour, so concerned with respect that realism was lost.

Just past the amphitheatre they angled to the left, off the main road. They followed a smaller way around the back of a temple with an elaborate portico, much more modern in style than the building it fronted. It ran between a stand of cypress trees and ended at a narrow cave mouth, just large enough to admit a man and utterly black. Nestor looked at it and found himself shivering. He didn't want to go in there.

Four priests stood in a line across the path. They stared in astonishment at the visitors, then turned angry eyes on their guide.

"Tynaeus?" one of them said. "What are you doing? These people aren't priests!"

"I know that," the man who'd brought them here said testily. "They are kings. The brawny one is Agamemnon of Mycenae."

"I don't care if he's the seventh son of Hermes," the other man retorted. "He shouldn't be here. What do you think you do?"

"They were... insistent," Tynaeus said. "Extremely so. I judged it wiser to allow them their way, and let Apollo decide if he is angered by their presumption. I rather suspect," he eyed Agamemnon with open dislike, "that he will be. But that's up to the god."

"That's not yours to decide," the guardian shot back. "Our task is to protect the god's silence here."

"As I have, for many years," Tynaeus said. "You know it as well as I. Don't insult my dedication."

"You insult it yourself," the man snapped.

The High King showed his teeth, his patience gone. "Take us to the Pythia, little man, as you promised to do."

"That is forbidden!" the cave guard shouted.

Agamemnon put a hand to his belt, where his sword hilt ought to have been. His expression darkened when he remembered it was no longer there. But Tynaeus was already moving forward, and for all his bluster the guard hesitated and then moved out of the way. Agamemnon followed, then Menelaus and hulking Ajax, leaving Diomedes and Nestor to stare at one another.

"I don't like this place," Diomedes said. Handsome warrior prince he may have been, but there was no colour in his face, and he might have aged ten years since they passed the Cronus-stone. His voice trembled. "The air is wrong here. Do you feel it?"

"I feel it," Nestor said. "But I'm going in. Men have never named me coward before and I'm not of a mind to let them start."

He forced his feet to move, and a moment later ducked his head as he entered the cave. He heard Diomedes sigh and then follow after.

Inside the others were waiting, taking time for their eyes to adjust to the darkness. It was almost totally black, a gloom relieved only by a tiny spark of light far ahead, thirty yards perhaps, though it was difficult to judge distance here. Nestor blinked, trying to clear a blur in his vision, but it wouldn't go.

"Go to the light," Tynaeus said. "When you reach it you'll be able to see another. There you will find the Pythia. I will not come with you. I've no desire to bring the god's anger down on my own head, however foolish you people might be."

"Thank you," Nestor said.

"You may find yourselves struggling to see," the priest added. "Or to hear, and your balance may desert you. That happens even to priests who have been here many times. I would tell you not to be concerned." This time it was he who bared his teeth to Agamemnon. "But given your presumption, you have every reason to fear punishment. Do not be surprised if you find it."

He turned and left them, ducking back through the cave entrance into the sunshine outside. Nestor could have joined him with two paces but the daylight still seemed a distant thing, too far away to reach. He looked at Diomedes again. The king of Argolis was pasty in the gloom, like a sick man somehow tottering to his feet in the night. Even Agamemnon and Menelaus were silent, unable to make themselves go on.

"Did we come so far just to stop?" Ajax rumbled. He strode into the darkness, his huge frame blotting out the distant candle.

The others followed, Diomedes dragging his feet at the rear. The floor of the cave turned out to be very smooth, made that way by the priests no doubt, who would not have enjoyed tripping every time they came to speak with the Pythia. Still, Nestor held a hand in front of him and moved carefully, unwilling to take a risk or walk into somebody in the dark. His bones were too old to risk a fall.

"There," he heard Ajax say, up ahead. He must have seen the second light. A moment later the big man moved off to the right, striding confidently along even in the near-total darkness. As Agamemnon and then Menelaus moved on Nestor passed the candle, a fat stick of tallow wedged into a crack in the rock where hundreds must have sat before; the stone was smeared with grease, layer on layer of it running down to the floor. He was sure it was scraped off from time to time, or else the cave would have been blocked long ago. But it still reminded him of the age of this place. He couldn't help shivering.

Past the light the tunnel sloped downwards, heading deeper into the heart of the mountain. The five men shuffled along in a line, trying not to step on the heels of the man in front, except for Ajax who still walked as confidently as he would in a meadow at midday. Perhaps he gained his confidence from seeing Diomedes so pale. Achilles aside, those two were the finest warriors in Greece, and Ajax would think that if he showed no nerves today he'd gain a measure of advantage over the other man.

The corridor turned sharply left, exactly where the second candle was, and opened into a round chamber with an angled floor. The men spread out along one side, not even Ajax willing to advance any further. When he reached the room Nestor saw why. The Pythia was there.

She wasn't as old as he'd expected, but he couldn't actually put an age to her. Perhaps twenty, perhaps twice that. She sat on a chair at the far wall, most of her face obscured by strings of matted hair, with dirt ingrained in the rest. Her fingernails were broken off short and caked with muck. She wore a long chiton, so old and filthy that Nestor wasn't sure what colour it had originally been. When she moved Nestor saw that she was chained to the seat, which in turn seemed to have been screwed into the rock. The sight made him grit his teeth. Nobody deserved to be kept this way, like an animal locked away for a lifetime.

From one wall water came in a fine spray, a few inches above the floor. It steamed gently, but you'd have to hold a cup for a long time before it filled. The air felt damp, clammy.

"No wonder the priests don't like outsiders to see their Oracle," he said to Diomedes. His voice sounded strange, as though the words were doubled.

"What?" the man said, and he realised it was Menelaus. The younger Atreide looked almost green in the wan light of a few candles mounted on the walls. "What did you say?"

"King of Sparta, lured away," the woman on the chair said abruptly. Almost sang it, in fact, crooning the words like a child talking to a beloved doll. "Lost your dearest treasure, and dream of her at night. In daylight, too. Dream of her. Touch. Taste of her mouth. Dream."

Menelaus grew even paler. He seemed about to speak but only swallowed, and Nestor understood completely. He felt bile in his own throat. Tynaeus had said they might feel peculiar in here, though Nestor couldn't remember his exact words now. His head felt stuffed with linen.

"High King, beloved daughter," the woman carolled. "Love her, lose her, send her away. Away to sorrow. Your sacrifice, or hers? Better that. Better that way. Your heart is sorrow."

"Ask her," Menelaus said, speaking for the first time all day. "Ask her, brother. My gorge is rising. If we have to stay here long I'll vomit on the floor."

Agamemnon nodded, and took a step forward. At once he swayed and fell back again, clutching at his throat. "Faugh! The air in here is foul!"

"Not the air," Nestor managed. "The water. There's something in the moisture that makes us sick."

"The Olympians know what it must have done to her," Diomedes said, with a jerk of his head towards the priestess.

Agamemnon had recovered a little of his composure now. He didn't advance again, but his voice came out stronger than the others were able to manage. "Pythia, hear my question! What will follow if Greece goes to war against Troy?"

The woman went still. Normally the priests read out questions written down by petitioners, and then interpreted her answers before carrying them back to the surface. It was that which Agamemnon had wanted to bypass; he didn't want a nameless cleric to change any of what the prophetess might say. He preferred to hear it himself. If he now had to ask the priests to translate it would be awfully embarrassing.

"Troy rises to power, but Troy may yet fall," the Pythia said. Her voice echoed in the cavern, seeming to come from many mouths at once. "Rise as Susa rises, fall as Hattusa falls. Troy's fate lies in the hands of the Greeks."

The words died away. Her chin rested on her chest.

"Does that mean," Menelaus began, and stopped, frowning.

"It means we will destroy Troy," Agamemnon said exultantly. "Didn't you hear her? *Troy's fate lies in the hands of the Greeks.* If we lead our armies there, we will conquer, brother."

"More I will say." The prophetess raised her head, and with a shock Nestor saw she was blind. He stumbled back a step, horrified by the dark holes where eyes should be. To his left Ajax made a choking sound and reeled away up the tunnel. A moment later Nestor heard the big man throwing up.

"More," the Pythia repeated. "If all Greece brings war to Troy, the greatest of heroes will fall on both sides. Fame will be won that rings down the ages. And the Euxine Sea will lie open to Greek ships, while Greece's name will be written in letters of fire that burn for thousands of years. This I foretell."

She fell silent again, her head falling forward. Nestor gulped down his own bile, fighting to stay upright. He thought he was swaying and wasn't sure. Tynaeus' words came back to him, clearly this time; *you may find yourself struggling to see, or to hear, and your balance may desert you.* He could still hear Ajax blundering his way towards the surface. "We should go. Before these fumes overwhelm us."

"Good idea," Diomedes agreed. He turned and hurried away, once turning his head to spit a great glob of phlegm against the passage wall. Menelaus was right behind him. In the chamber Nestor looked pityingly at the priestess.

"I wish we could help her," he said.

"Without her there would be no prophecies. And we have what we came for." Agamemnon still sounded jubilant. "A prophecy of Troy's defeat. Come. Let's join the others."

That isn't what she said, Nestor thought. He was already struggling to remember what she *had* said though. Troy may rise or may fall, and that fate is in the Greeks' hands; there will be glory and fallen heroes; and the trade routes of the east will lie open. Something like that. It did sound bad for Troy, he had to admit it, but the Pythia hadn't actually said the city would fall. Prophecies were notoriously slippery things. You might think they promised one thing when in fact they did not, and the reality was far different.

Best to deal with it on the surface. He turned and began to feel his way back up the tunnel, careful to avoid the slightly darker patch of floor where poor Ajax had emptied his stomach, and no doubt lost half his pride. He would be irritable for a long time because of that, easy to provoke to anger.

Nestor couldn't worry about that now. His head was ringing and he couldn't feel his feet. Whenever he blinked the single candle up ahead became three or four, and he stumbled into a wall trying to walk towards the wrong one. Finally he just felt his way along with one hand on the stone, and when he felt the first breath of fresh outdoors air on his face it was like new love to a lonesome man.

Chapter Twenty

Fame Will Be Won

"Perhaps you can tell us now," Nestor said later, "why you've been in such a foul mood since the Gathering."

The five of them were seated around a table partway down the mountain, in the town that provided accommodation and food for visitors to the Oracle. Far below the Pleistos river was a string of pale blue, splashed with white. On the far hillside deer browsed a slope patched with stands of trees, pines and cypress mostly, with wild grasses between.

Nestor could see twenty cairns from where he sat, easily. Most of them were simple piles of rock, only a few feet high; just enough to serve as markers, and no more. They appeared everywhere, some on the slope among the grazing deer, others by the road up from the river, more under the eaves of the woods. Each one marked where a god had been seen, or a dryad brushing her hair in the fading of the day. There was no holier site in the world than Delphi. Not even Egypt held a place so sacred.

"I suppose so," Agamemnon said, after a moment.

The High King didn't look well enough to argue for long. He was pale and his face drawn, as though he'd suffered a series of sleepless nights or a bout of dysentery that had left him weak. Menelaus was no better, and Diomedes was drinking wine at a prodigious rate, pouring straight from the jug with no water added at all. It was Ajax who was worst off though, slouching in his chair and not meeting anyone's eyes. He picked at the figs and olives but left the meats alone, and the wine. Nestor suspected the big man was afraid that if he ate properly he'd throw up again.

"Well?" he said.

"It's that goat-spawned devil in Crete," Agamemnon said. "Idomeneus. He sent his cousin to the Gathering in his place. It turns out he had a reason for that."

"Unrest in some of the villages, wasn't it?" Menelaus asked.

He really was slow sometimes. If there was nothing more to this than the story Meriones had told, Agamemnon wouldn't be so furious about it. The High King shook his head. "I don't think so, brother. That was just a tale spun to deceive us. Idomeneus has a higher aim."

"Which is?" Nestor asked. He was growing tired of teasing out words one by one, but he didn't dare push harder. Agamemnon might turn that temper onto him.

"First, he demanded equal authority with me over any army sent to Troy," Agamemnon said.

Ajax dropped a handful of raisins with a bellow. "What?"

"I don't think he was serious. He just wanted to remind me how badly I need those Cretan ships. And I do need them," Agamemnon admitted gloomily. "We can manage without, but it will take us longer to transport our troops, or else we'll have to spend a summer building enough galleys to take everyone in a single voyage. Either way, we lose time. Idomeneus knows it."

"Troy will use any time we give them to build their defences," Diomedes said. "To train soldiers, too, and to call for help from allies. We can't afford to gift them a year for it."

"I know that," Agamemnon said dangerously. "I am not a complete fool."

No, Nestor thought privately, *but you're making a good try at it.* Aloud he said, "So what was his real demand?"

"He wants to marry my daughter," Agamemnon said. "Iphigenia. He *demands* it, however courteous his words. That's his price. I will have to hand her to him if I want his ships."

"I'll tear his fawning tongue out with my hands!" Ajax erupted. "I'll pop his eyeballs like grapes! I'll – I'll –"

He tailed off, perhaps running out of words. Or perhaps he remembered that he was the one who'd vomited back in the Pythia's cave, and any threats from him just now sounded ridiculous.

Nestor looked out over the narrow valley, considering. Idomeneus had been one of those who hoped to marry Helen, before she picked Menelaus as her husband. The Cretan king had lost his wife some years ago, with no children to show for the union. He must be forty by now, and he looked it, a careworn and weary man entering middle age with no heir to groom to replace him. Those things made some men restless.

Idomeneus must be wondering why he fought so hard to hold power if he had no one to leave it to.

Iphigenia was young enough to give him children by the dozen, if he wanted so many, but she wasn't merely a brood mare. She would tie Idomeneus to the great families of mainland Greece, something Helen would also have given him. Any Cretan king would feel rather isolated from the stream of events in Greece, always on the outside looking in, and sometimes forgotten. Marriage into the Atreide dynasty would give Idomeneus a chance to change that.

This must be what the Pythia had meant in the cave. Nestor's memory had returned, once he was out of the cloying fumes of the cave and in the fresh air again. *Beloved daughter... love her, lose her. Send her away to sorrow.* The sacrifice Agamemnon must make, for the war he longed for.

"Clever of him," Nestor said.

Agamemnon glared, and then tossed his head like an angry bull. "Yes. I suppose it is."

"You don't have to accept the demand," Diomedes said. "Not from the mountain boar of Crete."

"I do if I want this war," Agamemnon said. "Because I need the ships, and because if Crete stands aside from the fighting we might destroy Troy, but at the cost of losing control of the Greensea to Idomeneus. We would trade one obstructive enemy for another. And I do want to destroy Troy, after what we heard in the cave. Do we agree on that?"

"Yes," Ajax and Menelaus said immediately, at the exact same time. Nestor said "No," and Diomedes only looked troubled.

"What do you mean, no?" Agamemnon demanded. "You heard the prophetess. Troy's fate is ours to control, we Greeks. If we go, Troy will fall."

"That's not quite what she said," Nestor replied. "No, High King, I don't mean to insult you. But we should be very clear on precisely what the Pythia said. I heard her say Troy's fate lies in the hands of the Greeks, but I did *not* hear her say the city will fall if we assault it. She said that Troy may rise, or she may fall. It's not the same thing."

"Troy may rise like Susa," Diomedes put in, "wherever that is. Has anyone heard of it?" None of them had. "Or fall like Hattusa, she said. But Hattusa hasn't fallen. I didn't understand that part."

"Neither did I," Menelaus agreed.

Agamemnon leaned forward. "We can't expect to comprehend every word she spoke. It was Apollo's words we heard, spoken through her mouth: that's the point of the Oracle, after all. But we can understand a lot. *Troy's fate lies in the hands of the Greeks,* she said. What more could we ask than that alone? If we go to Troy we lay our hands on the strings of destiny. *Our* hands, not Trojan ones. Isn't that reason enough to go?"

Diomedes was nodding, Nestor saw with dismay. He tried to speak but Agamemnon wasn't done, and the High King drove right over him.

"Fame will be won that rings down the ages," he said. Agamemnon's eyes were closed as he dredged the words out of his memory. "That should be enough too, but there's more. *Greece's name will be written in letters of fire that burn for thousands of years.* We're warriors, my friends. Our forefathers built these kingdoms with sweat and spears, and we're being told we can build a Greek empire that will last eternity. How can we turn away from a future like that?"

Diomedes was nodding again. Menelaus had been from the start, but then, he always agreed with his older brother. Nestor could remember when Agamemnon had first begun learning the spear, and little Menelaus had toddled into the tiltyard at Mycenae to watch, eager as a puppy to join in. As for Ajax, after his embarrassment in the cave he was always going to vote for war now, to prove he wasn't afraid. A man like him could do nothing else.

It all depended on Diomedes, just as Odysseus had said when he came to Nestor for help in forming a plan. If the king of Argolis opted against war, the lords here would be split three to two, and Agamemnon would have no mandate to launch his attack on Troy. If he voted for, then Nestor's would be the only dissenting voice, and the die would be cast. The Greeks would be going to war in Anatolia, for a prize he doubted they could win.

He tried desperately to think of an argument against it, and his mind snagged something the Pythia had told them. "She said this would only happen if *"all Greece"* joined the war. That means Achilles and the Myrmidons, and it means Crete too, I'm afraid."

"I know it," Agamemnon said, voice level.

He had decided, then. Agamemnon would send his young daughter to Greece to marry a middle-aged king he detested, in order to gain Cretan support for the struggle to come. The girl's mother would be livid; Clytemnestra was reputed to have a vicious temper, and it was an open secret that she believed Agamemnon saw their children more as tools than as people to be loved. This would not help change her mind. Agamemnon knew that, and he was going to do it anyway. Nestor felt a wave of dismay and fought it off. If there was still a chance to turn this Fate aside it had to be done now, before they left this little town.

He opened his mouth, and a voice behind him said, "My lord?"

It was one of Agamemnon's guards, a soldier clad in cuirass and helmet even here, in the most sacred place in Greece. He waited for his king's nod before he continued. "A messenger has come, my lord. From the east. He says he carries tidings for you."

Agamemnon nodded. "He has been searched?"

"Thoroughly, yes."

"Then bring him to me." The High King turned back to his companions. "News from Troy, I wager. Now we will see. Perhaps they are ready to give up, before we even raise a spear."

Nestor doubted it. The Trojans would not abduct Helen and then cave in so easily: it made no sense. He hoped he was wrong, if only because it would end this lunacy before it could begin... except that Agamemnon would be encouraged to believe there was nobody who could stand against Greece, and the next time someone upset him he'd demand revenge even more loudly than now. If it wasn't war on Troy it would be war in Egypt, or Phoenicia, or even far across the Greensea in wealthy Carthage. But all he could hope for was to win time. Prevent this war, and perhaps something else would happen to prevent the next, until finally Agamemnon died and a saner man became High King.

Nestor would be long dead by then. Most of the task would fall on Odysseus, and Menestheus in Attica. But Nestor had a feeling, as he watched the messenger approach, that they weren't going to have the chance.

A dove cried, right above the kings' table. Nestor turned his head in time to see it sweep away, a pale bird with black-barred wings, and his spirits sank even lower. Doves were sacred animals, always to be found where a god was present, or had been. That one had called out so close to the men had to mean the gods were watching what was about to happen.

He turned back to the messenger, hands suddenly cold.

"My King." The man knelt a few yards from Agamemnon, and Nestor felt his brows rise. Anatolians knelt, Carthaginians and Egyptians did, but Greeks were content to bow. But evidently Agamemnon had begun insisting that his servants kneel, as though before a foreign potentate. There were implications, if so. Perhaps Agamemnon believed that being High King entitled him to greater respect than an ordinary king.

And perhaps that would lead to trouble, one day. But not today. The messenger was still kneeling.

"What news?" Agamemnon asked.

"Word from the east," the man told him. "We've heard from two merchants now that there are stories of a great battle between the Hittites and Assyrians, fought somewhere beyond the mountains. One called the battle Sinjar, the other Keshad. Both agree the Hittites were defeated, and badly."

The High King leaned forward. "How badly?"

"It seems their entire chariot force was destroyed," the man said. "Trapped in narrow ground by ranks of spearmen, according to one of our people, though we can't confirm that. Half their spears were lost in the retreat – perhaps a good deal more than half. Word in Halicarnassus is that the Assyrians are advancing on Hattusa itself."

"By the Lord of the Black Cloud," Agamemnon breathed. "The Hittites are broken. This is an omen! A sign from Zeus himself."

Nestor closed his eyes for a moment. He knew now there was no point in further protest. Not just because Agamemnon would never listen, but because the gods were playing this game, beyond doubt. The dove removed any doubt of that. When the gods involved themselves there was nothing a mortal man could do but try to ride the storm, or he would be broken like a ship caught in surging currents. Menelaus and Ajax were watching the High King with shining eyes, convinced this meant the gods were on their side. Even Diomedes looked awed.

The gods were tricksters though, as likely to lure a man on and then betray him as they were to keep their faith. Agamemnon was a fool if he thought he could trust them. But saying so would gain nothing. Not anymore.

Agamemnon picked up his wine cup. Colour had returned to his face now, and he was smiling widely. "We go to Troy!"

"To Troy!" Menelaus repeated, ever the sycophant, and Ajax bellowed, "Troy shall fall!"

Diomedes echoed him a moment later. All the choices had run out. Nestor remembered abruptly the words spoken by the priest in Thessaly long before, over the body of the great boar Peleus had speared. *From this moment the world turns towards war.* Antenor of Troy had been there that day, to plead for the return of Hesione. That princess had become an open wound, dripping poison between Troy and Greece. Now here they were, preparing for war to rescue the woman Troy had stolen in desperate response.

He reached for his cup and held it up, managing a smile that he thought looked genuine. He supposed it didn't matter. Even Agamemnon hadn't yet tried to choose which thoughts he would allow a man to have, in the privacy of his own mind. What counted were a man's actions. In this case, whether he brought his ships and armies to the war in the east.

Nestor would do so. *Ride the storm, or be broken.*

"To Troy," he said.

*

She found him where she'd expected to, standing at the rampart of Ilos' Tower, at the western end of the Pergamos. The *Meltemi* had died away, leaving Troy calm and still, even this high up. He had sent the guard away. Usually there was only one, able to look out from here over the Plain and Bay of Troy, across the Hellespont and even into Thrace beyond.

Which was what Priam was doing, of course. He was fifty now, his hair more white than the sandy colour it had once been, his shoulders more rounded. Lines in the folds of his fingers and around his blue eyes. There were times when the light fell just so, and Hecuba would catch sight of Hector from the tail of her eye and think he was Priam, just for a moment. Priam as he had been, when they married. The years had been kind enough, until now. Until recently Hecuba had believed they would continue to be.

"I heard the news," she said.

He nodded, unsurprised by her voice, and went on staring west. The southern beach of the Bay was there, thick as ever with trading ships from across the Greensea. Hecuba could make out brown Phoenicians and black men from Egypt, sailors in kilts and others in trousers, in caps or hats or bare-headed, some in robes and some wearing shirts, or stripped to the waist. Visitors from the whole Greensea, come laden with trade goods but also come to wonder at Troy, its wealth and splendour.

From an eastern tower she would be able to see the caravans on the Trojan Road. Fewer of them than the ships, of course, but easier to see – or at least the dust trails they raised were. The men on the wagons might be Colchians or Zhykians, hard-eyed fighters from Sarmatia or even the pale, red-haired men who came from Rus, the land of great rivers north of the Euxine Sea. They might be Hittites or Assyrians just as easily, perhaps sent by their Great Kings to offer riches beyond measure for horses reared on the Trojan plains, *tarpans* trained by Trojan wranglers. This was not the centre of the world, not yet. But it was sometimes difficult to remember that.

"Well?" she asked.

He turned his head to look down at her. White hair and lines aside, his eyes were still the same, blue and bright and clear. *He* was still the same, older and more worn, but still the man she remembered.

"What is there to say?" he asked. "The Argives are mad. Only madmen would react as they have."

"You don't blame Paris?"

He shook his head. "Paris is what he's always been. It might be that Hector's right, and we indulged Paris too much as he grew. The youngest child is often loved too much, and spoiled."

"It was me who told you that," she said.

"I know," Priam said. No smile ghosted about his lips, as it usually did when she teased him. "But there's no point in blaming Paris. The plan was Antenor's, and since he first suggested it two years ago nobody has found anything to criticise in it. Not me, not Ucalegon or Hector or Aeneas. Not even you, my dear. If there's guilt here, we all share it."

She caught the note in his voice and responded to it. "But you don't believe there is."

"No. The plan was a good one, even after Paris... altered it. Faced with the loss of Helen, as well as punitive taxes on the Road, the Argives should have bargained. Any reasonable men would have done, but not them. I don't believe they know reason, not anymore. They truly are mad."

"They always were," she said. "Or else driven to their actions by capricious gods, which amounts to the same thing. We knew that. If the fault is ours to share, let us admit as much."

He sighed and nodded, hands on the parapet.

"It will be war, then," she prompted.

"So our agents tell us," Priam said. He sighed for a second time. "I will send to our allies and vassals tomorrow morning. Tell them to strengthen their walls and build new ones where none exist. And tell them Troy will need the aid they have promised, these past years."

He pointed past her, across the Plain with its clumps of grazing horses. "Do you see there?"

"What am I looking for?"

"Cradle Bay," he told her. "That's where they'll land. The Bay of Troy is too much of a risk, because when the *Meltemi* blows it will pin their ships to the strand. That will break up their supplies, and put them at risk if our warriors can reach their prows while the wind keeps them from putting to sea."

He shrugged under her penetrating gaze. "When I was a boy I tried to imagine how best to attack Troy by water. This is what

I worked out. Hector has reached the same conclusion now, though I've never spoken to him of the plan I made, all those years ago."

She studied him a moment longer, then reached up to place a soft kiss on his cheek. Priam touched his fingers to the place and frowned at her, obviously not understanding.

"For you," she said. "Because you *have* been a good shepherd to your people, all of your life. Whatever happens now."

He did smile then, just a flicker of movement at the corners of his mouth, but it would do. It would more than do, on this grim day. They were going to need laughter in the days ahead, if the Argives really were coming. And if they didn't baulk at their first sight of the mighty walls of Troy, rising out of the plain and seeming to hold up the sky. Hecuba didn't think they would, though she wished it. But then, if the Argives could be wished away the world would have been rid of them long ago, thanks to the sheer number of victims around the Greensea who prayed fervently that they would be swept away and lost.

"I would give it all away," he said, "whatever reputation I have, and such affection as I'm held in. I'd abandon it all, if it meant I could hand this city to Hector intact, and safe, when my time comes."

"You may yet," she said.

He smiled, but this time it was sad, and she said no more. They stood on Ilos' Tower and watched the ships in the Bay below, some sliding north and others south, their sails limp in the still air.

Caesura

There is an island in the Aegean, among the Cyclades, which men call Most Fair. Its proper name is Kallistē, named after a daughter of Poseidon who first walked on land there, and it takes the shape of a half moon. The smaller island of Therasia closes most of the open bay to the west. Both islands are steep and rocky, but both also have pockets of the most fertile soil in the world, where the most bone-fisted farmer can throw seeds on the ground and sit back to watch them grow.

Long ago, even before the time of Perseus, Kallistē and its companion were one island, or so the priests claim. The shining bay between them did not exist. Some people say a great bull was imprisoned beneath it in those days, a child of the sea-nymph herself, deformed into a half-animal form because of some unnamed sin committed by Kallistē in the past. When he raged against his confinement the island shook, and smoke rose from Mount Nievo.

Others tell a different story. The island was a Titan, they sat, an immortal giant made of stone, who curled himself up to hide from Zeus when Cronus was thrown down and left only his back above the waves. His name was Straeus, a brother of Cronus and more cunning than he, for neither Zeus nor the other gods could find him. Until one day Kallistē set her feet on his back, and so knew him, and Straeus realised his secret was betrayed.

Whether bull-man or Titan, the stories end the same way. The island exploded in a storm of smashed stone and dust, climbing into the sky like a giant hand. Straeus rising to challenge the sky, and throw down Olympus; or just the debris thrown out as the Minotaur sought to be free. In either case, stones and hot ash fell like rain in Greece, in Anatolia, even as far as Egypt. In Crete, directly south of Kallistē, the sea rose up in a great wave that smashed itself against the coast, shattering palaces and towns. Mallia, Kalami, Pelagia, Mochlos. Harbours and fleets were destroyed, farmland flooded, people washed away without trace.

The Kingdom of Minos fell, of course. Its stranglehold on shipping was broken, and its wealth was bleeding away long before Theseus arrived to kill the last king. People still speak of it, the common men as well as priests and kings. Whether the cause was a bull-man or a stone god, the tale reminds us that the gods can sometimes change our destinies for their own reasons, and wreak appalling destruction as they do.

*

Are all our actions thus Fated? Those of gods and men alike?

Once I believed as most men do, that it is the three sisters of Fate who control our destinies; the fine-armed Daughters of Night. Clothos the Spinner, who spools the thread of a life onto her spindle. Lachesis the Allotter, who measures the thread. And Atropos the Inexorable, who cuts the thread with her shears, and turns a deaf ear to all pleas. They cannot be persuaded, or bribed, or bargained with. They are implacable, and even gods die at their hands in the end.

I no longer believe so.

We choose our fates, we mortal men. More often than not it's we who set our own paths. And in choosing we condemn ourselves to blood and ruin, time and again as generations pass.

We did so in the years before Agamemnon called the Greek kings to war against Troy.

Telamon could have handed Hesione back, and been honoured for it. Instead he let himself be ruled by pride. Atreus, and later Agamemnon, could have pressured him to do so, and yet did not. Antenor could have shown more caution, Priam held out against the yearning of his heart to see his sister again. And so, and so; and step by step the world was dragged into the most ruinous war any of us had ever known, even in myth.

Could the gods have been involved in this? Guiding men's hearts, hastening their tongues, heating their blood? Perhaps. But events would have proceeded the same way without them, and so I tend now to believe events *did* proceed without them. We men are good at choosing ruin. We don't need gods to show us the way.

That winter messages ran through Greece, calling the kings and their armies to Aulis on the second full moon after the Festival of Anthesteria. At the same time similar missives spread across Troas and beyond, to the allies and friends of Troy. To Pandarus on Mount Ida, and Aeneas in Dardanos. South to king Crethon of Kolonia, Eetion in Thebe-under-Plakos, and further afield to Sarpedon of Lydia and Chromis of Mysia. Word ran back, promising aid when the attack came.

One other city was asked for aid. There was never any doubt what Miletos would do. It had suffered worse than any at Greek hands, and its king Danel sent back a vow to help Troy stand with all the strength he owned or could call on.

Meanwhile moats were cleaned out and deepened. Walls were rebuilt and made higher. Men were recruited as soldiers and trained. Fletchers produced barrels full of arrows, to be stacked on every rooftop and every tower; carpenters turned out spears by the thousand; metallurgists produced swords and points and buckles for cuirasses. Food was dried and stored carefully in jars.

The Greeks knew all this was happening but were powerless to prevent it. Ships do not sail the seas in winter. Those which try too often end wrecked on rocks, or simply vanish, swallowed by storm waves or dragged down by Nereids, the nymphs of the sea. But men trained in Greece too, while artisans churned out all the weaponry of war, and in the ports shipwrights worked day and night to make new galleys to carry the armies to Troy. I saw them myself that winter, in Attica where men laboured at the great harbour of the Piraeus. I even helped to carry a timber for a hull once, when one of the workers caught his foot and twisted the ankle too badly to walk.

"You've a sturdy heart," one of the men said to me afterwards, "but your body isn't strong enough for this, Thersites. Best leave it to us."

That was my contribution, during those long months of preparation. I carried one log to be split for planking. Hardly a hero's effort; but then, whoever heard of a hero like me?

But I should not be dismayed. I am still here, when so many heroes who went to Troy lie still in its black earth. That winter they yet lived, and prepared for what was to come.

I'm Ben Blake, and I hope you enjoyed the first volume of my version of the tale of Troy. The second volume, Heirs of Immortality, is due out in the autumn of 2014.

Feel free to contact me if you like, whether you liked the novel or not;

Facebook: https://www.facebook.com/benblakeauthor.

Blog: http://benblake.blogspot.co.uk/

Email: ben.blake@hotmail.co.uk

Also by Ben Blake

The Risen King
Blood and Gold (Songs of Sorrow volume 1)
The Gate of Angels (Songs of Sorrow volume 2)

Made in the USA
Charleston, SC
07 March 2014